WITCH'S BOUNTY

URBAN FANTASY ROMANCE

ANN GIMPEL

Edited by
ANGELA KELLY

Illustrated by
Sly Fox Cover Designs

CONTENTS

WITCH'S BOUNTY

DEMON ASSASSINS, BOOK ONE

**Urban Fantasy Romance With A Heaping Side of Hexes,
Spells, and Magick
By
Ann Gimpel**

BOOK DESCRIPTION: WITCH'S BOUNTY

One of three remaining demon assassin witches, Colleen is almost the last of her kind. Along with her familiar, a changeling spirit, she was hoping for a few months of quiet, running a small magicians' supply store in Fairbanks, Alaska. Peace isn't in the cards, though. Demons are raising hell in Seattle. She's on her way to kick some serious demon ass, when a Sidhe shows up and demands she accompany him to England to quell a demon uprising.

Gutsy, opinionated, and outspoken, Colleen refuses to come. Witches need her help, and they trump everything else. Despite breaking a prime Sidhe precept concerning non-interference in mortals' affairs, Duncan offers his assistance. Colleen fascinates him, and he wants to discover more about her. Lots more.

The Sidhe might be the best-looking man Colleen's ever stumbled over, but she doesn't have time for him—or much of anything else. She, Jenna, and Roz are Earth's only hedge against being overrun by Hell's minions. Even with help from a powerful magic wielder like Duncan, the odds aren't good and the demons know it.

Sensing victory is within their grasp, they close in for the kill.

...In the beginning, Ceridwen bent over her cauldron, stirring up the world. Sometimes the other Celts helped, but mostly they left her alone because she was so ill tempered. She created witches somewhere between Sidhe, dark fae, and Druids—borrowing a pinch of this, and a bit of that, to give them an eclectic mix of magic.

Gwydion dropped by one day and leaned over her shoulder, peering into the large, black pot. "You've made the witches far too powerful," he complained.

Ceridwen shrugged. She pulled her staff out of the sludge simmering before her, dark eyes flashing dangerously. "Do you want this job?"

The master enchanter shook his head. Blond hair wafted in steam from the cauldron. "No, but you'll rue the day you didn't temper their magic."

The goddess narrowed her eyes. "Does Bran, god of prophecy, know you've taken over his job?"

Gwydion bristled. "Damn my eyes, woman, you've made witches as strong as the Sidhe."

She got to her feet, faced the other god, and thumped his chest with her long-nailed forefinger. "One day we may need that strength."

Gwydion looked as if he wanted to say something. Instead, his broad-shouldered form shimmered and disappeared.

"Humph. Good riddance." Ceridwen sank into a cross-legged sit next to her cauldron and went back to stirring. She'd die before admitting this to the other Celtic gods, but out of all her creations, witches were her favorite…

CHAPTER 1

Rain worsened from a steady drizzle to a pounding, punishing deluge of icy sleet. Colleen Kelly strengthened the spell around herself. It sizzled where it ran up against the droplets. At least she wasn't quite as wet as she would have been without its protection. Pavement glistened wetly in the last of the day's light. It was just past three in the afternoon, but December days were short in the northern latitudes and Fairbanks was pretty far north.

"At least it's not snowing," she muttered as she pushed through a nearby glass-fronted door into the magicians' supply store she owned with two other witches in the older part of downtown. Bells hanging around the door pealed discordantly. She sent a small jolt of magic to silence them.

"I heard that. Not the bells, but you. It's supposed to snow this time of year. How could you possibly be pleased the weather patterns have gone to hell?"

Jenna Neil stalked over to the coatrack where Colleen stood. Blonde hair, hacked off at shoulder level, framed a gamine's face and shrewd, hazel eyes. Jenna towered over

Colleen's six foot height by a good four inches, and her broad shoulders would've made most men jealous. Between her trademark high-heeled boots and a scruffy embroidered red cloak tossed over skintight blue jeans, she looked as exotic as the anti-hex hoop earrings dangling from each ear.

Colleen rolled her eyes, shook out her coat, and hung it on the rack. "Spare me your lecture about global warming, okay? It's cold enough to snow. It just isn't, for some reason."

"Mmph." The line of Jenna's jaw tensed.

Indian spices wafted through the air, mingling with the scents of herbs, dried flowers, and desiccated body parts from small animals. Colleen's stomach growled. Breakfast had been at six that morning—a long time ago. Pretty bad when even dried newt smelled like food.

"Did you cook something?" she asked. "And if you did, is there any left?"

A terse nod. Jenna turned away, walking fast. Colleen lengthened her normal stride to catch up. "Hey, sweetie. What happened? You can't be in this big a snit over the weather."

Jenna kept walking, heading for the small kitchen at the back of the store. "A lot of things. I was just having a cup of tea. Shop's been dead today." She disappeared behind a curtain.

Colleen glanced over one shoulder at the empty store. The phalanx of bells around the door would alert them if anyone stopped in. The minute she tugged the heavy, upholstery fabric that served as a kitchen door aside, the pungent tang of Irish whiskey made her eyes water. "You said tea."

"Yeah, well I spiked it."

Colleen grunted. "Smells like you took a bath in booze. What the fuck happened?" She grabbed the larger woman and spun her so they faced one another.

"We got another pay-your-tithe-or-die e-mail from our Coven." Jenna's nostrils flared in annoyance.

"So? That's like the tenth one." There were new policies none of them agreed with, so they'd joined with about twenty other witches and stopped paying the monthly stipend that supported their Coven's hierarchy.

"It's not what's bothering me." Jenna pulled free from Colleen, tipped her cup, and took a slug of what smelled like mostly liquor.

Colleen fought a desire to swat her. Getting to the point quickly had never been one of Jenna's talents. She clamped her jaws together. "What is?"

"Roz called with…problems." Jenna turned and started toward the steep staircase ladder leading to her bedroom above the shop.

"You can't just drop that bomb and leave." Colleen made another grab for Jenna to keep her in the kitchen. Worry for their friend ate at her. Of the three of them, Roz was by far the most volatile. "What happened? I thought she was in Missouri, or maybe it was Oklahoma, visiting that dishy dude she met online."

"Didn't work out." The corners of Jenna's mouth twisted downward.

Colleen quirked a brow, urging her friend to say more.

Jenna plowed on. "He only wanted her for her magic. Turned out he preferred men."

"Aw, shit." Colleen blew out a breath. "She must've been disappointed."

Half a snorting laugh bubbled past Jenna's lips. "Maybe now she is. At the time, furious would've been closer to the mark."

Colleen's throat tightened. "Crap! What'd she do? She didn't hurt him, did she?"

"Not directly. She turned him over to the local Coven."

"Thank God!" Colleen let go of Jenna and laid a hand over

her heart. Roxanne Lantry was more than capable of killing anyone who pissed her off. It was how she ended up in Alaska. Roz hadn't exactly been caught when her cheating husband and his two girlfriends went missing, but she hadn't stuck around to encourage the authorities to question her, either.

Colleen and Jenna had already left Seattle when that little incident went down. Roz repressed her antipathy for Alaska's legendary foul weather and joined them. Magically, she was strong as an ox, and she had a hell of a temper.

Colleen's stomach growled again. Louder this time. It didn't give a good goddamn about anything other than its empty state. She pushed past Jenna to the stove, lifted a lid, and peered into a battered aluminum pot. Curry blasted her. The spicy odor stung her eyes and made her nose run.

"Whew. Potent. Mind if I help myself?"

"Go ahead." Jenna sat heavily in one of two chairs with a rickety wooden table between them. She picked up her mug and took another long swallow.

Dish in hand, Colleen slapped it on the table in front of the other chair and went in search of a mug of her own. There weren't any clean ones, so she plucked one out of the sink and rinsed it. Back at the stove, she tipped the teakettle. Thick, amber liquid spilled from its stubby snout into her waiting mug. Jenna waggled the whiskey bottle in her direction.

"Nah." Colleen settled at the table. "It would go right to my head. Maybe after I get some food on board." She tucked in. After the first few mouthfuls, when the curry powder nearly annihilated her taste buds, the pea, potato, and ham mixture wasn't half-bad.

Jenna drank steadily, not offering anything by way of conversation.

When Colleen's dish was empty, she refilled her mug with

tea, filched a couple of biscuits from the cupboard, and sat back down. "Are you going to talk to me?"

"I suppose so." Jenna's words slurred slightly.

Colleen cocked her head to one side. "I suggest you start now, before you forget how."

"Oh, please." Jenna blew out a breath, showering the small space with whiskey fumes. Colleen waited. The other witch could be stubborn. Wheedling, cajoling, or urging wouldn't work until she was good and ready to talk.

Finally, after so long Colleen had nearly chewed a hole in her cheek, Jenna finally muttered, "Roz called."

Colleen ground her teeth together. "You already said that. It's how you knew what happened with the guy."

Jenna nodded. "There's more." She picked up the whiskey, started to pour it into her mug, then apparently changed her mind and drank right from the bottle. "She's in Seattle. Checked in with Witches' Northwest, just to say hello, and because she wanted to touch base with people she's known for a long time."

Another long pause. Colleen batted back a compulsion spell. It wasn't nice to use those on your friends. She shoved her hands under her bottom to reduce the temptation.

Jenna lowered her voice until Colleen had to strain to hear. "The Irichna demons are back."

"But our last confrontation wasn't all that long ago. Only a few months. Sometimes when we best them, they've stayed gone for years."

Colleen shook her head. Even the sound of the word, *Irichna*, crackled against her ears, making them tingle unpleasantly. Irichna demons were the worst. Hands down, no contest. They worked for Abbadon, Demon of the Abyss. Evil didn't get much worse than that. No wonder Jenna was drinking. Colleen held her hand out for the bottle—suddenly a drink seemed like a most excellent idea—and picked her words with care. "Did Roz actually sight one?"

"Yeah. She also asked if we could come and help. More than asked. She came as close to begging as I've ever heard her."

"Erk. They have a whole Coven there. Several if you count all the ones in western Washington. Why do they need us?" Colleen belted back a stiff mouthful of whiskey. It burned a track all the way to her stomach where it did battle with all the curry she'd eaten.

Jenna just shot her a look. "You know why."

Colleen swallowed again, hoping for oblivion, except it couldn't come quick enough. She knew exactly why, but the answer stuck in her craw and threatened to choke her. The three of them were the last of a long line of demon assassins, witches with specialized powers, able to lure demons, immobilize them, and send them packing to the netherworld.

When things worked right.

They often didn't, though, which was what killed off the other demon assassin witches. It didn't help that demons as a group had been gathering power these last fifty years or so. Witches lived for a long time, but they were far from immortal, and demon assassin ability was genetic. She, Jenna, or Roz would have to produce children or that strain of magic would die out. So far, none of them had come anywhere close to identifying a guy who looked like husband material…

Colleen looked at her hands. Even absent a husband, none of them had a shred of domesticity. Certainly not enough to saddle themselves with offspring.

"What's the matter?" Jenna grinned wickedly, clearly more than a little drunk. "Cat got your tongue too?"

As if on cue, a blood-curdling meow rose from a shadowed corner of the kitchen and Bubba, Colleen's resident familiar, padded forward. When he was halfway to them, he gathered his haunches beneath him and sprang to the table. It rocked alarmingly, and Jenna made a grab for her cup. The large black cat skinned his lips back from his upper teeth, bared his incisors, and hissed.

"Oh, all right." Colleen clamped her jaws tight and summoned the magic to shift Bubba to his primary form, a gnarled three-foot changeling.

The air shimmered around him. Before it cleared, he swiped the liquor out of her hand and drained the bottle.

"Would've been a good reason to leave you a cat," Jenna mumbled.

He stood on the table and glared at both of them, elbows akimbo, bottle still dangling from his oversized fingers. "If you're going to fight demons, you have to take me with you."

"No, we don't," Colleen countered.

"You don't follow directions well," Jenna said pointedly.

"Isn't that the truth?" Colleen rotated her head from side to side, starting to feel the whiskey. At least once when they'd humored the changeling, he'd almost gotten all of them killed. Problem was she couldn't predict when he'd follow her orders, and when he'd decide on a different tack altogether. Then there were the times his fearlessness had saved them all.

Bubba might be a wildcard, but he was *her* wildcard.

"You forgot when I welcomed your spirit into my body— and kept it alive—while the healers worked on you." Bubba eyed Colleen, sounding smug.

"If you hadn't decided to play hero, and needed to be rescued, the demons wouldn't have injured me." Colleen winced at the sour undertone in her voice. That incident had happened five years before. Maybe it was time she got over it.

"Nevertheless." He tossed his shaggy head, thick with hair as black as the cat's. "When you conjured me from the barrows of Ireland, and bound me, we became a unit. You can't go off and leave me here. It would be like leaving a part of yourself behind." His dark eyes glittered with challenge.

"I hate to admit it—" Jenna sounded a little less drunk "—but he's right."

"See." Bubba leered at them, jumped off the table, and waddled over to the stove with his bowlegged gait. Once there, he opened the oven, climbed onto its door, and peeked into the pot. He started to stick a hand inside.

"Hold it right there, bud." Colleen got to her feet, covered the distance to the stove, and dished him up some of the curry mixture. "Get some clothes on and you can have this."

He clambered down from his perch and over to several colorful canisters scattered around the house where she stashed outfits for him. Keeping Bubba clothed had been a huge problem until she'd hatched up a plan, and sewn him several pant and shirt combos with Velcro closures, since he didn't like buttons or zippers.

The changeling dressed quickly and took the bowl from her. "I could've gotten my own food."

"Better for the rest of us if you keep your paws out of the cook pot." Jenna stood a bit unsteadily. "I'll be right back."

Bubba stuffed food into his mouth with his fingers. "Where's she going?" His words came out garbled as he chewed open-mouthed.

Colleen looked away. "Probably to pee. Maybe to throw up. Um, look, Bubba, it might be wiser if we took a quick side trip to Ireland and released you."

She glanced sidelong at the changeling spirit she'd summoned during a major demon war forty years before. He'd been truly helpful then, especially after he'd mastered English, which hadn't taken him all that long. In the intervening time, he'd mostly clung to his feline form, eating and keeping their shop free of mice and rats. They'd lived in Seattle the first ten years or so after he joined them, relocating to Alaska to conceal their longevity. She dragged the heels of her hands down her face, feeling tired. It was getting close to time to move again, but she didn't want to think about it.

Bubba shook his head emphatically. Food flew from the sides of his mouth. He scooped a glob off the floor and ate it anyway. "I have to agree to being released. I don't want to go back to my barrow. I like it much better here."

Colleen sucked in a hollow breath, blew it out, and did it again. Bubba was right. Rules were rules. He'd had a choice at the front end. He could've refused her. Witches respected all living creatures. The ones on the good side of the road, anyway. No forced servitude for their familiars, despite rumors to the contrary.

Jenna lurched back into the kitchen looking a little green. "You okay?" Colleen asked.

"Yeah. I drank too much, that's all." She rinsed her mug at the sink, refilled it with tap water, and sat back down. "Did you two come up with a plan?"

"I'm going." Bubba left his dish on the floor and vaulted back onto the table.

Jenna rolled red-rimmed eyes. "That was the discussion when I left."

"Your point?" Colleen swallowed irritation.

"Nothing." The other witch sounded sullen, but maybe she just didn't feel well.

"I offered to free him—" Colleen began.

"I refused," Bubba cut in. He shook his head. "No recognition for all my years of loyal service. Tsk. You should be—"

"Stuff it." Jenna glared at him. "We have bigger problems than your wounded ego."

He stuck out his lower lip, looking injured as only a changeling spirit could, but he didn't say anything else.

"I suppose we have to go to Seattle," Colleen muttered, half to herself.

"Don't see any way around it." Jenna worried her lower lip between her teeth.

"What exactly did Roz say?"

"We didn't talk long. Her cellphone battery was almost dead." A muscle twitched beneath Jenna's eye. "She'd just stopped in at Coven Headquarters and the group mobbed her. Said we had to come. They've already lost about twenty witches to stealth demon attacks."

Colleen's heart skipped a few beats. Twenty witches was a lot. Maybe a quarter of the Witches' Northwest Coven. "Crap. When did the attacks start?"

"Only a few days ago. They'd planned to call us, but saw it as goddess intervention when Roz showed up."

"Damn that Oklahoma cowboy." Colleen pounded a fist into her open palm. "If his Coven doesn't flatten him, I will."

"He wasn't a cowboy." Jenna's voice held a flat, dead sound. "He was supposed to be a witch. You know, like us."

"Doesn't matter."

"Do you want to close things up here, or should I try to get someone from our Coven to fill in at the shop?" Jenna looked pale, but the tipsy aspect had left her face.

Colleen shook her head. "We haven't sold enough in the last few weeks to make it worthwhile to pay someone to clerk for us."

"Okay." Jenna's hazel eyes clouded with worry. "When do you want to leave?"

"If you asked Witches' Northwest, we probably should've left three days ago."

"How are we getting there?" Bubba squared his hunched shoulders as much as he could and eyed Colleen.

"Excellent question." Jenna looked at Colleen too.

She raised her hands in front of her face, palms out. "Stop it, you two. I can't deal with the pressure." Colleen clamped her jaws together and considered their options. Roz already had a car in Seattle. It didn't make sense to drive their other one down, plus it would take too long. Flying with Bubba was impossible. He looked too odd in his gnome form and his cat form didn't do well with the pressure changes. They had to teleport, which would seriously deplete their magic and mean they couldn't fight so much as a disembodied spirit for at least twenty-four hours after they arrived.

Jenna screwed her face into an apologetic scowl, apparently having come to the same conclusion. "Look, I'm sorry I'm not more help. There's something about that particular mix of earth, fire, and air that I always bungle."

Air whistled through Colleen's teeth. It had been so long since they'd teleported anywhere, she'd almost forgotten Jenna's ineptitude with the requisite spell. "How about this? You go down to the basement and practice. I'll get a few things together…"

"What do you want me to do?" Bubba asked.

"You can help me," Jenna said. "I'll do better if I have an object to practice with."

The changeling scrunched his low forehead into a mass of wrinkles. "Just don't get me lost."

"Even if she does, I'll be able to find you." Colleen tried to sound reassuring. She was fond of her familiar. In many ways, he was very childlike.

Heh! Maybe that's why I've been so reluctant to have a kid. I already have one who'll never grow up.

The bells around the shop door clanged a discordant riot of notes. "Crap!" Jenna shot to her feet. "First customer in two days. I should've locked the damn door."

"Back to cat form." Colleen flicked her fingers at Bubba,

who shrank obligingly and slithered out of clothing, which puddled around him. She snatched up his shirt and pants and dropped them back into the canister.

"I say," a strongly accented male voice called out. "Is anyone here?"

"I'll take care of the Brit," Colleen mouthed. "Take Bubba to the basement and practice."

She got to her feet and stepped past the curtain. "Yes?" She gazed around the dimly lit store for their customer.

A tall, powerfully built man, wearing dark slacks and a dark turtleneck, strode toward her, a woolen greatcoat slung over one arm. His white-blond hair was drawn back into a queue. Arresting facial bones—sculpted cheeks, strong jaw, high forehead—captured her attention and stole her breath. He was quite possibly the most gorgeous man she'd ever laid eyes on. Discerning green eyes zeroed in on her face, caught her gaze, and held it. Magic danced around him in a numinous shroud. Strong magic.

What was he?

And then she knew. Daoine Sidhe. The man had to be Sidhe royalty. No wonder he was so stunning it almost hurt to look at him.

Colleen held her ground. She placed her feet shoulder width apart and crossed her arms over her chest. "What can I help you with?"

"Colleen Kelly?"

Okay, so he knows who I am. Doesn't mean a thing. He's Sidhe. Could've plucked my name right out of my head.

"That would be me. How can I help you?" she repeated, burying a desire to lick nervously at her lips.

"Time is short. I've been hunting you for a while now. Come closer, witch. We need to talk."

CHAPTER 2

Duncan Regis eyed the grim-faced woman standing in front of him. She was quite striking with such stunning bone structure—high cheekbones, square jaw—she could have been a runway model. Her unwavering pale blue eyes held his gaze. Dressed in brown wool slacks, a multicolored sweater, and scuffed leather boots, she had auburn curls that cascaded to waist level. A scattering of freckles coated her upturned nose. Her lips would've been full if they weren't pursed into a hard line.

He knew he was staring, but couldn't help himself. Colleen was tall for a woman, close to six feet, with well-defined shoulders, generous breasts, and a slender waist that flared to trim hips. He smelled her apprehension and was pleased she cloaked it so well with a defiant angle to her chin and challenge mirrored in her icy stare.

Despite his earlier command, she didn't move. Annoyance coiled in his gut. He could summon magic and force her, but he wanted—no, make that needed—her cooperation. Compulsion spells had a way of engendering lingering resentments.

He smiled, but it felt fake so he gave it up. "I like women with spirit, but I'm used to being obeyed."

She frowned and tilted her chin another notch. "I'll just bet you are. I'm not coming one angstrom closer until you tell me why a Sidhe is hunting for me."

Surprise registered. He tried to mask it, just as he'd attempted to disguise himself in a human glamour. Duncan tamped down a wry grin, wondering if his second ploy had worked any better than his first.

"Not really." She tapped one booted toe. "I read minds. You'll have to do a better job warding yours, if you want to keep me out." Colleen exhaled briskly. "Look. Maybe it would be easier if you just told me why you're here. I'm sort of busy just now, and I don't have a bunch of time to spar with you."

"You don't have any choice."

"Oh yes I do." Anger wafted from her in thick clouds. Along with it a spicy, rose scent, tinged with jasmine, tickled his nostrils and did disconcerting things to his nether regions. He resisted an urge to rearrange his suddenly erect cock.

Colleen unfolded her arms, extended one, and pointed toward the door. "Out. Now."

"You're making a terrible mistake—"

"Maybe so, but this is my turf. If you force me with your magic, you'll have broken the rules that bind your kind. The covenant among magic-wielders is quite clear in that regard. No being with greater magic shall force one with lesser to—"

"I know what it says," he snarled. "I helped write it."

Duncan's temper kindled, but it didn't dampen the lust seeping along his nerve endings. Rules be damned. He could flatten this persnickety witch, or better yet, weave a love spell and bind her to him that way. Maybe he should do just that and have done with things. He clasped his hands behind him to quash the temptation to call magic. The movement stretched his trousers across his erection, making it obvious if she chose to look down.

Something dark streaked from the back of the shop and planted itself in front of him, hissing and spitting.

Gaia's tits. A cat.

He stared hard at it, but something didn't feel right. Maybe it wasn't a cat after all. Duncan reached outward with a tendril of magic. Before it reached the creature, Colleen bent and scooped it into her arms. The not-a-cat wriggled and growled, but she held fast.

"Leave him alone," she said through clenched teeth. "He's mine."

Duncan narrowed his eyes in sudden understanding. "Damn if it isn't a changeling. How'd he end up with you?"

Colleen tapped the scarred wooden floor with her boot toe, the beat so regular it could've been a metronome. "I asked you a whole lot of questions." She took a step backward. "But the only one I want to know the answer to is—"

"What the fuck are you doing?" Jenna wavered into view, having teleported in from somewhere. Her gaze landed on the cat. "Thank Christ! For a minute there I thought the little bastard got away from me."

"Jenna." Colleen snapped her fingers in front of the other woman's face. "The Sidhe have deigned to call."

Jenna straightened her shoulders and stared at Duncan. He stared back. What was it with these witches? Had they taken some sort of potion to supersize themselves? The new arrival made Colleen appear positively petite. As Jenna sidled closer to Colleen, he noticed part of her height came from high heels, but she was still an imposing woman.

"What does he want?" Jenna growled with all the warmth of a cornered alley cat.

Duncan cleared his throat. "I'm right here. You can ask me."

"Fine." Jenna put her hands on her hips. "What are you doing here?"

"How do you know I want anything?" he countered, trying to buy time to figure out what to do now. He hadn't counted on two witches—and a changeling.

Jenna cast a scornful glance his way. "Because if you didn't, Colleen would've shooed you out of here by now. You really do need to leave. We're busy."

He snorted. "Yes. Colleen made that abundantly clear." He looked from one witch to the other. At least his erection was fading. Crowds always had a dampening effect on his libido. Many other Sidhe thrived on group sex, but he'd never appreciated its appeal.

"Either tell us what you want right now—" Colleen moved toward him, cat still in her arms "—or leave. I'm going to count to three—"

"Maeve's teeth, witch! We're on the same side," he sputtered, nonplussed by her dismissal.

"Generally speaking—" Jenna exhaled briskly, dousing him in whiskey fumes "—that's probably true, but the Sidhe have never helped us."

Colleen quirked a brow. "No, they haven't." She narrowed her eyes to slits. "And I have this prescient feeling that Sidhe-boy here is about to ask for a pretty big favor."

"Sidhe-boy?" The dregs of his lust scattered, and he scrunched his hands into fists. "Show some respect."

"You're not respecting me," Colleen retorted. "I've asked you to leave—twice. No, make that three times." The not-a-cat finally twisted free. He skimmed over the distance to Duncan and buried his claws in his leg.

"Why you changeling bastard!" Duncan shook his leg. The thing didn't budge. Duncan bent, curled his hands around the furred body, and tugged. The thing bit him. Anger flashed.

Magic followed. The changeling howled and fell into a heap on the floor.

"Goddammit!" Colleen shrieked. "He was just trying to protect me. If you've killed him…"

"I didn't. He's only stunned." Duncan rubbed his ankle, glanced at the puncture wounds on his hand, and directed healing magic to both places.

Colleen sprang forward and gathered the creature into her arms. Duncan felt her magic quest into its small body. She blew out an audible breath. Cradled against her, shrouded by her long hair, the changeling mewled softly.

Duncan shook his head. He'd hoped to be subtle, accommodating, encouraging, so the witch would at least hear him out with an open mind. The time for that was long past.

"All right." He spread his hands in front of him. The flesh wounds on the one were already nearly closed. "I'm here because we've had problems with Irichna demons—"

"Christ on a fucking crutch," Jenna cut in. "Seems like they're on everyone's mind these days. We were just—"

Colleen rounded on her. "Shut up!"

"Oops. Sorry." Jenna held out her arms for the changeling. "I'll just take him and—"

"No." Colleen's voice was more like a growl. "You'll stay right here." She placed the changeling in the other witch's arms and turned to face Duncan. "I know you're Sidhe, but who are you?"

"Duncan Regis." He held out a hand. She ignored it, so he let it drop to his side.

"Regis, Regis," she mumbled, her forehead scrunched in thought. "Ruling class from somewhere in Scotland."

He nodded, impressed. "Northern England, at the moment, but the border has moved around a bit over the years. I do lay claim to Scottish roots. I didn't know witches studied our family lines."

"Witches don't, but I did."

"Any particular reason?" He was almost sorry he'd asked. She had strong feelings about the Sidhe, and he was about to find out why.

The changeling yowled, obviously recovered from his semi-comatose state. Jenna cursed and set him down. "Damn it! He scratched me."

Duncan thought about saying something cheery, like *welcome to the club*, but bit back the words.

Colleen rolled her eyes. "He wants to talk. There'll be no peace until he shifts." She flicked magic toward the creature winding itself between her booted feet. The air shimmered and a rather large gnome took form.

He rocked toward Duncan with a bow-legged gait that made him look like a drunken sailor. His open mouth displayed squared off teeth. "I'll tell you why she knows about you." The changeling drew himself to his full height of about three-and-a-half feet. "She came to the Old Country looking for help during the last demon war. You Sidhe were too high and mighty to get your hands dirty, so she had to settle for me."

Colleen snickered. "Not exactly the way I might have described it, but close enough. Hey, Bubba! Get some clothes on."

"Later," the changeling snapped without looking at her.

"Which of us did you approach?" Duncan made the question casual. Whoever turned Colleen down had broken another tenant of the covenant binding magic-wielders to come to one another's aid in times of need. He wondered if she knew.

"Of course I do." She sneered. "Your thoughts are as transparent as a child's. Even Bubba here—" she pointed to the changeling "—does a better job masking his mental machinations when he puts his mind to it."

"Thanks." The changeling glowered at her before transferring his attention back to Duncan.

"What kind of name is Bubba?" Duncan linked to the changeling, and was surprised by the complexity of his thoughts. Maybe the witches had been a good influence.

"You didn't have to just push your way in." The changeling screwed up his seamed face in disgust, but didn't draw back. "My true name is Niall Eoghan."

"Clothes," Colleen reminded him.

Bubba made a face at her, turned, and walked behind one of the display cases. When he emerged, he wore wide-bottomed green trousers and a black shirt.

"Irish." Puzzle pieces clicked into place, and Duncan transferred his attention back to Colleen. "You never did tell me who you'd asked for help. It appears they not only turned you down, but chased you across the Irish Sea."

"We left voluntarily," Jenna said.

Colleen's lips twisted in distaste. Whatever she remembered apparently didn't sit well. "We spoke with two Sidhe at Inverlochy Castle outside Inverness. They refused to give us their names, but said they were princes over your people. They heard us out and sent us packing. Gave us twenty-four hours to leave Scottish soil."

"I was all for staying," Jenna chimed in. "After all, we had passports."

"Was it just the two of you?" Duncan asked.

"Roz was with us," Colleen said.

Understanding washed through him. "Three. You brought three to maximize your power."

Colleen's full mouth split into a chilly smile. "We were under attack by the Irichna. Would you have done any less?"

"Probably not. So after we, that is, the Sidhe—"

"*We* worked fine," Bubba said flatly. "Unless you've decided to renounce your heritage."

Duncan traded pointed looks with the changeling. "Speaking of magic, you're stronger than any changeling I've ever come across."

"That's because you're used to our feeble Scottish cousins. They were stronger before you stripped their magic and diverted it for your own purposes."

"Enough." Colleen snapped her fingers. "Or I'll change you back into a cat. We don't need a history lesson just now." She shook her hair over her shoulders. The movement strained her sweater tighter across her breasts.

Duncan dragged his gaze elsewhere. "About the Irichna—" he began.

"We can't help you," Colleen said flatly.

"Why not? We'd pay you well."

"It's not a matter of money, although I'm not sure you could afford us."

"We have an, um, previous engagement," Jenna offered.

"Whoever it is, we need you more than they do." He looked from one witch to the other.

Colleen transferred her gaze to her boots and rubbed the bridge of her nose between her thumb and index fingers. When she looked up, the skin around her eyes was pinched with worry. "I'm not sure it's a matter of who needs whom more." She speared him with her pale blue eyes. "Do the Sidhe know why the demons are so much more active here of late?"

He debated how much to tell her. Given her ability to burrow inside his head, it was unlikely he'd be able to hide much. If he told her everything, though, it would certainly piss her off. Hell's bells, it annoyed the crap out of him.

"You haven't answered me," she pressed.

"No, we don't know. Not exactly."

Her nostrils flared. "You can do better than that. If you can't, the door is behind you." She folded her arms beneath her breasts. "Talk now or leave now. It's all the same to me."

"Not to me," Bubba grunted. "I think he should leave. Changelings in Scotland are weak because the Sidhe drained their magic to avoid another uprising."

Duncan drew the smallest of spells in hopes the topic would die. The changeling was correct, but it wouldn't be productive to haul that particular bone out to gnaw on. "That's very old history," he said mildly.

"And not the least bit relevant right now," Jenna snapped. "Colleen's right. Either spit out the truth, or get out of here."

"One," Colleen counted. "Two…"

"All right. All right." He spread his hands in front of him. "What do you know about demon history?"

"The Irichna work for Abbadon. Insofar as I know, they always have. Do things like that even have histories?" Colleen asked.

"Irichna are the only ones we've ever worried about," Jenna chimed in. "The other demons are more of an annoyance than life-threatening."

"Next question." Duncan swallowed hard, and embarrassment tightened his chest. "Do you understand why you have the power to corral the Irichna?"

Both witches stared at him. When they didn't say anything, he forced himself to keep talking. Heat rose to his face and the discomfort in his chest intensified. "It used to be us, but when the Irichnas' power cycle intensified about two hundred years ago, we recognized they were in one of their upswings."

An unpleasant light gleamed in Colleen's eyes. "I could guess the rest, but I don't have to because I see it in your mind. You foisted the demons off onto us."

He gritted his teeth, determined to tell them the truth, no matter what it cost his pride. "It's actually a little worse than that. We tried to get some other takers, but the Druids, undead, and weres turned us down, so we didn't ask the next candidate."

"You lily-livered bastards." Jenna pounded a fist into the nearest object. It happened to be a display case. Glass shattered.

"Guess Great-Gran's tale about being shanghaied by the Sidhe was truer than we ever guessed." Spots of color splotched Colleen's cheeks. She looked like she wanted to kill him, and Duncan didn't blame her. "What exactly did you people do to her?"

"Gene splicing. We actually augmented her power with our own, using a dominant pattern so all her offspring would have at least some level of power." Duncan cringed at the defensive tone beneath his words. At the time, he'd bought into the concept wholeheartedly.

Today, he castigated himself for being a fool.

Colleen looked right through him. "You broke the covenant. It says we get to choose something like that—not have it stuffed down our throats."

He swallowed shame. It tasted acrid, bitter. "I'm sorry. It seemed like a win-win. Witches got more power and we—"

"Offloaded one of the Sidhe's major responsibilities, which is to keep Earth safe from demons," Bubba spoke up.

Duncan felt as if he'd been shot through the soul. Out of the mouth of a changeling... "I can't change what's happened. How many of you are there?"

"You mean of great-Gran's descendants?" Colleen quirked a brow. He nodded. "Three."

"That's all?" Duncan didn't even try to modulate the shock waves roiling through him. The Sidhe council had been certain there'd be more like forty or fifty. "What happened to all of you? You don't live as long as we do, but still…"

"What do you think?" Jenna flapped her fisted hand at him. "Demons killed us."

Guilt smote him, joining shame and remorse. "I'll help you."

"It's a little late for that," Colleen muttered. "Even Sidhe can't raise the dead."

Duncan shook his head. "When I first got here, you tried to get rid of me, said you had something important to do. I'll go with you. Help you. It's the least I can do to make up for…for…"

He couldn't get the words out. Sidhe meddling had set the altered witches up for what looked a whole lot like genocide. Because he couldn't bear the fury and accusation in their eyes, he looked away. Even the changeling hated him, with good reason.

He could almost hear gears turning in Colleen's head. She drew near him and he left himself undefended, wards down. She placed a hand on his head and sent magic auguring into him. Her touch was deft, if not terribly gentle. When she moved her hand, he fought an urge to grab it back.

"You told the truth," she said, sounding surprised. "You can come with us. If things are as bad as I think they are, we'll need all the help we can get."

"I don't agree," Jenna spoke up.

Colleen's mouth twisted as if she'd tasted something bitter. "Beggars can't be choosers. If we're not careful, there won't be any demon assassins left."

Not on my watch. Duncan made a silent vow between himself and the gods before bowing formally toward both witches. "Thank you. I will do everything I can to ease your burden."

And see it shifted back onto my people, where it belongs.

CHAPTER 3

"Sit if you'd like." Colleen pointed at a chair. "Jenna and I need to get a few things together and then we'll leave. How are you with teleporting?"

He shrugged. "Fine. How far are we going?"

"Seattle."

"Piece of cake."

He grinned. It transformed his face into something boyish and quite beautiful. Colleen blinked and looked away. If she didn't keep her guard up, Duncan just might inveigle his way past barriers she'd had up for longer than she cared to think about. As it was, a warm, fluttery feeling started in her belly and spread outward. She warded herself so he wouldn't notice.

Jenna made a grab for her arm. "Come on," she growled, voice gravelly. Colleen gritted her teeth. Maybe the other witch had intuited her thoughts.

"I'm going with you," Bubba announced. "Who knows what *he'll* do to me if I stay here." He stared meaningfully at Duncan. The Sidhe looked away and settled himself in a leather easy chair next to one of the display cases.

"Are you done talking?" Colleen eyed Bubba.

The changeling looked solemn. "It's easier to transport me when I'm a cat, huh."

"Much."

"Okay. I'll chase down a mouse or two while you and Jenna get what you need. At least that way, I won't be hungry when we get there."

"Fat chance." Jenna rolled her eyes. "You're always hungry."

Colleen flicked magic his way before he could come up with a snappy retort, watching to make sure the transformation was complete. She picked up his clothes, wondering why she bothered keeping him covered. The changeling didn't mind being naked. Someday, she'd ask Bubba why the Sidhe had felt the need to drain the Scottish changelings' magic, but today wasn't the day. Tomorrow wouldn't be, either. Until they got the Irichna on the run, there wouldn't be time for anything else.

"Colleen." Jenna's voice vibrated with impatience, and Colleen understood the other witch wanted her alone so they could talk.

"Coming." She trailed after Jenna across the shop and through the kitchen curtain, pulling magic as she went to shield their conversation that hadn't happened yet. Jenna headed for the narrow, hanging ladder staircase that led to a bedroom nested beneath the old building's eaves. Colleen followed her up. By the time she got there, Jenna was half-naked and in the midst of changing into traveling clothes.

Not a bad idea. Colleen opened the two drawers where she kept a few things, and eyed their contents. She and Roz shared a ratty, older house on the southern outskirts of Fairbanks. Jenna lived above the shop. For all her earlier hurry, Jenna remained ominously silent as she dressed and chucked a few things into a rucksack.

Colleen unlaced her boots and toed them off. She pulled on warmer pants and a long john top, layering fleece over it. "You wanted to talk about something. What?" She stuffed a stout rain jacket into a small pack and bent to get her boots back on.

Jenna stalked to where Colleen stood and bent so close Colleen saw her shoulder muscles bunch. "We. Do. Not. Need. Him." She bit off each word. If she'd been a cat, every hair would've stood on end. "Besides, you want to fuck him."

Defensiveness tightened her stomach into a sour ball. "So what if I do? He's gorgeous. Any woman would want him, plus I can't remember the last time I got laid."

"I can. Beltane."

Colleen counted on her fingers. "Okay. Six months, give or take a few days. And the last time before that was the Beltane before. It's not exactly like I'm a slut."

Jenna shook her head. "That's not it. I wouldn't care if you entertained a different man every night." She crossed her arms over her chest and winked lewdly. "It might actually improve your disposition. You're not thinking, Colleen. The Sidhe is a complication. We're stretched so thin, we don't need anything else to deal with right now."

Colleen blew out a tired breath. "He may be a complication, but we need some kind of help," she countered. "I wanted to talk about this before Roz left, but somehow the opportunity never presented itself. Besides, when the demons aren't very visible, I suppose I always pretend they're gone for good."

"Talk about what?" Jenna's mouth curled suspiciously.

"The Irichna. We know they've been getting stronger. Especially after that last skirmish in California a few months back, where they killed five of us." She scrubbed the heels of her hands down her face and gazed at Jenna. "Bottom line is they want us dead. All of us. Once we are, they'll have free rein here on Earth."

Something flickered in the depths of Jenna's hazel eyes. It was gone so fast, Colleen couldn't name it, but it might've been fear. The other witch straightened. "I still say we can get all the help we need from other witches."

"Christ! Be reasonable, Jenn. Other witches are great, but they're helpless against Irichna. The demons may have killed five of us, but thirty other witches died defending us in that disaster."

"I haven't forgotten."

Colleen's temper, never on a long fuse, stirred to life. They needed to leave, not have a philosophical discussion about what the demons were up to. It went against the grain to force her will on anyone, but she focused her gaze so Jenna had to look at her.

"Once we're not in their way anymore," Colleen enunciated every word, words that could've doubled as shards of glass in her throat, "the Irichna will open Abbadon's gates, and all those hideous creatures will flood Earth. Panic will overcome everyone and everything. World governments will declare martial law—"

"And it won't make a fuck's worth of difference at that point, because we'll be dead. Goddammit, Colleen, I know all that. So does Bubba. He's worried changelings will be the first ones targeted."

"What?" Shock raced through her. Bile splashed the back of her raw throat, and she swallowed painfully.

Jenna nodded. She looked more sad than angry, and lines formed around her eyes like wagon wheel spokes. "He told me that all the old creatures were vulnerable. Virtually all of them have demon blood, and it's a two-edged sword. It makes them valuable allies when we battle the Irichna, but it also draws demons to them like a lodestone."

"Why didn't he tell me?"

Jenna shrugged. "I think he tried, but you soft-soaped him."

A confusing welter of feelings rocked her, but the one that swam to the top was guilt. Sometimes months went by when she didn't pay much attention to the changeling, beyond making certain he had food.

"Yeah." She had to take a breath to force the rest of the words out. "I can see where I haven't been very present for him." She squeezed her eyes shut. Damn good thing she didn't have kids. She'd probably end up on some sort of Child Welfare list for being a crappy mother.

"I'm ready to go." Jenna draped the strap of her bag over one shoulder. "About the Sidhe… I don't trust him. They hung us out to dry. He as much as admitted it."

"Yes, I went into his head. He didn't fight me at all. He feels bad about what happened to us, almost as shitty as I do about ignoring Bubba."

"Maybe he made it up. He could have ulterior motives."

Colleen tossed a couple more tops into her bag, zipped it shut, and shouldered it. "No, he was telling the truth. What kind of ulterior motives could he possibly have?"

Jenna raised a hand, waved it around in the air, and shrugged. "I don't know. Maybe he'll divert our teleportation spell."

"Not likely. If you understood that spell better, you'd know it has zilch in the way of stealth elements. I'd know immediately if he were trying to route us back to the U.K."

Color rose to Jenna's face and stained her sharp-boned features. "Touché."

Colleen grunted. "We've been up here so long, he may have given up on us and left."

"A girl can dream. Let's go. I'd like to get there while Roz is still alive."

Colleen's eyes widened. "That bad?"

"I couldn't tell, but when's the last time you remember her asking for help?"

"Good point. She's not the type." Colleen walked to the trap door, faced inward, and grasped the sides of the ladder. She slithered down it, hurrying so Jenna, who was right above her, didn't step on her hands.

"I'll spell the place," Jenna muttered and raised her arms with her hands positioned palms up. "Won't take but a minute, and it should keep most everybody but a really strong mage out." She chanted softly, calling on the four directions and four elements to protect their shop. Colleen tossed some magic into the mix. Jenna didn't need any help with simple spells like this one, but nervous energy frizzled Colleen's nerves, and it felt better to do something beyond simply standing there.

Bubba rocketed out of a dark corner. He meowed loudly and wove around their feet. Still feeling remorseful, Colleen bent and scooped him into her arms. He purred loudly and leaned into her as she straightened. Jenna dropped her arms.

"Ready?" Colleen asked.

Jenna didn't answer. She pushed past Colleen and strode through the curtain into the main part of the shop. Colleen heard muffled cursing and wondered if it was because Duncan had left —or because he was still there. She sent a thread of magic questing outward, and was ridiculously pleased to sense the Sidhe's energy.

Stop! Just stop. He's probably got half a dozen paramours back in the U.K. waiting for him to come home.

She clutched Bubba closer, made sure her bag was solidly around her shoulder, and followed Jenna into the front room. "We're all set," she said brightly.

"Excellent." Duncan flowed to his feet. The mage light hovering near him flickered and went out. "How do you want to do this?" He quirked a brow.

"Huh?" Confusion rocked her. "Do what?"

"You asked for my help with teleporting. Are you just coming along for the ride, or—"

"Sorry," she cut in, voice brusque to mask her sudden feelings of stupidity. "I was hoping you'd lend power to my spell since I know where we're going."

He walked two paces closer, his green gaze boring into her. "I don't mind doing the whole thing. Send me an image of our destination, and I'll run with it."

She tried to look away and couldn't. *Damn!* His magic was hella strong this close. Because she hadn't been careful, he'd mired her in a spell. Fury vied with helplessness, and she gritted out, "Stop that right now." Bubba writhed in her arms and hissed.

Duncan had the grace to look embarrassed. "Sorry." The aura dancing around him shrank to a pale glow.

Jenna stalked between them, glowering. "I told you this was a shit-for-brains idea. He just tried to force you with compulsion."

Colleen rounded on the other witch. "You think I can't recognize a spell I just got trapped in?"

Duncan rolled his eyes. "Oh for the love of Titania, would the two of you back off. Yes, I drew magic." He threw his hands in the air. "Guilty as charged, but my motives were pure. It takes a lot of magic to teleport. It will deplete you far faster than me. You didn't say much about why you're racing to Seattle, but you don't have to. What if the Irichna are lurking where we exit? If you drain a great deal of your own power getting there, you're dead ducks."

Colleen felt her face heat. She'd worried about exactly the same thing. "Thanks," she mumbled.

"Why are you thanking him?" Jenna demanded. "If it

weren't for the Sidhe, we wouldn't be in this mess. He as much as admitted it."

"I wish you wouldn't talk about me as if I wasn't standing right here." Duncan's tone sharpened and he sounded annoyed. "The operative pronoun is *you*, not *he*."

"Now who's splitting hairs?" The air around Jenna crackled with suppressed power.

"I thanked him because he's trying to take care of us, me in particular," Colleen ground out. Bubba flexed his claws. One caught her forearm and she yelped.

"Bubba doesn't like anything about this," Jenna observed.

"He's reacting to the tension in this room," Colleen retorted. She shifted the cat to her other arm to free a hand and rubbed her temple where a headache had started. "And he's right. We're headed off to do battle with something ancient and powerful. We all need to be on the same page, or it's as good as showing up wearing signs that say, *Just Kill Me Now*."

"Good you understand that," Duncan muttered. He turned to Jenna, sheathed the remainder of his magic, and bowed formally. "I understand why you don't trust me. You have many reasons not to. Exigencies make unlikely bedfellows. I honor the covenant betwixt magic wielders. It's why I offered my assistance. There are other Sidhe like me, honorable mages I can call upon for help. I was waiting until we arrived at our destination before I did so." He hesitated a beat, and then went on. "It is unwise to marshal troops before one knows exactly what is needed."

Jenna crossed her arms over her chest. "Why are you doing this?"

Duncan looked askance at her. "I've asked myself the same question. Actually, I spent the time the two of you were upstairs considering why I didn't just get up and leave."

"What'd you come up with?" Colleen asked.

Bubba leaned toward the Sidhe as if his answer was important. The changeling had always had good instincts. Colleen tuned in with her third ear to listen carefully. Sidhe were notorious for trick answers, multi-layered affairs that were meant to obfuscate and blur things, while sounding perfectly reasonable on the surface.

"Several things." Duncan held up a finger. "One. I had no idea there were so few demon assassins left. Two—" a second finger joined the first "—I, er, finally understood that my people hung you out to dry and it annoys the hell out of me."

"So it would've sat better if there were still forty of us?" Jenna cut in. "Or fifty?"

Color stained Duncan's bronzed skin. "To be brutally honest, probably." He held up a hand. "Let me finish. It would mean the Sidhes' genetic manipulations weren't responsible for killing off so many of you."

"If it killed even one of us, would that have been acceptable?" Colleen couldn't help it. She leapt into the fray.

Duncan made a fist and pounded it into his open hand. "No." He narrowed his eyes. "What we did was wrong. I see that now. Mind you, many of my fellows won't agree with me. They view all humans, even those with magic, as expendable, but we will have allies among the Sidhe too."

Colleen rolled his last statement around in her head. "*We,* huh? You make it sound as if you've signed on for the long haul."

"I have." He cleared his throat. "I never finished giving you the reasons I didn't simply walk out of your shop. If the Irichna win—and they nearly have—we'll all face the consequences. I fear it will be the end of magic here on Earth. As it is, many Sidhe have faded into the *Dreaming,* or taken up residence on the borderworlds."

"Scarcely the end of magic." Colleen clanked her teeth together, so pissed off she wanted to kill something. Bubba twisted in her arms and she loosened her hold, realizing she must have been squashing him. "Merely the end of *good* magic. The Irichna and their minions have plenty of the other sort."

"Exactly what I meant." Duncan inclined his head toward her. "Thank you for the clarification. I came here hoping to gather maybe ten or twelve of you to deal with a fairly major Irichna uprising in Cumbria." The muscles in his jaw worked. Colleen wasn't sure if he was angry or embarrassed, or maybe a little of both. "Sidhe have always been fairly insular. We don't pay much attention to the goings on in the human world."

"So you didn't know how strong the Irichna had gotten," Colleen said flatly. "Or how depleted our ranks were."

"In a word, no. I'm shocked, furious, dismayed…" He blew out a breath. "None of that matters. Feelings are an indulgence. What's important is figuring out how to get those bastards on the run. It didn't make sense for me to leave two of the three remaining demon assassins alone to face what might be Armageddon, while I teleported back to the Old Country, hat in hand, to solicit aid on your behalf."

"Maybe I misjudged you," Jenna muttered. Her face and voice had lost their closed-off aspect.

A corner of his mouth turned downward. "Actions speak louder than words, witch."

Colleen snorted. "Yup, and talk is cheap. I've been chafing at the bit to get out of here, but these last few minutes were time well spent."

"Agreed." He aped a Scottish brogue. "Ye canna fight alongside a man ye doona trust." Duncan held out a hand. Both witches shook it. Bubba walked to the Sidhe on the land bridge formed by their arms and cuddled against him before jumping to the floor.

"What's that? An old Celtic saying?" Jenna asked, but she was smiling.

"You might say that." Duncan straightened his shoulders. "Now send me an image of where we're going."

"You do that—" Jenna trotted to the door "—and I'll lock up."

Colleen slapped her forehead with a palm. With everything that had happened, the last thing on her mind was securing the shop. "Thanks," she murmured and sent a mental picture of the Witches' Northwest headquarters to Duncan.

CHAPTER 4

uncan gathered his spell and waited for Jenna to return, so he could drape it around all of them. More than anything, the changeling's vote of confidence touched his heart. He made himself a vow to be worthy of the creature's trust, particularly in light of what he'd always considered a heavy-handed reaction to the Scottish changelings' very minor rebellion. The Sidhe could have opted for a stern talking-to. Even at the time, he'd thought draining their magic more than a little draconian.

Colleen clucked to Bubba, and he leapt into her outstretched hands. Jenna killed the dim shop lights and took her place between him and Colleen.

"Double check our destination." Duncan fired his mage light so he could see their faces, and sent an image to both witches. At their nods, he launched his casting and felt the weightlessness he associated with teleporting. Though it was risky, he planned to bring them out in the basement boiler room of the multi-story structure that housed the Witches' Northwest Coven headquarters.

He'd considered an outdoor location, but he wasn't familiar enough with the area to guarantee someone wouldn't see them pop out of the ether. If that happened, the sort of panic it would engender was sure to attract the Irichna, if they were as close as Colleen and Jenna thought.

Too late, he considered weaponry. Seraph blades were ideal. There were several in the Sidhe armory, deep beneath Penrith. In a pinch, an iron blade dipped in holy water worked almost as well, but not for the Sidhe. Iron was poison to them. He wondered what the witches used. Meanwhile, brick walls formed around them. Water dripped down the bricks in a steamy cascade. Duncan held his spell in place, ready to whisk them away if he sensed danger.

"It's okay," Colleen whispered into his ear. "Only us here."

"How'd you determine that so fast?" Impressed by her ability, he kept his voice low and reeled in his casting. The basement looked to be one large room. Perched in one corner like a prehistoric beast, an ancient boiler creaked, snapped, and groaned as it sent steam heat elsewhere in the building through an elaborate ducting system that disappeared through the low ceiling.

"Demons have a particular stink about them," Colleen said. "You can't not notice it."

"Isn't that the truth?" Jenna muttered. She turned in a tight circle and ended up facing Duncan. "I'm guessing you've never actually confronted one."

She hadn't asked a question, she'd told him. Duncan winced, mostly because she was right. He tried to modulate defensiveness that rose to the fore. "I've fought other enemies."

"But not Irichna." Colleen glommed onto Jenna's insinuation like a homing pigeon. The skin around her eyes furrowed with worry. "We've fought other enemies too. Nothing ever quite prepares you for the reality of an Irichna demon."

Duncan sent his magic spinning outward. Not only were there no demons anywhere near, they had the entire basement level to themselves. Bubba wriggled in Colleen's grasp, and she set him down. He streaked to a far corner of the boiler room. Muted squeaks from the hapless mouse he'd caught told the rest of the story.

"We're not in any immediate danger," Duncan said. "Take a few minutes and sketch out what I need to know about the Irichna."

He felt Colleen draw a ward about them and was glad he'd spared her what would've been a magic-draining teleport. Jenna moved beyond the ward's invisible circle. "I don't need to hear. I already know about them."

Despite her warding, which was solid, Colleen moved close enough to talk into his ear, and she kept her voice so low he had to focus his power to hear her.

"Abbadon works under Ba'al. Together, they rule every level of Hell but the ninth. The Irichna are their henchmen, created from spirits of the worst humans. Some of the dead beg to become Irichna because they crave power, even in death, and they glory in sowing pain and dissent. The murderers, rapists, sadists, and those utterly lacking a conscience. Abbadon picks a few and they become Irichna."

"But if they're already dead, how—?"

"Oh, they don't remain in Hell. Abbadon moves them to one of the borderworlds as soon as they've been created. They wreak their havoc from there."

"I don't understand. Abbadon rules in Hell. Why wouldn't he want his minions near at hand?"

She waved him to silence. "Stop asking questions and listen. Irichna are impervious to pain. They fear nothing. The sole way to get rid of them is to drive them into the lowest circle of

Hell. It's the only one Abbadon and Ba'al haven't been able to get their claws into.

Duncan nodded. "I get it. Abbadon doesn't keep Irichna in the underworld because they'd be right next to their doom in the Ninth Circle."

She gave him a thumbs-up sign, but her eyes held a flat, hard edge. "Righto. It's too bad. They'd be ever so much easier to get rid of if we didn't have to drag them all the way through Hell every single time. Anyway, there's a gateman guarding the lowest circle…" She paused to take a breath. The skin between her eyebrows creased, forming a vertical line. "I can't tell you his name, it isn't allowed, but he knows Jenna, Roz, and me. When we show up, he opens an iron portcullis and helps us trap the demon inside." She pursed her lips. "Once the gate slams shut, we're done, and we head back up to try to trap another one."

"I was thinking maybe a Seraph blade…"

She shrugged. "Might work for you. That's a Sidhe tool."

"Oh, come now. We're not the only ones who use them."

"That's true. Druids and priests like them. They never caught on with witches, probably because we can handle iron, so we don't need magic knives. Besides, the only sure way to get rid of an Irichna is in the lowest pit in Hell. Maybe a blade could help immobilize them, so they aren't such a pain in the ass on the way down." She shook her head. "If it only shut them up, it would help. I swear, it's like listening to a Siren's song sometimes. Take your average compulsion spell, and ratchet it up tenfold."

She shuddered. He resisted an impulse to wrap his arms around her, although she wasn't asking for comfort. A day might come when she'd turn to him for solace, but it certainly wasn't happening now.

"Thank you." He inclined his head. "That was helpful. Most

of what I know about them comes from the borderworlds they control."

"You'll have to tell me sometime. Not now. I know less than nothing about that aspect of their existence." Colleen ground her teeth together. "Fuckers. Maybe they'll all die out, so I'll never have to concern myself with them ever again."

Duncan didn't think it likely, but he kept his thoughts to himself.

"All done?" Jenna inquired much too cheerily for the words that had passed between him and Colleen.

Colleen nodded. "He got the basics, but nothing will prepare him for the reality of an Irichna, other than facing one down without puking, fainting, or turning tail and running like hell."

Duncan squared his shoulders. He was so convinced he wouldn't do any of the above, he didn't dignify her words with a comment.

"You think I'm joking?" Colleen's face was scant inches from his, and her warm breath seared him. He shook his head. "Good, because I'm not. All of us have done all those things. Fortunately, it was when there were a few more demon assassin witches to bail us out until we got our shit together."

"Enough." He spread his hands in front of him. "We need to see if we can locate your friend."

"She's not here," Jenna said flatly. "I looked while the two of you were talking."

"Do you have a way to track her down?" Duncan asked.

Colleen grinned and pulled a cell phone out of her pocket. "Pretty low tech stuff in the midst of magic, but the Irichna don't understand cellular technology."

"Thank Oberon for small favors," he muttered and watched while she moved beneath one of the high windows that dotted the basement's brick walls and punched numbers on the small display, including the speaker key so everyone could be included in the conversation. He followed her so he could hear over the noise the boiler made, without drawing additional magic. From the sound of things, he'd need every ounce of power at his disposal. It wouldn't be wise to squander any magic unnecessarily.

Roz picked up on the first ring. "Holy godhead," she shouted. "It took you two fucking long enough to get here. What'd you do, jump the slow boat to China?"

"Behave yourself, sweetie," Jenna called as she walked closer. "We have company."

"What? Who? Is that why it took you hours to show up?"

"We, um, found a Sidhe along the way. Or he found us. Showed up in our shop." Colleen held the phone a little farther away and turned its volume down.

"They're the reason we ended up demon assassins in the first place." Roz's voice was shrill. "Send him back to wherever the fuck you found him."

"I don't think he'll want to go," Colleen said. "At least you could reserve judgment until—"

"Why the hell would I want to do that? The only good Sidhe is a dead Sidhe."

"Goddammit, Roz." Jenna stepped right next to the phone. "You don't like it much when people say that about us. And they do."

"Where are you?" Colleen cut in.

"Right where I told you I'd be. At Coven HQ."

"But I tried to find you, and couldn't," Jenna protested.

"I would hope not. I have personal wards deployed, and I'm in a warded room."

"We're in the basement. Which floor are you on?" Colleen asked.

"Top one. There's a conference room in the attic." Roz sounded slightly less surly.

"Be there soon." Colleen tapped the end call button and pocketed her phone. "Interesting that Roz knew about the Sidhes' role in our demon assassin abilities." She shot Jenna a puzzled look.

"Humph." The other witch snorted. "Even more interesting she never mentioned it to us before."

Duncan started to gather magic to teleport up a couple of levels, but reconsidered. It would probably be better to walk. That way, he could get a sense of how the building was laid out.

When Colleen caught his eye and nodded, he realized she'd been in his head again. It was eerie how she could manage it without him knowing. Usually, even full-blooded Sidhes had trouble catching him unaware.

She made a clucking noise with her tongue against her teeth, and Bubba came at a dead run. He threaded his body around her legs, purring furiously. "You'll be safer as a cat until we get past the first floor," she told him. The changeling retreated with a short hiss that seemed to indicate he didn't agree.

"It must be frustrating for him when he can't talk," Duncan ventured.

"And frustrating for us when he can," Jenna cut it. "He has opinions about everything." Bubba meowed furiously and took a swipe at her ankle, but she jumped out of the way.

"Come on." Colleen beckoned. "Let's see if we can't find a back staircase or something. As I remember this building, the whole front of the main floor is leaded glass windows, tucked in between Victorian fancywork and turrets, with a clear view of the street. It would be better if we could avoid it."

Duncan gazed around the basement and saw two doors. One sat atop a half staircase and clearly led to the outside. He headed toward the other and depressed the latch. The door rattled against its stops, but didn't move. Locked. He sent magic snaking outward and the deadbolt withdrew from its hidey-hole in the doorframe.

"Neat trick," Colleen murmured.

"Yeah, we'll have to look him up next time we decide to case a joint." Jenna smirked.

"Ssht." He shot a meaningful glace at both witches. Bubba was right next to where the door would open. "You too." He tapped the cat's back. "No racing off anywhere on your own. You stay with us."

He eased the door open and swept the part of the hallway he could see with seeking magic, tuned to sense fell creatures. Satisfied nothing lurked nearby, he pushed power beyond his immediate visual range. A faint tinge of evil pinged back at him, but it was days' old. He stepped onto a linoleum-floored hallway, lined with cinderblock walls. Florescent lights recessed into the ceiling every twenty feet or so cast a sickish yellow pall over everything.

The building smelled old. Nothing like buildings in the U.K., but mold, mildew, and disrepair were evident. Apparently building maintenance wasn't high on the witches' list of priorities.

"Watch it, sweetie," Colleen hissed into his ear. "If you criticize anyone, they'll force you to leave."

He made a grab for her arm and tried telepathic speech, unsure if she'd be able to hear him. *"Why are you living in my mind?"*

"Because I'm still not positive you won't betray us."

He bristled at the implication he'd be anything less than honorable. He'd offered himself up in an honest effort to right old wrongs, and her attitude grated. "If you'd rather, I can leave right now," he said stiffly.

"Bully idea," Jenna muttered, but Bubba clawed his way up Duncan's side and settled in the crook of one arm.

Colleen shook her head. "No. Like I said before, we need all the help we can get. Besides, Bubba seems to trust him and he doesn't give that away lightly."

"Maybe the changeling's just pissed at you," Jenna said, "and hoping for better luck with the Sidhe." The cat hissed, snarled, and reached a paw toward Jenna, claws extended. "All right, all right." She took a step back. "I didn't mean it."

Duncan blew out a tense breath. Though he'd tossed out the option of ditching them, the last thing he wanted was to leave Colleen's side. To avoid further arguments, he started down the hall, still holding the changeling. The creature felt warm against his side.

"How'd you know to go left?" Jenna asked. "Supposedly, you haven't been here before."

"I haven't. Another door at the far end of the boiler room looked like it went outside. If we're hunting for an inner staircase…" he let his words trail off. Duncan wasn't used to justifying himself to anyone, but then no Sidhe did much explaining, no matter what their social standing.

He came to an opening where risers led upward and sent magic ahead, checking for danger. Witch energy bombarded him. "Looks like your friend got tired of waiting."

"Patience never was her long suit." Colleen snorted back what sounded like laughter.

Privately, Duncan didn't think any of the three witches could be poster children for anything that smacked of submissiveness, but he kept his mouth shut and hoped to hell Colleen wasn't in his thoughts.

Heavy soled boots sounded on the bare, wooden stairs. A

woman with black hair so long it reached her knees came into view. Strong Native American features, with high cheekbones and a beak of a nose, graced her ageless face. She was the same height as Jenna, which pegged her around six feet four, but she had a much more slender build. Discerning dark eyes caught his gaze and held it. She wiped her hands on the sides of her tattered blue jeans and tugged a nondescript, gray sweater lower around her hips.

"Yeah, baby." Roz licked her lips suggestively. "I can see why they didn't toss you out on your ass. Colleen didn't say you were drop dead gorgeous."

"Give it a rest, Roz." Jenna pushed in next to Duncan. "They all are."

"You're doing it again," Duncan said through gritted teeth.

"Doing what?"

"Talking about me as if I were an object and wasn't here."

"Really? Was that what I was doing?" She swept her upper body into a mock bow. "Can you ever forgive me, Sidhe, sir?"

"Can we just go on upstairs?" Colleen's voice held a weary note. "There's an enemy here, and it's not us."

"It's why I came down." Roz turned and headed back up the stairs. "To show you this staircase."

Except I found it just fine without you.

Duncan muffled his thoughts. If Colleen could invade his mind like a stealth fighter, no doubt these other two could also. Hadn't they said Roz was more powerful than both of them put together? He thought about it and realized they hadn't actually said that. He'd plucked it out of Colleen's head.

Duncan followed Roz's swinging hips up the stairs. Apparently Colleen wasn't the only one guilty of mind eavesdropping. He considered apologizing, but since she hadn't been aware of him culling through her thoughts, maybe he should leave well enough alone. Bubba curved closer to his body, purring. Colleen's energy pulsed behind him, and he felt Jenna drawing up the rear.

They passed landing after landing. When the stairs stopped on the fifth one, Roz pushed a banded metal door open. He felt the iron from several inches away. Good thing witches weren't sensitive to it. It made his stomach roil and his nerve endings scream.

The witch held the door open far enough that he could scrunch through without actually touching it. He fought back nausea and muttered, "Keeps the demons out, huh?"

Roz eyed him sharply. "Yes. And other riff-raff too."

He bit back a pointed retort. He was here as the witches' guest, sort of, but not a particularly welcome one. It would behoove him to remember that. Roz led the way down a short hallway. The farther he got from that goddess-blasted metal door, the better he felt. Maybe when it was time to leave, he'd teleport out of here and avoid the door altogether.

"In here." Roz pointed through a curved doorway. Mercifully, this door was plain old wood.

Duncan walked through and stopped. The large room tucked beneath the old house's eaves might have been cozy, with its dark wainscoting and a bevy of colorful cushions scattered about, if a dozen witches dripping power weren't staring malevolently.

An aged crone with long, gray braids and a seamed face stood and pointed a gnarled finger at him. Black robes flowed around her as if they had a life of their own. "Start talking, Sidhe, and I warn you. Anything less than the unvarnished truth in response to our questions will earn you a session in an iron clad room with the Irichna we just caught."

He looked from one hostile face to the next and kicked himself for his impetuous Sir Galahad moment back in Colleen and Jenna's shop. Duncan squared his shoulders. "I will do my best, but if you ask for things my people hold secret, I will not be able to oblige you."

The witches looked from one to the other. Something passed among them, but magic barred him from their minds. "We shall see." The crone thrust her chin out. "First question: Roz said you showed up at her magicians' supply shop in Alaska. Why? What's really going on in the Old Country?"

"That was two questions."

"So?" She tilted her head. Rheumy, dark eyes pierced him. "Answer them in order."

CHAPTER 5

Colleen took Bubba from Duncan. She used the opportunity of snagging the cat from his arms to touch him briefly and infuse confidence he'd get through the interrogation. She knew better than to go up against Mathilde, head of the Witches' Northwest Coven and one of the most powerful mages Colleen had ever known.

She set Bubba down and released him from his cat form. The changeling capered around the floor until Mathilde pointed a finger at him and he shrank to Colleen's side, wrapping an arm around her leg. She dug in her bag and handed Bubba a set of clothes. He made a sour face, but clambered into them.

Duncan responded to a spate of questions. Some had to do with why he'd come hunting for her, but others went way back to the original Sidhe decision to conscript witches for what had originally been Sidhe dirty work: keeping Earth free of demons. *Crap!* Had she and Jenna been the only witches who didn't know about that? Apparently tired of standing, Mathilde sank back onto her chair, but kept the questions coming.

Something tugged at Colleen's innards. With a shock, she realized she felt proud of Duncan. Not only was he holding his own in an intimidating environment, but he was also doing his best to be as forthright as he could. This time, he had to know she was inside his head because she made her presence obvious, but he hadn't chastised her or chased her out. No, he'd accepted her. A warm glow started in her belly. To her surprise, she welcomed it.

"So." Mathilde's harsh rasp of a voice dragged Colleen from her musings. "Let me make certain I've got this right, Sidhe. One lousy Irichna demon showed up in the Cumbrian countryside, and your kinsmen panicked and sent you after a demon assassin witch."

Color stained Duncan's cheeks; a muscle twitched in his tight jaw. He looked the witch square in the eyes and nodded. "There were actually five demons, but close enough. And I have kinswomen as well."

"Pfft." Mathilde waved a dismissive hand. "Why couldn't you take care of the demons yourself?"

"Because we gave that power to you."

"Explain." Mathilde bit off the word.

"I thought I already did. We gave certain witches the genetic ability to herd demons into Hell."

Mathilde narrowed her eyes. "Yet you didn't retain it for yourselves?"

"No. Apparently not."

"Why?"

Duncan breathed out a tense sigh. Colleen saw in his mind that he was grateful he didn't actually know. "I wasn't privy to that part of the discussion."

"Would you have agreed with it if you had been?"

Duncan spread his hands in front of him. "I'm not sure how

that's relevant. I was a different man two hundred years ago. I might have agreed, or not. I can't extrapolate backward." His forehead crinkled. "As I recall, there was something about shape shifting ability that went along with that particular genetic sequence. The Sidhe have never been comfortable with altering our forms. Besides, we have other magic we can potentially tap to fight demons. It's somewhat unpleasant, though, and hard to control, so none of us have used it for a long time."

Bubba sidled to Duncan's side and faced the witches ranged in a semicircle. "I trust him. He's sorry about what happened to the changelings."

"Ach." Mathilde made a chopping motion. "You're like a child, swayed by the first bit of kindness tossed your way."

Colleen felt Bubba's anger flare. She made a dive for him, but was a hair too late. The changeling launched himself onto a heavy oak table right in front of Mathilde. "Do you know what changelings are?" he demanded, waving a clenched fist in the witch's face. "How we came to be?"

Colleen scooped him up. He writhed in her arms. "Not now," she snapped and handed him to Duncan, who'd stepped to her side, hands extended.

Colleen's temper was growing thin. She moved between Duncan and the witches' tribunal. "We're wasting time. An Irichna requires transport out of here. How many others have you seen? What's the body count, and is it just here that demons have targeted us, or are there other locations?"

Mathilde furled her gray brows, apparently surprised by Colleen's sudden barrage of questions. "The attack seems widespread throughout the northwest corridor, even up into British Columbia. As of yesterday, forty of us were dead all through the region, half from this Coven. Other than the demon we captured, five more have been spotted—we think. They change form so frequently, it's impossible to be certain."

"Which means there are probably more than five," Jenna, who'd been uncharacteristically silent, murmured.

"At least two are lurking close by," Roz said. "I did a little reconnaissance after I talked with Jenna earlier."

"Are you certain the one you have bound is still here?" Colleen asked.

Mathilde nodded. "It's trussed with iron manacles in an iron clad room. Last I looked in on it, it was moaning we'd flayed the skin off its bones."

"I thought you said they didn't feel pain." Duncan quirked a brow at Colleen.

"They don't," she said shortly. "That was just a ploy on its part. Maybe someone would feel sorry enough to unshackle it."

"We should get it out of here," Jenna said.

"Right," Roz seconded. "Sooner the better. Then we can concentrate on the pair I sensed in the park across the street."

An idea took form. Colleen said. "How about this? It certainly won't take all of us to shepherd one Irichna into Hell. I'll take Duncan and Bubba. It can be a practice run for our new Sidhe ally. I'll be able to see, up close and personal, how he feels about the ability his people foisted onto us."

She shot him an appraising glance. Duncan tipped his head her way, obviously rising to the challenge. Bubba worked his way out of Duncan's grasp and ran to her, his pique at Mathilde apparently forgotten, or at least shoved aside for now.

"I didn't release the Sidhe," Mathilde pointed out. Getting back to her feet, she crossed her arms over her chest.

"I wasn't aware I was your prisoner." Duncan kept his voice mild, but his hands curled into fists.

Colleen clenched her jaw in frustration. Hell no, Duncan

wasn't the witches' prisoner, or even a detainee. She wanted to slap Mathilde. Anything to wipe the smirk off her face. Her questions were an indulgence. She had to know as much. They had more important fish to fry. Besides, she, Roz, and Jenna weren't part of the Witches' Northwest Coven, so technically, they didn't owe any particular allegiance to Mathilde, or her witches.

Forcing a direct confrontation would be a mistake, though, no matter how badly Colleen wanted to tell Mathilde off. Instead, she half bowed to the other witch. "Please consider releasing him. I'm certain Duncan will make time for further questions, as your *guest*, once the immediate danger has been defused."

Mathilde smiled dangerously with lots of teeth and zero warmth. "I will hold you to that, Sidhe." She jabbed a finger toward Duncan.

Colleen held her breath, afraid Duncan would argue that her offer of a further brain-picking session didn't bind him to anything. All he did was nod noncommittally and say, "Ready whenever you are, Colleen."

Bubba trotted toward the door. Duncan sauntered after him, and Colleen followed. Out in the hallway, he half-turned. "Which way are we going?"

"One floor down." She shepherded them back through the iron door to the stairwell, noting how Duncan cringed away from it.

"Pretty intense group," Duncan said. "Reminds me of Sidhe gatherings."

She swallowed a snort of laughter. "Magic wielders never were known for having a sense of humor."

"Some of us do," Bubba piped up as he trotted between them. "We'll have to get the demon out of the metal room without Duncan," he went on. "Iron makes him sick too."

"Why doesn't it bother you?" Duncan asked the changeling.

"It did. The thing with being a changeling, is that part of our makeup is, well, changeable. Colleen infused enough witchiness into me, I lost my sensitivity to iron."

"He wouldn't have been much good as a demon-hunting sidekick if he got sick every time we got near metal," she said and pushed open the door to the hallway leading to the demon containment area. "Say—" she shot an appraising glance Duncan's way "—maybe that was the real reason your kin wanted out from under Irichna hunting so badly."

"Probably not. We have seraph blades." Duncan sucked in a breath. "Tell me what to do so I'll be a help, not a hindrance."

Part of her was pleased he recognized the wisdom of asking for help in a situation he'd never faced before. Her estimation of him edged up several notches. Most men, regardless of species, would rather die than ask for assistance.

He chuckled, obviously having read her thoughts. She blushed. "Sorry," she murmured. "That might have been slightly sexist."

"Maybe, but truer words, er thoughts, were never spoken. On a more serious note, you'll have your hands full, and I don't want to be a burden."

"Thanks. Bubba and I have done this enough, we'll have things under control, but it won't feel that way. That shape shifting element you recalled earlier?" He nodded and she went on. "Expect me to change form, probably several times. The Irichna can morph into an infinite variety of things. If I couldn't match them, form for form, I'd be dead meat."

"Me too." Bubba sounded excited. "I can be lots of things besides a stupid cat."

Colleen kept them at the end of the hallway—as far from the iron-shielded room as she could—for Duncan's sake. She needed to tell him a couple more things before they packaged the Irichna for transport.

"Ward yourself." She swallowed hard. "And then ward yourself again. Be ready for anything. The Irichna will recognize you for what you are, and it will see you as the weak link in the chain. It'll turn itself inside out trying to seduce you. If that doesn't work, it'll tug hard on whatever sets you off. Ignore it. No matter what."

"Got it."

Colleen shook her head. "No. You only think you do. Wait for the main event to unfold before you pat yourself on the back—about anything."

She thumped her index finger into his chest. "If you let any part of the demon inside your mind for any length of time, you'll never be quite sane again, not even after it's buried in the bottom of Hell."

Colleen watched Duncan's face, gratified when fear flickered in the back of his clear, green eyes. She jabbed him again with her finger. "It's good for you to be afraid. Never, never underestimate an Irichna. The demon will delve for your weaknesses. Once it finds them, it'll exploit your weak underbelly."

"But you're immune?"

"Of course not. I just have more practice than you. And I can shape shift. My animal forms aren't as susceptible to demon flattery—or insults. Bubba and I will herd the demon. This would go a lot faster if you kept your wits intact and teleported us to the gates of Hell."

"I can do that."

Colleen lifted her chin. "Excellent. Once we pass the first gatekeeper, you can follow us down, but stay out of the way. Demons become frantic the closer they get to their doom. They know there's no exit from where we're taking them."

"Got it," he repeated somewhat stiffly. "I'm to ward myself and provide transport."

"What else?" She fought an irrational impulse to draw him close to her. He was so beautiful, and so vulnerable. He'd never be the same after today, but she didn't have the heart—or the words—to tell him. Besides, he'd never believe her. Until afterward.

"I'm supposed to ignore the demon. How hard could that be?"

"You'll be surprised." She began stripping off her clothes. The changeling did too.

"What are you doing?" His gaze roamed over her appreciatively. Lust darkened his eyes to emerald.

"Stop leering at me. I'm not doing this because I want sex. I'll be shape shifting. I don't want to rip my things to shreds. This way, I'll have something to put on once we're done—and so will Bubba."

She held out her hands for the changeling's clothes, stuffed everything into her small rucksack, slipped it around her neck, and pushed it out of the way so it hung down her back.

"Come on sweetie." She clucked to Bubba and headed down the hall. "Let's get this show on the road."

DUNCAN WATCHED HER WALK AWAY. He wound wards about himself and tried to move past the tightness in his gut and throat. He should be protecting Colleen, not the other way around. The longer he spent with her, the more he admired her courage and wanted to stake his claim as her mate. The other Sidhe would pitch a fit. They didn't mate outside the blood, but he didn't care. He'd never found a woman he felt anything for except momentary sexual release. Colleen was bright, funny, brave, and knew how to use her mind. She'd done a hell of a job maximizing what he'd always considered inferior magic too.

Maybe it's not as inferior as I thought.

A door clanged shut. Iron filings wafted down the hall. Despite his antipathy for iron, he hoped the demon was still manacled. Duncan's eyes widened. Walking—no, make that sashaying—next to Colleen, was an unbelievably beautiful woman. Blonde curls framed a perfect face. Soft blue eyes were bordered by thick, dark lashes. A sheer, gossamer gown billowed about her, giving him a clear view of high, taut breasts tipped by rosy nipples, and a lithe form. Blonde curls nestled in the vee between her legs.

"Sidhe." She reached for him. "One of the beautiful ones. Come to me, sweetling. It's been long since I've had a man. I can fulfill your every desire." Her mouth curved into a lascivious smile. "And perhaps a few you didn't even know you had."

Duncan's libido was still raw from Colleen's nudity. His cock sprang to life. As hard as it ever got, it strained against the front of his trousers. His fingers itched to cup the blonde's breasts and slip into the moistness hiding between those luscious thighs. Heart beating triple time, he stood rooted in place, his mind an absolute blank. Everything fled but the need to fuck the woman cooing to him.

"Duncan!" Colleen's voice cut like a bullwhip. Why couldn't she sound more like the lissome blonde? "The traveling spell? Now, goddammit!"

His mind was fuzzy. He tried to ask Colleen what traveling spell, but his tongue felt thick and stupid. Despite the blonde still being twenty feet from him, she had some way to caress his cock. He felt her gripping him, stroking him. He'd never been so hot. All he could think about was release...

"Oh for Christ's fucking sake!" Colleen growled and flicked her fingers at him.

His cock jerked in his pants, and semen pulsed out in burning gouts. It happened so fast, he could scarcely believe it. He hadn't lost control of his penis since he was a very young man. His head cleared immediately. Chagrin followed as soon as he could think straight.

Colleen rolled her eyes. "Men! You are so fucking weak. Tighten your ward. If you think the Irichna actually looks like a blonde bombshell, think again, buddy. It scented you from the other end of the hall, hid its own stench, and arranged its appearance accordingly. Hell, even I don't know what these things really look like."

Shame swamped him. He amped up his wards until he just barely had enough power to teleport them. Maybe his wet crotch would remind him to pull himself together. "I'm sorry," he mumbled, and readied a traveling spell.

"Hurry." Bubba nipped at the blonde's feet. "It's about to change again."

Duncan tossed a spell around them and herded the group through a rough portal. Once they were inside the small space, things disintegrated rapidly. The Irichna grew. Scales formed. Its beautiful face turned reptilian, along with the rest of its body. Duncan understood its bite was deadly poison without being told.

Colleen shifted right along with it. In moments, two dinosaur-like creatures hissed and spat at one another. Bubba puffed into some variant of a scaled creature Duncan had never seen. It had a snake's body and four arms with pincers. Bubba curved himself around the Irichna and cut through its scaled hide with his pincers. The demon screamed as black blood jetted out, drenching all of them.

Duncan poured more power into his teleport spell. The

sooner they got this thing delivered to Hell, the better. He thought about how easy it had been to divert him from their goal and felt ill. Colleen was right. Men could be slaves to their cocks. He shook off disgust with himself. No excuses. Despite everything she'd told him, he hadn't been ready for the reality of evil incarnate. Watching the scaled creatures do battle with each other while avoiding being whipped with talons, tails, or horns, fine-tuned his focus damned fast.

The black edges of their traveling portal grayed out. He sent a prayer to Danu they'd come out at the right place, that the Irichna hadn't somehow subverted his spell, along with his manhood. He'd only been to Hell's entrance once, but he never forgot it. The river Styx had run black with blood after a battle where the Sidhe mowed through wargs and trolls. The cries of the dead still haunted him.

He checked his coordinates as the gray lightened and breathed a small sigh. Not relief, not yet. That would come once they were shut of the demon. But at least the next things they should see were the huge wooden gateposts that marked the border between the land of the living and the land of the dead.

"Good job." Colleen spoke into his head.

Duncan was certain her reptilian mouth was incapable of speech. Her tail lashed from side to side, and she gripped the Irichna with both forelegs. The demon buried its fangs in Colleen's shoulder. Blood flowed, staining her scales red.

"Nooooo," Duncan shrieked and sent a killing blow right at the demon.

It bellowed in pain, but didn't let go. Duncan struck again. All he could think about was stopping the demon from pumping more poison into Colleen. Bubba slithered to where the demon's mouth held Colleen's shoulder and attacked it with his pincers. It let go with a grunt and tried to swipe

Bubba off, but the changeling managed to stay out of the demon's grasp with a string of creative maneuvers.

Colleen straightened. She clapped a taloned foreleg over her wound and it began to close before his eyes. Duncan started breathing again. She could heal herself in beast form, apparently even from poisoned bites. Thank the gods. He sent jolts of power zinging toward the Irichna to keep it occupied while Colleen got her bleeding under control.

She focused her odd, reptilian eyes on him. *Its bite would kill you. Stay away from it. I'm good. I can take over again.*

With everything that was going on, she was still trying to take care of him. Duncan wanted to hug her, scales and all. *"Thanks."*

She was obviously still in his mind. *"Wait until I'm human again."*

The gates of Hell opened inward, creaking and groaning. A robed and cowled figure, with a dead haze where eyes should have been, motioned them through. Colleen and Bubba tag-teamed the demon, herding him. The gatekeeper helped, and Duncan funneled magic at the demon's hindquarters. It seemed to do the trick. The abomination stumbled through with Duncan on its heels.

He remembered what Colleen said about things escalating between here and the bottom and gritted his teeth. He didn't see how they could get much worse, but she'd been right about the demon being more evil than his worst imaginings, so likely she was right about this too.

The gates screeched shut behind them. What would happen if the demon got loose in Hell? "I bloody, fucking well don't want to find out," he muttered and adapted his vision to the ever-present dimness of the underworld.

The demon morphed back to the blonde again. This time he was ready for it and shuttered himself against its honeyed tones. Colleen regained her human form, except for her eyes, which blazed with a fey light. Bubba stayed a snake. He moved like lightning, able to defeat the demon's efforts to drag him from its body.

Their trip through the circles of Hell lasted forever, and was over in moments. Time shifted crazily. The demon shrieked and clawed and tore at whatever it could lay its long-nailed hands on. The dead cawed protests in return. Shades coated the demon, but it tore its way through all of them, as it shifted from bear to wolf to cougar to a sleek, black jaguar. Colleen shifted right along with it, doing her best to shield the dead from further harm.

The big cat was beautiful, as beautiful as the blonde had been in its own way. Duncan recognized how dangerous his thoughts were and what a slippery slope they led to. "It's not a cat. Not beautiful." He repeated the words through clenched teeth.

He was still saying them when the creak of another gate grated loud in his ears. Colleen, Bubba, and the gatekeeper, another robed and hooded figure, forced the demon to his doom.

"You can still save me, beautiful man."

Duncan stared through the gloom at a goddess incarnate. Titania, queen of the Faerie Court, beckoned to him through a shroud of silver hair. He fought a compulsion spell, stronger than any he'd ever known. Finally, just when he feared he was lost, he managed to tear his gaze away. The gate slammed into deep holes in the ground. Duncan half turned, gasping to move air past a thick place in his throat. His palms ached and he realized he'd clenched his hands into fists so hard, his nails had drawn blood.

"Come on." Herself again, Colleen motioned to Bubba. The changeling glittered, shifted back into his gnome's body, and ran to her. She gathered him into her arms and turned to Duncan. "Ready to leave?" Weariness underscored her words, but at least the madness had left her eyes.

"More than ready." He reached for her hand. She grasped it and together they floated upward. He knew better than to try to deploy a teleportation spell from the bowels of Hell. It would boomerang right back at them.

CHAPTER 6

Hell ejected them in short order. The underworld knew who belonged there—and who didn't. Colleen caught her breath as the enormous wooden entrance gates swung shut behind them.

"Let's get away from here," she murmured as she shucked her small backpack, pulled clothes from it, handed Bubba's to him, and dressed. "We don't have to go far, but…"

"I understand." Duncan nodded. He drew a ragged spell about them. "How about if I aim for the nearest point where Earth coincides with this borderworld?"

"Fine by me." Because the borderworlds weren't static, they could come out anywhere, but it didn't matter so long as they put some distance between themselves and Hell.

One of her fears had always been that the gatekeeper to the Ninth Circle would tire of his role as jailer and come after her before she'd cleared the underworld, demon in tow, shrieking, "Take it with you." She had no idea what would happen if she refused, and she didn't want to find out.

Colleen picked Bubba up again and moved to Duncan's

side. The changeling's body shuddered against hers. "You were a hero," she told him.

"This one was hard," Bubba said.

Colleen nodded. The changeling was right. This had been the most difficult trip she'd ever made to Hell with a demon. Were they getting stronger? If that was true, she didn't like thinking what it might mean for her, Roz, and Jenna. Duncan's magic rose around them. A sun swept vista, dramatic counterpoint to Hell's dusky atmosphere, appeared almost immediately.

She gazed at sagebrush, rolling hills, and dried, packed earth. "Thank God. No people."

"I'm not sure why," Duncan sounded almost as wiped out as she felt, "but it worked that way last time I left Hell too. Maybe the gods want to make certain mortals don't discover too much about the kingdom of the dead."

"Maybe so." She sank onto warm earth, glorying in how alive the dirt felt against her body. Insects buzzed and birds chirped in the near distance. Bubba wriggled and she let him go. The changeling staggered a few steps away, lay down, and curled onto his side. He'd sleep until they were ready to leave, which was fine. He'd earned it.

Duncan settled into a cross-legged sit across from her, his face serious. "First off, I'm ashamed about my poor showing when you escorted the demon down that hallway at the witches' headquarters." He shook his head and the corners of his mouth curved into a disgusted moue. "I don't fully understand what happened, but I couldn't think about anything except..." His cheeks splotched with color and his voice trailed off.

"Getting laid," she filled in for him. "Yes, I know. I've been there. The Irichna are incorrigible. They'll use any tool they think will turn us into instruments that dance to their bidding."

Should I tell him?

Colleen felt her face heat and figured she was almost as rosy as Duncan. "Er, it was me who made you come. Not the demon. I figured if you got it over with, there was at least a slender hope I'd still be able to bring you with us."

Humiliation scored his features, and lines formed around his eyes. "You would have left me behind." At her nod, his jaw tightened. "I don't blame you. You had a hell of a time with that thing. You didn't need me mucking up the works."

"Look." She held his gaze. "I've been there. I've puked. I've nearly caved in to their manipulations. The first time I saw one, I was with a dozen other witches. I bolted. They had to haul me back and force me to face the thing. I was shaking so hard, it was all I could do to remain upright."

Admiration kindled behind his eyes. "Even knowing that, you took a chance on me." His lips curved into a soft smile. "Thank you."

Colleen bit back a snort. "You came very close to making me sorry."

"I'll do better next time."

Her eyes widened at his words because she understood there would, indeed, be a next time. "Does that mean you're still volunteering to help? I thought surely after...well, after actually coming into contact with those bastards—"

"—I'd exit stage left with a bunch of convenient excuses?" he cut in. Duncan edged closer and took one of her hands in his. "I'm not that easy to get rid of." An odd expression flitted across his face, but it was gone before she could interpret it. "I've never fancied myself a coward. How could I live with myself if I fled back to my nice safe life, knowing I left you to face those...abominations by yourself?"

She bristled and tried to draw her hand away, but he held

fast. "Bubba and I, along with Roz and Jenna, have been doing just fine. I don't need crumbs from your table."

He tipped her chin with his other hand so she had to look at him. "Well now, you don't have a choice in the matter. It's not *crumbs from my table*. You're an amazing woman. I haven't been able to think of anything but you since you emerged from that curtain at the rear of your shop."

Her stomach did an odd little flip-flop. "What exactly are you saying?" Her lips trembled. She smushed them together, hoping he hadn't noticed.

He brushed a knuckle over her mouth. "I'm starting to care about you, Colleen. A lot. I admire your courage, and your mind. You're beautiful and strong and fearless. I can't tell you how panicked I was when the Irichna bit you."

"My animal forms have power. It took me years to discover just how much."

"I noticed." He tightened his hold on her hand. "You can heal yourself."

She nodded. "Most of their poisons don't bother me, either."

"Like I said, beautiful, strong, and fearless."

His words sent shivers racing down her spine, but she shook her head. "Scarcely fearless. It's just I've figured out how to function when I'm so scared I can't see straight."

"Doesn't matter."

He caressed her lips again and then moved closer. His mouth hovered over hers, and she understood he was giving her a choice to push him away, to say no. His warm breath soothed and excited her at the same time. Despite a tiny voice telling her that maybe this wasn't such a good idea, she tilted her mouth upward.

He closed his lips over hers in a kiss so sweet and so electric, it set her soul ablaze with all the feelings she'd denied for most of her adult life. Colleen wound her arms around his neck and pulled him close. She opened her mouth to his questing tongue and sparred with it, enjoying the taste and feel of him. He had a musky, exotic scent that eddied about them. It stoked her lust, and she inhaled hungrily, anxious for more of what felt like an aphrodisiac.

He wrapped her in an embrace and held on as if she were the only thing that mattered in the world. From time to time, he lifted his mouth from hers and murmured Gaelic endearments. At least she supposed that was what they were, since she didn't speak the language, beyond what she needed to cast spells.

Heat rose in her nether regions, and her nipples pebbled into peaks. Duncan drew her onto the sandy ground so she lay next to him, never breaking their kiss. He ran his hands down her back and cupped her ass, pulling her close. She felt the hard length of him press her thigh and positioned herself so she could rub against him. Desire pierced her, so hot and yet so sweet, she didn't fully recognize what she was feeling. She understood sex, pure and simple, but this felt like the beginnings of ever so much more. Duncan wasn't a man she could fuck and forget.

Alarm bells sounded deep in her mind. She wriggled away, gasping and panting, as she tried to sort her jumbled thoughts. "Can't," she managed.

He reached for her, his green eyes blazing with desire. "Why not? You're scarcely a maid."

Colleen rolled to her hands and knees and then tucked her legs under her and sat, trying to ignore the insistent throbbing between her legs. "That's not it. I never cared about any of them."

A soft, slow smile spread over his face, intensifying his beauty until she had to look away. "It's more than just caring about you." His breath hitched. "If I were honest, I'm falling in love."

Alarm bells rang louder. She held up both hands, palms out. "No. Not a good idea. What I do is dangerous. I may not be alive next month. Hell, I may not be alive tomorrow."

"Colleen." He moved close enough to drag one of her hands out of the air and enclose it in his. "You don't get it. I want to share your life. All of it. Today was a proving ground. I'll face down the Irichna with you. And I'll do my damnedest to get some of my people to help. Gene splicing is a two way street. We can take back the sequence we foisted off onto you." His expression turned thoughtful. "It would be a hell of a lot quicker than the three of you who are left trying to make new witches, and then waiting for them to grow up."

She twisted her mouth into a wry grin. "No shit. Not that any of us ever got anywhere close to having babies."

He shook his head. "It doesn't appear your witch ancestors did, either. The ones who died didn't leave progeny, or at least not many. Why?"

"At first they did, or there'd have been even fewer of us. At least potentially, we live a long time, nothing like the Sidhe, but still..." She shifted to a more comfortable sit, but kept holding his hand. "Think about it. How could any of us be out of the action for the nine months it would take to be pregnant? Let alone the years required to care for a babe?"

A familiar sadness flashed through her. For the first time, she dared to acknowledge it. Before, she'd always shoved it aside as an indulgence. She scrubbed the heel of her free hand up her forehead. "I suppose I never expected to live out a witch's four or five hundred years." She winced, but kept going, determined to tell Duncan the truth. "I didn't even think I'd live long enough to risk becoming a mother." She leveled her gaze at him. "Today was hard. Harder than it's ever been.

I'm not certain I would have had enough power to teleport Bubba, the demon, and me into Hell and fight with it too. If you wouldn't have been there, today may well have sealed my doom. Depends how generous the gatekeepers were feeling. Sometimes they've helped me."

He nodded solemnly. "We're not certain quite why, but the Irichna have grown much more aggressive—and stronger too. That's one of the reasons I searched you out, although I was shocked by how few you were once I found you. We, witches and Sidhe, need to work together. I'll impress that on the Sidhe council. The days when witches alone could hold Earth safe from the Irichna have passed."

"Yesterday, I might've argued with you. Today, not so much." She paused for a beat, so used to being alone, it was a struggle to ask for help in any form, let alone consider accepting it. When she'd hatched up her idea to bring Duncan along on today's journey, she'd assumed he'd decide dealing with demons was too hard...

He quirked a brow. "So you set me up to get rid of me?"

"Yes. No. For God's sake, stay out of my head!"

"But it's instructive to know what you're thinking." He tightened his hand around hers and she started. She'd nearly forgotten he was touching her.

"My thoughts are a jumble. I'm not sure what I'm thinking."

Duncan narrowed his eyes. "I know what's in your head—and heart." She opened her mouth to protest, but he shook his head. "Let me finish. You're a lot like me. Stubborn, willful, determined. I've never been one to let anyone close enough to either help me or hurt me. You're the same way. It's why we'll make a good pair. We understand one another."

She did a quick soul-search and recognized wisdom in his words. Colleen glanced up and was snared by his gaze. She tried to look away, and then realized she didn't want to. Being lost in Duncan's beautiful green eyes was exactly where she belonged.

"You're right that I'm torn," she murmured. "Part of me wants to snap up your offer and another part is scared to death that once I do, I'll be vulnerable and lose the edge I need to be effective against the Irichna."

"Maybe we'll be stronger as a pair." Something danced behind his eyes. A challenge.

She rose to it instinctively. "I'm willing to find out." Colleen clapped a hand over her mouth. "I can't believe I just said that."

He grinned. "I can."

~

Duncan scooted closer and wrapped his arms around Colleen. She leaned into him. The feel of her firmly muscled body was unbelievable. He buried his face in her rich auburn hair and inhaled the jasmine-rose scent of her. He held her for long moments, letting the rest of the world drop away. They'd have little enough in the way of time to explore one another until the demons were banished. It felt important to maximize right now, nestled in each other's arms.

She splayed her hands across her shoulders and turned her full lips up for a kiss. Because he couldn't resist, he closed his mouth over hers and explored her mouth with his tongue.

His cock hardened, reminding him of his earlier fall from grace. He wanted Colleen with all his heart and soul, but he wanted their first lovemaking to be perfect, not a byproduct of having survived by the skin of their teeth. He chuckled. Nothing like a near brush with death to drive desire.

She pulled away from his kiss. "What's so funny?" Her mouth was soft, eyes dreamy with heat-lust. She reached between them and cradled the bulge of his erection in her hand. He groaned and pushed against her, wanting nothing more than to strip off her pants and bury himself deep inside her body.

"I'm just happy." He reached down and uncoiled her fingers from him.

She quirked a mischievous brow. "I could make you happier. This time, I'd let nature run its course."

He swallowed hard. Her offer was damn near irresistible, but… With enormous difficulty, he moved a few inches away. "I want you. Never doubt that."

Her eyes clouded, and the line of her mouth hardened. "There's a *but* in there. But, what?" She drew back, pale blue eyes never leaving his face. He sensed a truth spell hovering between them.

"Guess I can't sugarcoat anything."

"That was the idea." She curved two fingers and waggled them. "Out with it. I'm a big girl. I can deal with the truth—whatever it is."

He took a steadying breath, and then another one. "I want to court you, make you my mate—"

Joy lit her face, followed by uncertainty. "But you hardly know me."

"I know you better than you think. More importantly, I know myself. I'm slightly over a thousand years old. If I haven't come to a level of self-knowledge where I recognize my life's mate when she finally shows up, then I should be ashamed of myself."

She cocked her head to one side. "There's a mutual attraction between us. A damn strong one. So we need to spend time together to figure out if it's real and has the stuff to go the distance."

"There are those elements," he agreed, "and a few more

you're not aware of." The truth spell deepened until it pricked him. "Hey! I've told the truth."

"Not all of it," she prodded.

No, not all of it.

He glanced down, and then shook his head and looked at her again. "Sidhe don't tend to look on matings outside our blood favorably." She gestured for him to go on. "I have to return to the Old Country for two reasons. To try to secure assistance with the demons, and to lay my heart at Titania's feet and ask for her blessings on our marriage."

"Don't you think you might want to wait on that last until we're certain we want to get married?" A corner of her mouth twitched. "For one thing, you haven't asked me, nor have I accepted." She sucked in a breath. "And I wouldn't right this minute. Not until we've put in more time together."

Heat swept from his chest to the top of his head. For a moment, he felt like a bumbling youth. "I want to do this right. To do that, I must be free to court you." He shut his eyes for a moment and then opened them, begging her to understand.

She didn't disappoint him. "What if Titania refuses?"

"Then I have some hard decisions to make. It would mean I'd have to walk away from my people, be an outcast. It would also end my immortality. Not immediately. I'd still have a few hundred years, give or take."

"Kind of a lot to give up." Her eyes shone with unshed tears, but she blinked them away. Her truth spell scattered like so much dust.

Fierce possessiveness rocked him. He never wanted to be a source of pain for Colleen. Never. He leaned forward and crushed her to him. "No matter what. We'll work something out." He stroked her hair. "Believe in me."

"I want to." Her voice was muffled against his neck. "It's hard. I've spent years only believing in myself."

"That would make two of us." He tightened his hold on her. "I don't know why we found one another now, but it feels like a gift and I'll do whatever I can to hold onto it." He peeked into her mind and answered her next thoughts. "Despite the fact we barely know one another, you're who I've been waiting for. You're the reason I don't already have a mate."

"I want to believe you so much, it's scary." She drew away, her eyes shiny with unshed tears, and squared her shoulders. "Enough emotional stuff for now. We need to firm up our plans. You're going to the U.K., and I'm going back to Seattle with Bubba."

"Will you stay there?"

Her forehead creased in thought. "I'm not sure. I'm not overly fond of Mathilde, but it would be political suicide to shine her when she's asking for our help. Witches stick together."

He swallowed a snort. "Yeah, just like the Sidhe. We'll tear one another to shreds, but let an outsider utter one disparaging word…"

"…and everybody jumps him." She offered him a crooked smile.

Her mouth looked so inviting, he kissed her, but lightly. She was correct, it was past time to leave. He tapped the tip of her nose with a finger. "How about if you give me your cell number?"

"What? No telepathy?"

"All magic draws attention."

She grinned and rattled off a string of numbers that he committed to memory before giving her his number in return.

CHAPTER 7

Colleen hugged the sleeping changeling closer. For once, she'd left him a gnome during teleport because she hadn't wanted to wake him. They'd just come out in front of the Witches' Northwest compound, an impressive restored Victorian, complete with turrets and a tower. Thank God it was dark. No shrieks, so her sudden appearance hadn't startled any mortals. From the position of the moon and stars, she guessed it was long past midnight. She'd planned to emerge inside the building, but she was tired and her casting had gone slightly awry.

At least I got us to the right place—sort of.

Bubba stirred in her arms. She placed her mouth against his ear and told him to be quiet. He nodded against her chest and wrapped his arms around her neck. After a rocky beginning when she'd first coaxed him into joining her, the changeling had come to trust her. She laid her cheek against the top of his thick hair and inhaled his clean, earthy scent. Bubba was like a cross between a protective pet and an adolescent child. They had the occasional tense moment, but she hoped he didn't harbor misgivings about throwing in his lot with her.

Colleen sent what little magic she had left spinning in a rough circle and breathed a ragged sigh when she didn't sense a demon. Maybe the pair Roz found had left—or they'd been captured while she was gone. That would be even better, so long as one of the other women escorted them to Hell.

"Pssst."

Colleen spun around. Frantic, heart pounding, she raked the darkness and settled on the open front door of the huge Victorian. "Roz. You scared the crap out of me."

"Get in here," the other witch snapped. "What the fuck are you doing outside our wards?"

"It's a long story." Colleen trudged up the wooden staircase to the front door. *Christ!* There must be fifty steps. Some of them might've been illusion, but she was breathing hard when she got to the top.

Roz grabbed her arm and almost chucked her inside, slamming the door behind them. Bubba snarled and Colleen set him down. He immediately latched onto Roz's tatty jeans with a grimy hand and said, "You should be nice to Colleen. We had a hard time."

Roz cocked her head to one side and nailed Colleen with her dark gaze. "What happened?"

Colleen shrugged. "What didn't? Do you mind if I sit down?" Without waiting for an answer, she pushed past the other witch into a well-appointed living room that matched the building's Victorian exterior, and fell onto a plush, padded sofa with needlepoint upholstery. Bubba followed her, staying close. Her head spun from weariness, and she bent to unlace her boots, toeing them off so she could lie down. She'd no sooner plumped an occasional pillow beneath her head when Roz dragged a chair close, but the other witch didn't sit.

"Be back in a minute," she said.

Colleen must've dozed because time slid away before Roz returned bearing a tray with a bottle of whiskey, two glasses, and fruit and cheese chopped into uneven pieces on a china platter. The corners of Colleen's mouth twitched as she wondered just what Roz's foray into domesticity had cost her. Of the three of them, Roz was most likely to buy all her meals out.

"Don't say anything," Roz warned as she dropped the tray onto a nearby coffee table.

"How about thanks?" Colleen made a sleepy grab for a cheese wedge and stuffed it into her mouth. Bubba closed a grubby fist over several food items, all of which found their way to his mouth.

"Humph. I'd forgotten how much you eat." Roz patted the changeling's shoulder and trotted away. "I'll be back with more cheese and some bread."

"Double thanks, Roz," Colleen called after her. "Bubba saved my bacon. He deserves anything he wants."

"Got it."

In less than five minutes, Roz was back with enough food for a small army. She set an overflowing plate in front of the changeling, along with a bottle of beer. Colleen poured herself a couple fingers of whiskey. The liquor warmed her. She was just as wiped out, but didn't care as much.

"Where's Jenna?" she asked.

"Asleep," Roz said shortly. "Good thing. Mathilde and her crew are pretty hard to take." She shook her head. "Tell me how things went with the demon—and the Sidhe. I notice he's not with you." She shot a meaningful glance at Colleen.

"Great observational powers." Colleen winced at the acid in her voice. "Sorry, Roz. None of this has been easy." She pushed to a sit and raked her fingers through her tangled hair. "Let me start at the beginning…"

Half an hour later, the platters of food were picked down to nothing, and she'd drunk another few fingers of Irish whiskey. Colleen was a bit tipsy, but she felt decidedly better than she had when she and Bubba first arrived. After a total pig-out, the changeling had fallen asleep in an overstuffed chair, with his long fingers intertwined over his belly.

"So you're what? Engaged?" Roz's normally deep voice cracked on the last word.

Colleen threw her hands into the air. "I don't know." She gathered her scattered thoughts. "I thought it would be better for us to spend a bunch of time together, decide what we want… But he just sounded so formal. Said he wanted to do things right, to court me, and that he needed permission from Titania, or something like that."

"Is that why you didn't fuck him yet?"

Colleen's cheeks warmed. Roz had a forthright aspect that took some getting used to. "Let's just say it wasn't because I didn't offer." Tired as she was, heat licked at her nether regions, and she pressed her thighs together.

Roz drew her dark brows inward. They looked like startled bird's wings cutting across her tanned face. "Do you love him?"

"I think I could, given time. God knows, he's hot enough to set any woman's blood on fire. He kisses like an angel. And I can't wait to run my fingers over his body. Between those shoulders and that high, tight ass—"

Roz grunted and made a chopping motion with one hand, but she was smiling. "TMI, even for me. Does he have any traits that make you think he might be useful out of bed?"

"Now that you mention it, he made a good recovery after that inauspicious start I told you about. I was really proud of him."

"Sounds like he did a hell of a lot better than you did the first time you faced an Irichna."

Colleen rolled her eyes. That was the trouble with family and close friends. They remembered all of your faux pas. "Thanks. As if I needed a reminder. I actually told him the same thing."

"You admitted you squalled like a Banshee and took off as if all the dogs of Hell were after you?" When Colleen nodded, Roz said, "Son of a bitch, must be love if you'd disclose something like that."

"Enough about me." Colleen stretched out full length on the sofa again, sighing with pleasure at being prone. "Tell me what happened here and then I need to catch a couple hours' sleep."

Roz pinched the bridge of her nose between her thumb and forefinger. "Mathilde pretty much ordered us to chase down the demons I'd sensed. Jenna refused. Said we'd be better off waiting until you got back. They got into a hell of a shouting match."

"Not good." Colleen narrowed her eyes. "I'm surprised you're still here."

"We wouldn't be except a cadre of Mathilde's witches dragged her off to God-only-knows-where and drummed some sense into her. She didn't exactly apologize to Jenna, but she did allow as to how we could remain here until the current problems were resolved."

"We could, or we have to?"

"Yeah." Roz drained her glass and reached for the whiskey bottle to refill it. "I saw it as more of an order than a choice, but we don't answer to her."

"Probably not how she sees it."

Roz blew out an exasperated breath. "No shit. In Mathilde's worldview, we all answer to her. Mortals, witches, hell probably even Druids, changelings, weres, and the Sidhe. Switching gears here, I have a room a couple of floors up. There's an extra bed in it."

Colleen stretched her arms over her head. "I'm pretty comfy right where I am. Looks as if Bubba is too. Just kill the lights."

"Will do." The other witch extinguished her mage light. She got to her feet and laid a hand on Colleen's shoulder. "You did good today, sister."

"Thanks. See you in the morning."

Roz's heavy tread faded as she crossed the room and mounted a nearby staircase. Colleen was certain she'd pass out immediately, but her thoughts turned to Duncan. In a drowsy twilight of not quite asleep, but not quite awake, either, an image of him floated before her in the darkness.

She drank in his white-blonde hair and emerald eyes. In her vision, his hair was unbound and came halfway down his chest. He extended his hands to her in a clear invitation to join him, and she understood he walked the Dreamers' Paths. Some witches, those with strong precognitive ability, had access to the dream world. Because of her demon assassin blood, she hadn't had the time, or energy, to fine-tune other parts of her magic. From the time her power first rose, in conjunction with her menses, she'd been closeted with other demon assassins, except there had been a whole lot more of them then...

"*Colleen. I don't want you to be sad. Come walk with me.*" A dream, yet not. Duncan smiled just for her and crooked a finger. "*There's a moonlit glade not far from here.*"

She gazed at him and realized he was naked. His golden-hued skin shimmered as if lit from within. Hard and proud, his cock jutted from a mat of golden curls. Desire, sharp and shockingly present, speared her. She got to her feet, unzipped her jacket, and dropped it onto the sofa she'd just vacated.

Next, she pulled her sweater over her head and unclipped her bra. Both slithered to the floor.

She heard him gasp, followed by, *"Hurry, darling. I need to feel you in my arms."*

She undid the fastenings on her pants and let them slither down her hips. A small push and her black thong followed. Colleen shook her hair behind her shoulders. *"Tell me how to enter the dream world."*

"You've never been here?"

She shook her head.

"Open your mind to me, and I will make a path. Once it forms, walk toward me. Don't stop until you feel my arms around you."

She ached for him, wanted him, but entering the Dreamers' Paths obviously employed magic she wasn't familiar with, so she had to ask, *"Will I be able to return?"*

"Returning is never a problem."

It was good enough for her. She pushed her magic outward, seeking him, and felt him latch onto her. A glowing thread began at her feet and extended into mist. It pulsed and broadened. Once it was wide enough to walk on, she started down it and was immediately swallowed by mist.

Things bumped against her in that thick, nearly opaque vapor. Not demons, but fell things just the same. For one long, awful moment, she wondered if the dream sending had been an Irichna trick, designed to separate her from her changeling, Jenna, and Roz. She tried to ward herself, but couldn't. All her magic was drawn into the shining path beneath her feet. Fear pounded through her, but she kept walking. If it had really been Duncan on the Dreamers' Paths, he'd said not to stop until he held her in his arms.

Or until the Irichna rip me to shreds, she thought sourly, nerves jangling from tension.

Colleen lost all sense of time. The creatures in the mist became more aggressive. Teeth nipped at her. Fire scored her back and she hastened her steps. She'd nearly decided to pull out all the stops, turn around, and make a dash back along the magical trail, when Duncan's familiar scent filled her nostrils. Relief, so intense it made her knees weak, washed through her.

He pulled her to him. She hooked her arms around his shoulders and clung for dear life, heart pounding against her ribs. "Why didn't you tell me how rough it would be?" she demanded, voice garbled because her mouth was pressed against his neck.

"I couldn't. Like all magic, the Dreamers' Paths hold their own secrets. I gave you what you needed to reach me safely, and you did." He buried his mouth in her hair and kissed the top of her head.

"What were all those…things?"

He pushed slightly away and tipped her chin up so their eyes met. "The stuff of nightmares. They have to live somewhere." He kissed the tip of her nose. "We don't have much time. The Dreamers' Paths don't allow much, and I don't want to waste what little we have talking. The journey here is different for each of us. Those spirits in the mist are your worst fears."

He kept one arm protectively around her and led her a little way forward. The moonlit glade he'd mentioned came into view with a deep, still pool surrounded by inviting looking tussocks of grass. She didn't see a moon in the sky, yet one was reflected in the water's depths. At the pool's far end, two nightingales perched atop a weeping willow. Duncan sent magic spiraling their way. The birds tipped their heads back and began a song so poignant and tinged with love that Colleen's heart cracked open and spilled over.

He led her to a spot near the water's edge where soft blankets were spread. Sitting on them, he drew her onto his lap and traced the lines of her face with tender fingers. She laced her fingers behind his neck and pulled him into a kiss.

She wanted to ask a million things, like had Titania blessed their mating, but she didn't want to ruin the moments they had with words. He'd said there wasn't much time. She wondered what happened when the Dreamers' Paths decided to eject you and wished she'd paid more attention when some of the other witches had talked about it.

He trailed kisses down her neck, and positioned their bodies so she lay on her back on the sweet-smelling woolen blankets. Colleen arched her spine when he captured her nipple in his mouth and suckled it. He rolled the other nipple between knowing fingers and then switched sides.

She felt a climax spool deep in her belly and reached for his erect cock. She could come without much of anything else, but she wanted to feel him inside her. He was so huge it took both her hands to fully span his girth. Anticipating how he'd feel plumbing her depths, stretching her, sent shivers of delight through her body. The reality of his skin beneath her fingertips was even more sensuous than she'd expected. Simply touching him was enough to drive her mad, between his heady scent and the silky feel of him, velvet skin stretched taut over hard muscle.

He moaned and pressed himself into her hands. She moved her other hand to his hip and urged him between her legs. He knelt over her and took his cock in one hand, guiding it so his cockhead pressed against her entrance. She drew her legs up, placed a hand on each side of his hips, and tugged.

He pressed inside, but only a little, and moved himself in small circles. Her hips bucked in frustration. "Please."

"Since you asked so nicely." His voice was rough with passion, but he sank in a little farther.

Colleen hooked her legs around his waist and pulled. With an inchoate moan, he sank into her. She came when he hit bottom, nails digging into his back as spasms ripped through her. Colleen heard herself shrieking, her cries mingling with the nightingales' courting song.

He drew back, ever so slowly, and sank into her again.

"You are so beautiful," she murmured, tracing a finger down his perfect chest and the planes of muscle cutting through his stomach.

"Not as beautiful as you, darling." He flexed his cock inside her, and she tightened around him.

Colleen blinked. Duncan's body had developed a translucent quality, as if he were fading. "No." She made a grab for his arms, but her fingers closed together as if his body wasn't there.

"It's all right. I'll try to come for you tomorrow night. Soon after that, I'll…" But he was gone, beyond her reach.

She wrapped a blanket around herself and sat on the banks of the pool, listening to the nightingales. Duncan's scent lingered in the air. The feel of him was all over her body. She'd just begun wondering how the hell she'd find her way back without him, when the dream world shattered around her and she landed with a thud next to her couch in the Witches' Northwest living room.

Dawn was breaking. The sky outside the living room's leaded glass panes shone pearlescent gray with pale pink streaks. Bubba rolled off his chair and moved to her side. "I was wondering where you were. I just woke up and was getting ready to hunt for you." He crinkled his nose. "I smell sex. Where'd you get that blanket?"

Colleen's mouth twisted into half a smile when she realized

the cushy ivory blanket was still wrapped around her. "I was in the dream world," she told the changeling. "With Duncan."

"How? Did the Dream Guardian request your presence?"

Colleen shook her head. "I don't know much about that magic, but it's sounding like you do." She patted the floor next to her. "How about if you cozy up and tell me?"

CHAPTER 8

*D*uncan shook his head in frustration as the familiar walls of his eighteenth century manor house bedchamber closed about him. His cock was so engorged, it ached. Of all the blasted times for the dream world to decide his time was up…

His hand strayed to his cock. He had to come or he wouldn't be good for anything. Colleen's scent embraced him, the musk of her arousal so intense, he could almost pretend she was still next to him.

Without even bothering to lie down, he gripped himself and stroked his throbbing shaft, imagining Colleen's high, firm breasts with their strawberry nipples. He remembered the feel of them in his mouth, how they hardened as he sucked on them. And the sensation of her body closing around him, all fire and heat and wanting. He imagined sinking his length into her again and pumping hard.

His cock erupted, geysering semen into the air. He gasped and shoved himself into his hand, until the last spasms died. Duncan sank to the carpeted floor, panting. He made a grab for a discarded shirt and made a token effort to mop up after himself. Sidhe homes, most of them anyway, were spelled to be self-cleaning. Sure enough, the damp spots on the thick, Aubusson carpet got smaller, and then disappeared entirely.

He pulled a pillow off a nearby chair, shoved it beneath his head, and waited for his heart rate to return to normal. It had been a risk, luring Colleen onto the Dreamers' Paths. He hadn't realized how big a risk until she told him she'd never been there before. But he had to see her. Their separation cut into him.

Now that she knows the way—and to ignore the monsters—we can meet there every night.

At least until the Dream Guardian decides we need to declare our love before the real world too.

Duncan blew out a breath. The Dreamers' Paths were a boon to magic wielders. They provided both an escape, and a way to focus and hone power, but the ancient spirit who controlled them wouldn't tolerate his realm being used to deceive.

"Is that what I'm doing?" Duncan murmured. "Sidestepping my confrontation with Titania?"

He hadn't been back for more than a few hours, and he'd spent the entire time sending the word out to convene their council. Duncan lurched to his feet, strode to a richly carved armoire, and pulled out a pale green linen shirt, a pair of black trousers, and fresh underclothes. He layered a black jacket over everything, picked up and discarded several ties, and finally decided he didn't need one. Most Sidhe from his era still dressed in ceremonial robes, at least at council meetings, but Duncan had gotten rid of all his a hundred years ago because they'd seemed hopelessly archaic. He snapped a brush off the dresser, ran it through his hair, and formed several thick plaits close to his skull. He worked automatically, only realizing when he was nearly finished that he'd done his hair in the ancient Celtic warrior pattern.

Guess I'm expecting a confrontation.

He caught a glimpse of himself, sporting a wry grin, in the huge mirror mounted on the wall opposite his bed and chuckled. Sidhe were a dried-up, humorless lot. Even though it might make things more contentious, he found himself hoping they'd show a bit of spirit today.

He glanced at a grandfather clock and hurried out the door, down two flights of stairs, and through the great room that took up most of the bottom floor of the manor. Usually, his collection of artwork, sculpture, books, scrolls, and highly polished mahogany and ash furniture soothed him, but not today. He barely glanced at anything as he pushed the ten-foot-tall front door open and barked words to ward his home. From habit, he started for the carriage house he'd converted into a garage, but drew up short. He'd never be able to drive to this destination. It was either teleport, or don't go at all.

Hissing his frustration to the four winds, he summoned a teleport spell.

Moments later, the marble and crystal of the Sidhe meeting hall formed around him. After the disaster of two world wars, his people had set up an alternative castle on a borderworld close to Earth, so they'd be safe from prying, mortal eyes in the event of an atomic catastrophe.

Duncan gazed about him and nodded. The lavishly furnished room, with its long table and comfortably padded chairs, comprised the top floor of a three-story structure. The bottom was sunk into bedrock, so only the upper two floors had windows that admitted the continuous light of this off-Earth location. Two suns, one bright, one dim, tag-teamed their way across the sky in perpetual motion. The lack of a true night, coupled with a climate so arid growing anything would've proven damn near impossible without a huge assist from magic, was probably why this world had remained deserted.

He was first to arrive, which was good. It would give him time to organize what he wanted to say. It had been at least ten years since one of them convened a council meeting. They only happened when something important needed discussion. Because the Sidhe lived forever, many of them expended vast amounts of energy pretending they were normal. Part of *normal* didn't include being faced with other immortal beings, outside one's immediate family. The Sidhe might not like one another very much, but their blood thickened if an outsider dared utter a withering comment.

He felt sad for his kind. Keeping demons at bay had been their last important task, and one which forced them to work together. Once they'd foisted that responsibility onto the witches—for a host of poorly thought out reasons—they'd lost even the small interconnections that bound them.

Duncan took a seat at the head of the long table. As an elder, he had a right to one of those six chairs. He steepled his fingers together, rested his chin on them, and considered how best to address his fellows. He was still thinking when they began to trickle in, generally alone, but occasional pairs and triads popped out of the ether. They bowed to one another, scrupulously polite, as always.

As he watched his people assemble, Duncan was awed by their beauty. Perfect faces. Perfect forms. They should have lived perfect lives, but something had gone awry somewhere along the way. Most were like him, clinging to an existence that had little meaning, though they'd go to great lengths to avoid admitting it.

"Thank you all for coming." Duncan glanced from one Sidhe to another and received cool nods in return.

A man with dark hair, hanging loose past his shoulders, and shrewd blue eyes stood. "Things are bad in Manchester. Those damned Irichnas have killed ten people. Of course the mortals think it's a resurrection of Jack the Ripper, but we know better. Did you bring one of those witches back to help us?"

Duncan answered Ronin's question with one of his own. "Did you know there are only three left?"

"No, but I scarcely see where that's relevant. All we need is one."

Duncan cleared his throat. "What happens when there aren't any left?"

A woman, who took after Aphrodite, with lush, blonde hair, flapped an indifferent hand. "We can simply make more of them."

"If we wished to do that—" Ronin looked temporarily uncomfortable "—I suppose we should begin now while we have some living genetic material to work with."

"Aye." Another Sidhe with a strong Irish lilt spoke up. "If we wait too long, 'tis cadavers we'll have to deal with, and I fear we may not meet with our previous success."

Duncan hated to bring it up, but he'd always been curious. "I wasn't involved with this part of things, but did you leave any of us with demon assassin ability?"

Krystal, the Aphrodite lookalike, showed him a mouthful of teeth. "Why do you want to know?"

"It seems important," he hedged.

"You never did acknowledge if you secured a witch for us," Ronin pressed.

"They need our help."

"We need theirs. Seems like a quid pro quo to me." Krystal got to her feet and strode next to Duncan. He felt her net him with a truth spell. "What exactly happened when you went after the witches, and why did you draw us together?"

A hot rush of anger buffeted him. "How dare you?" He surged to his feet and balled his hands into fists. "What? You think I'd lie to you in our very council chambers?"

She shrugged. "Anything is possible. We share blood, yet none of us are close."

If he backed down now, he was finished. Worse, every Sidhe in the room knew it. Duncan stuck his face inches from hers. "Sit down and take your spell with you." He shifted his gaze to the hundred or so Sidhe ranged about the room. "If any here do not trust me, leave now."

Grumbling, Krystal found her way back to her seat, and her casting dissolved into swirling golden motes. No one else stirred. Duncan drew in a breath. There was still a huge divide to cross, but at least he hadn't lost the first battle. "Hear me out. Wait until I'm done for discussion. Agreed?" After a long pause, heads bobbed and he began talking.

"...So after the witch and I returned from Hell, I teleported back here because I needed to talk with all of you." Duncan drew himself up and infused compulsion into his words. "Demons were always our responsibility. Oberon and Titania tasked us with keeping all demons, but especially the Irichna, under control. Don't answer me right now, but I expect you to do some soul searching.

"Everyone needs a reason to exist. A lot of our reason evaporated once we scuttled out from under our responsibilities."

Ronin opened his mouth, but Duncan held up a hand. "I'm nearly done. If we don't recapture the gene sequence that allows us to escort demons into Hell, at the very least, we have to help the witches. They're nearly extinct. The demons are stronger than they used to be. I tell you, the one I faced was worse than my expectations by a factor of about ten.

"The last thing I want to leave you with is this: it's time to allow the changelings sovereignty again. We don't need their magic. We never did. They could be staunch allies against the demons, and they never were much of a threat to us—or anyone else."

Duncan sank into his seat. The ebb and flow of musical Sidhe voices eddied about him. He'd done his part. The group would come to a decision in their own time and their own way. There was nothing more for him to do or say. It was hard not to continue to argue for what he wanted, but he bit back further words.

Nothing to do now but wait.

He got to his feet and walked to a side table where someone had thoughtfully provided carafes of water and mead. He poured himself a cup of water and washed it down with spirits, thinking of Colleen, Jenna, and Roz. It pained him to admit it, but the three witches were braver and more resourceful than this roomful of Sidhe. They didn't question their destiny. No. They stepped up to the plate and took care of business.

"Duncan!"

He turned and stared at his fellows, wondering who'd called him.

Krystal stepped away from the group. "We've been trying to get your attention for the last few minutes. We've come to a decision."

He set down his cup, walked briskly back to his place at the head of the table, and waited. No matter what happened, he'd given it his best shot. If the Sidhe refused him, he'd already decided to return to Colleen's side and help her, Jenna, and Roz.

"There is merit in your argument," Ronin said. "We shall see about sharing responsibility for corralling the Irichna, at least until this current problem is over."

"Yes, then we shall seek a more permanent solution," Krystal added.

"We'll be requirin' blood from one of the witches." The Sidhe with the Irish accent sat straighter in his chair.

"I'll see you get it." Duncan spoke crisply. He wanted to whoop and turn handsprings, but he could celebrate later. He wished he'd paid closer attention to the discussion that netted him what he wanted, but he'd been so certain the tide would flow the other way, he'd held himself aloof on purpose.

So he didn't bash any of those perfect, Sidhe faces to a pulp.

He gathered magic to teleport away from their meeting place, but Ronin laid a hand on his arm. "You need to hear the rest. We will reconvene at my home on the outskirts of Penrith in one week's time. The witches need to be there. Your task is to see that they are."

"Will you allow them to have a voice in our plans?" Duncan asked and then kicked himself for not keeping a tighter rein on his mouth.

Another female Sidhe, with a riot of red curls framing her alabaster skin, drew near, brows quirked. "A bit protective of an inferior species, aren't you?"

Duncan swallowed angry words. Up until very recently, he'd viewed witches the same way, so shaming the speaker wouldn't change her mind. Instead, he said, "I merely thought I should let them know what to expect."

"Mmph." Helena stalked closer. Duncan clapped wards around his mind, which earned him a knowing smile. "I suspect it might be a wee bit more than that."

Duncan poured more magic into his warding and waited, but Helena turned and walked away. He exhaled, but quietly, and turned back to Ronin. "I shall do my best, but it's possible they won't want to come."

"Compel them."

Duncan bristled. "That's how we secured their cooperation in the first place. It wasn't right then and it's not right now."

Ronin made a clicking sound with his tongue and teeth. "Tsk. Tsk. When did you become such a champion of magical underdogs...brother?"

Ever since we decided Sidhe should rule the magical world.

"I'm not sure that's what I am, but I haven't totally lost my sense of fairness."

Ronin drew his arched brows into a disapproving line. Duncan felt the other Sidhe's resentment spark and held up his hands, palms out. "Let's not fight. We need to save our energy for what's important."

The other Sidhe clacked his jaws shut. "Just remember whose blood flows in your veins."

As if I could forget.

"A week is a long time. Are you going to do anything about those Irichna before they call in reinforcements?" Duncan asked blandly.

Ronin glared through narrowed eyes. "I suppose so. The Celtic gods owe us a favor or two. We'll call in our chips."

"Good idea." Duncan clapped him on the back with faux cheer. "I knew there was a reason you were our leader."

Ronin snarled, but before he could come up with a snappy retort, Duncan summoned magic and teleported to the last place he remembered Oberon and Titania's palace had been. The pair moved often and shrouded their location by magic, so locating them was often a challenge. Not that anyone looked very hard these days. He'd heard rumors Oberon had faded from all worlds, leaving Titania to rule for both of them.

Duncan knew Oberon and Titania weren't there the moment he landed at their last known location. For one thing, the world had gone dark. For another he couldn't sense their royal energy.

He searched three different borderworlds in quick succession and was hungry, tired, and close to giving up. Besides, now that he'd gotten a bit of distance from it, he needed to sort through what had happened at the council meeting. The Sidhe had agreed, but it felt like a temporary concession with something behind it he couldn't quite grasp. Perhaps the reason he'd been lost in thought by the refreshment table was because the others had snared him in a mild ensorcellment.

That last thought chilled him.

"I'll try once more," he muttered and teleported to a borderworld he'd only heard about, but never visited. The royal castle rose before him, in pastel hues, with flags flying. He girded himself for what would come next. He'd wanted to find his sovereigns, but they could kill his dreams with a word. A triple sun floated lazily overhead. Butterflies clustered thickly, and birds trilled. Hummingbirds landed on his arms, small wings beating in staccato time.

Duncan floated up the steps and into the castle. Gravity was mild here, its tug so minimal he had to use magic to force contact with the marble steps and entryway. He wasn't surprised to find the castle deserted as he wandered through it in search of a throne room. Servants were summoned when needed. Magical creations, they faded to invisibility the rest of the time.

Rich, meaty smells came from the kitchens. Duncan detoured, intent on dishing up a bowl of whatever was cooking, and found Titania, skirts rucked up, her bare feet propped on a table. Silver hair cascaded about her and pooled on the floor. Her unlined face could've belonged to a young woman, but for her world-weary eyes. The queen had always been tall, but now she was so thin her skin held a translucent quality. Duncan wondered if she'd begun the process of fading into the *Dreaming*. It happened to all of them when they'd had enough of immortality.

"Duncan!" She waved a gravy-soaked heel of bread at him.

"Dear boy. Come share a meal with me. It does get terribly lonely here."

He bowed, nodded his thanks, and filled a bowl for himself before settling at the table across from his queen. "Thank you, Your Highness. I should have asked before I sat, but may I get you anything?"

She smiled and handed him an empty glass. "There's a mead cask in the far corner. Feel free to help yourself."

By the time he returned to the table, he'd ordered his thoughts and come to a decision. It was manipulative as hell, but he spent the next hour eating and making small talk with Titania. It was obvious she was starved for companionship, and so they talked of people they'd known and places they'd been. He thought about asking where Oberon was, but decided not to since the queen hadn't mentioned him.

At length, she set her glass down and speared him with her pale blue gaze. "This has been delightful, but I'm through deluding myself that this was a social visit. You went to a great deal of trouble to run me down. Why?"

Duncan squared his shoulders. This was it. He couldn't beat around the bush in the face of Titania's frank stare. "I've fallen in love with a mortal, a witch, and—"

She made a chopping motion with one hand. The beautiful planes of her face twisted into something so unpleasant Duncan looked away. "Fuck her all you want," the queen snapped, "but I will not see our blood further diluted by matings outside our line."

He opened his mouth to protest. The air sharpened with magic so ancient, it scoured his skin, burning him. Duncan summoned a ward. By the time it was in place, Titania had vanished.

CHAPTER 9

Colleen pushed to her feet, keeping the blanket wrapped around her. Her clothes were right where she'd left them, and she stuffed them into her small backpack and slung it over a shoulder. Despite having had very little sleep, she felt surprisingly alert.

Bubba tugged on the blanket. "I told you about the Dream Guardian. I want breakfast."

"Me too." She grinned at the changeling. "But first I'm going to take a shower and get dressed. Maybe by then, Roz and Jenna will be up."

"Do you think anyone would mind if I scouted through the kitchen?"

Colleen thought about Mathilde and decided the crone would probably mind very much, particularly since Bubba wasn't known for being neat. "How about this?" She cocked her head to one side. "This is an old house. There have to be lots of mice. Remember that nice fat one you caught in the basement?"

"Oh, all right." Bubba made a face. "I know where this

conversation is heading." He spread his arms wide in mock surrender and bowed to her.

"I swear, you missed your calling. You could have had quite a career on the stage." She flicked magic his way. He shrank into his black cat form and paced out of the room with dignity, tail held high.

She picked up his clothes and followed, but by the time she made the main hallway, he was nowhere in sight. Colleen sent a silent prayer to whoever might be listening that the changeling wouldn't get himself into trouble and mounted the broad, formal staircase leading to the home's upper floors.

Bubba's depiction of the Dream Guardian had been chilling. An ancient creature, older even than the gods, he ruled his realm with an iron fist. Since he held nightmares at bay, he couldn't afford to pussyfoot around. Long ago, he'd welcomed all with magic to cavort in his kingdom, but too many took advantage of his generosity and weren't careful to bar his gates on leaving. Now he picked and chose. That he'd allowed Colleen entry was an unexpected boon, at least according to Bubba.

When she'd asked what might have happened, the changeling looked away, and she understood. The creatures that had nipped at her would've gone farther. Much farther. They'd have yanked her off the path and ripped her to bits.

Surely Duncan knew that. Maybe he kept me safe...

It didn't take long to find a bathroom with a deep, claw foot tub and a shower attachment. She'd just soaped herself when someone barreled into the bathroom, letting in a cloud of cold air. Colleen threw magic outward and recognized Jenna's energy.

"Thank Christ you weren't bothering to mute your aura when you came in here," the other witch said. "Hurry up."

Colleen's heart jolted into overdrive. She peeked around

the curtained tub into the steamy bathroom. "Why? What's happened?"

"Roz scented the Irichnas from the other day."

Colleen dunked her head under the shower spray and rinsed shampoo from her hair as fast as she could. Water running down her body took care of the rest of her. She flipped the taps off and grabbed a large, fluffy blue towel she'd laid next to the tub.

"I've got to go." Jenna turned toward the door. "Meet us in the foyer downstairs."

"Could you round up Bubba?"

"I suppose so. Where'd you see him last?"

"Downstairs hall. Um, he's a cat. His pants and shirt are on the floor, right in front of you. If you could change him back, and…"

"Crap!" Jenna grabbed Bubba's clothes and hustled through the door, not bothering to shut it. "If he's a cat, he could be anywhere. We don't have any time to spare."

Cold air continued to swoosh into the bathroom. Colleen pulled on underwear, pants, top, and jacket over her still-damp skin. She tested her magic while she laced her boots. *Damn!* It hadn't fully recovered from yesterday's trip to the underworld.

"Why are you still here?" Mathilde stood in the open door, hands on her hips.

"Because I was taking a shower." Colleen zipped her jacket and blew out an exasperated breath. "I thought this was a bathroom, not a gathering place." She snatched up her rucksack and slung it over one shoulder.

"Get going." Magic flashed from the crone's hands. Colleen sidestepped it, all but for the smallest jolt, which zapped her leg.

Her temper raced to the fore. She warded herself and stalked forward until she was scant inches from the other witch. "If you want my help—or Roz's or Jenna's—you will never deploy hostile magic against me again. Do you understand?"

"I do what I deem necessary. Right now you're slowing down progress," Mathilde barked. Power bounced off Colleen's ward.

"You bitch! Stop that immediately, or I'll be forced to fight back."

"You can't talk to me like that." Mathilde wove her fingers together. The next blast of power buffeted Colleen, making her stagger slightly.

"I just did." Colleen pushed past her and trotted down the hall.

"Ha! It worked. At least you're on your way to get rid of those demons."

Colleen skidded to a halt and spun to face Mathilde, standing twenty feet away down the long hallway. "No. For the record, I'm not. I'm going to get Roz, Jenna, and my changeling, and we're leaving. I told you what would happen if you raised your magic against me. You didn't listen. Catch the demon yourself. I'm done."

"You can't just leave." Mathilde materialized by Colleen's side, her dark eyes alight with fury.

For a moment, Colleen was confused, and then she understood the other witch must have teleported. She hadn't known it was possible over such a short distance. "Watch me," Colleen gritted through clenched teeth.

"I outrank you. I order you to—"

"You missed something, sweetie. I'm not part of your Coven. Rank doesn't come into play here." Colleen wasn't interested in trading barbs with Mathilde. She skittered down the long, curving staircase and nearly barreled into Roz and Jenna. Bubba, in gnome form again, raced to her.

"Finally," Roz muttered. "Come on. Let's get going before the old bat that runs this place gets hold of us."

"Old bat is it?" Mathilde shrieked as she catapulted down the stairs.

"Did I say that? I have no recollection of any such thing." Roz's voice held persuasion.

Half a dozen witches, including a couple of men, marched out of one of the downstairs rooms, formed a circle around Mathilde and herded her, still shrieking epithets, away from them. "Sorry about that," one of them called over a shoulder. "Just get going. For some reason, your presence riles her."

"We're going all right," Colleen said. "We're leaving."

Roz laid a hand on Colleen's forehead, as if testing for fever. "There're two demons out there. Hunting them is what we do."

"I don't care." Colleen hastily summoned a teleport spell. "Do you all have everything? We can sort this out back in Fairbanks."

"What about my car?" Roz asked.

"Shit! I forgot about it. Where's it parked?" Colleen asked.

"Around back," Jenna answered.

"I found a couple of different back doors." Bubba sounded proud of himself.

"Lead the way," Colleen told him. When Jenna and Roz hung back, she grabbed each of their arms. "Come on! Mathilde attacked me. We can talk about this in the car. It's a long drive back home. Or maybe I'll think of a better alternative when I'm not so pissed off."

Jenna narrowed her eyes. Roz's eyebrows drew together, but at least the other witches took off after the changeling at a dead run. Colleen drew up the rear. Moments later, they piled into Roz's battered Subaru Outback and headed toward Interstate 5, going north.

"She's going to complain to Coven Central about us," Roz predicted from the back seat, after they'd been driving for a while.

"We might get a chance to tell our part of things. Depends who's presiding," Jenna said. She and Bubba sat up front with Colleen, who was driving.

"Oh, for criminy sakes." Colleen tightened her hands around the wheel. She ferried the car across a couple of lanes, onto an off-ramp, and into a Starbuck's parking lot. Once the car came to a stop, she lowered her forehead and rested it on her hands, folded atop the steering wheel. "None of that matters. What matters is getting back to Fairbanks and our own Coven, and the closest thing we have to a power base."

"What exactly did Mathilde do?" Roz asked.

"Attacked me with magic because I wasn't out hunting down Irichna fast enough to suit her."

"Was it an actual attack?" Jenna asked.

"If I wouldn't have warded myself, I'd probably be dead."

Bubba threw himself into her lap and hugged her tight. Colleen stroked his head. "It's okay. It all worked out. Something's definitely wrong with Mathilde. I thought she was… odd while she questioned Duncan, and today pretty much capped it. I've met her a time or two before and she was always a crusty, old thing, but reasonable. It's almost as if she's possessed."

"Mmph." Jenna nodded. "Maybe that's why Roz's sense of the Irichna faded in and out before we got there."

"It would explain a lot," Roz murmured. "Including Mathilde's stalling while she grilled Duncan. Um, are we going after coffees?"

"Yes. Anyone want a breakfast sandwich, or a sweet roll?" Colleen asked.

"How about if we all just go inside. We're far enough from

Witches' Northwest, we could probably risk the few minutes it will take to get coffee and food." Jenna pushed her car door open and got out.

"I'll stay here with Bubba," Roz said. "Get me a large black coffee and that maple scone thing they have."

"But I want to go," Bubba protested.

Colleen disentangled his arms from her shoulders. "I know, sweetie, but your appearance is odd enough people would remember you, and we want to slip in and out unnoticed."

"We need to practice me taking a form that looks more normal."

"We do, but not right now. When a demon is around, you borrow from their energy to shift. So far, you and I have only managed your cat form, but we'll work on doing better than that. I promise. Tell me what you want from inside."

The changeling bowed his head, looking sad. "Breakfast sandwich with bacon, large latte coffee, and two sweet rolls."

"You got it." Colleen set him on the passenger seat and ruffled his hair before getting out.

By the time she walked across the parking lot and into the coffee shop, Jenna was halfway through a long line. Colleen sidled up next to her. "I've been thinking."

Jenna snorted. "Could be dangerous."

"Not this time. It's something like twenty-two hundred miles to Fairbanks. Even if we manage five hundred miles a day, it will take the better part of five days."

"Roz isn't going to take kindly to abandoning the car." Jenna followed the queue as it inched forward. "Do you have a better idea?"

"Yeah, I do. We can put the car on a ferry in Bellingham, with instructions for them to park it at the ferry dock in Haines."

Jenna's face lit with understanding. "Which is only about six hundred fifty miles from Fairbanks."

"Um-hum. We could drive it in a very long day, since the roads aren't all that great. Maybe a day-and-a-half."

They finally reached the counter, placed their orders, and had the barista put their coffees into a cardboard carrier. Colleen moved to the small counter with cream, sugar, and powdered flavorings. She doctored her coffee and Bubba's. Jenna hovered, waiting for their food order.

Cups and bags in hand, they pushed through the swinging door and started for the car. "Won't it take the ferry a few days to get to Haines?" Jenna asked.

"Three, if I remember right."

"So we'd go home and just teleport back to pick up the car?"

Colleen set the coffees on the car's hood and opened the door. "That was my plan, let's see what Roz thinks of it."

"Let's see what Roz thinks of what?" the other witch demanded and held out a hand for her coffee and scone.

Colleen mapped out her plan while sipping coffee and munching on her English muffin sandwich.

Roz mopped sugary crumbs from her mouth with a paper napkin. "I like it better than driving for the next week."

"We might actually get a few things done in Fairbanks." Jenna tipped the last of her coffee into her mouth and gathered wrappers. "May as well ditch our trash since we're still here. This isn't quite all of it, but good enough." She got out of the car and jogged to a nearby garbage can.

Once she was back inside, Colleen started the car, rolled into a gas station right next door, and filled the tank. She turned their plan around in her mind, hunting for flaws. Once they were headed north again, she said, "The only possible glitch is if the ferry doesn't have room."

"Or maybe finding someone to move the car from the

Bellingham ferry—once it hits the end of the line in Ketchikan —to the one that goes into Haines," Jenna said.

"Maybe we can, um, persuade them," Roz said. Colleen glanced in the rearview mirror. The other witch was grinning.

"If they're full, do you expect they'll offload someone else's car into the Pacific?" Colleen asked.

"If I ask nicely, that's exactly what they'll do." Roz sounded smug.

"Enough." Jenna's tone was sharp, but Colleen knew her well enough to understand she was worried. "Coming up with a game plan for the car was a piece of cake. What are we going to do about the Irichna? And about having alienated Mathilde?"

Bubba looked up from his breakfast. "When those other witches raced out and grabbed her, it didn't look like they agreed with her."

"No, it sure didn't." Colleen worried her lower lip between her teeth. "I was surprised she allowed them to herd her."

"She's very old and very powerful," Roz said. "Strong enough to flatten that entire house and everyone in it."

"Her witches probably know that," Colleen murmured, "which is why they won't even attempt to corral her with magic."

"What will they do?" Bubba crumpled the paper that had held his sandwich and threw in on the floor.

"Pick that up and put it in the trash bag, honey," Colleen told him.

"The other witches were giving us a chance to get out of there," Jenna said.

"Probably so," Colleen agreed. "Once they sensed we were gone, I'm sure they stopped humoring Mathilde and turned her loose."

"Which means she could be waiting for us in Fairbanks," Roz pointed out, her voice sour.

Colleen hadn't considered that, but it made sense. Mathilde had been close to apoplectic. For one witch to send killing magic after another for any infraction, let alone something as minor as not moving quite quickly enough, was unheard of. "Not much we can do about it," she said.

"Like hell there's not," Roz cut in. "I'm not going to let her, or anyone else, run me out of my home or my business."

"Why would she know where the house is?" Bubba asked.

"Good thinking. She wouldn't." Colleen jumped on the changeling's question. "She could always track us with magic, but she's never been there."

"We can surround the place with an invisibility spell," Jenna mumbled, "so long as we get there first."

"All righty." Colleen glanced at a passing highway sign that said Bellingham was another twenty miles. "That'll be our first order of business, once we get rid of the car. It'll freak the neighbors out, but what the hell."

"What the hell, indeed." Roz chortled. "They think we're odder than a flock of geese in the dead of winter as it is."

CHAPTER 10

"What do you mean she's not here?" Duncan thundered. He stuffed his booted foot in the front door of the Witches' Northwest headquarters to discourage the male witch on the other side from slamming it in his face.

"She and the other two, and their creature, left early this morning." The witch kept his voice mild. Duncan sensed a placating spell beneath the words. "Please." The slightly built man bent toward him, talking low. Brown hair chopped to uneven lengths fell over his hazel eyes. He looked truly young, maybe not much over eighteen.

"Please what?" Duncan matched the witch's muted tones.

"Things are a little difficult just now. It would be best if you left before Mathilde—"

"Oh no you don't," a strident female voice called from somewhere upstairs. "Mistress said she was particularly interested in the Sidhe if he came back." Footsteps sounded on the risers.

Duncan drew his boot out of the way and moved off to one

side. The male witch nodded tersely and pushed the door closed. His words, "It's not what you think," would have been muffled by the thick, glass-fronted door, but Duncan had exceptional hearing.

"What do you mean, it's not what I think?" the woman demanded. "I sense Sidhe magic."

"Well, I don't. You must be mistaken, Adrienne."

Duncan pulled invisibility about himself and settled in to eavesdrop. Something had happened here after Colleen returned around dawn. He wanted to know what it was.

The male witch went on, "It wasn't the Sidhe. It was just the religious right hawking pamphlets. They've somehow decided we're evil incarnate."

Adrienne brayed laughter.

Understanding what the young male was trying to do, Duncan intercepted bits of his spell and added to it. The youngster's work was far from elegant, but the other witch didn't realize she was being hornswoggled.

"How's Mistress doing?" the male asked.

"Eh. So-so. She's gotten over her snit from this morning, but she just doesn't seem like herself."

"Not to me, either." The male witch paused a beat. "I'm pretty new here. Do you have any idea what's wrong?"

Adrienne exhaled breathily and murmured. "Not exactly, but things began changing several months ago when she developed a fascination with the Irichna. At first, she talked about joining up with the trio from Alaska to hunt them, but that didn't last long."

"Curious."

"That's one word," Adrienne said. "The one I'd pick, though, is disturbing. We're all bound to obey Mathilde. I've known her for over twenty years, and it feels like she's lost her mind.

In my worst moments, I think she's in league with the demons."

"Possessed?" The male witch's voice was a hoarse, horrified whisper.

"Possibly, but don't breathe a word. Her magic is so strong it's scary. If she's not one hundred percent on top of things, she could do huge amounts of damage."

"Maybe I'll come up with a plausible excuse," the male witch said a bit shakily. "Leave for a while…"

"Humph. Not a bad idea. Perhaps I'll join you. Mathilde has the right to kill us if we're accused of breaking any major tenets of the covenant. That could be a problem if she starts seeing things that aren't there. You should've heard her this morning. She actually attacked one of the Alaska witches. The one with long, reddish hair."

Duncan stopped breathing. He balled his hands into fists. If Mathilde had harmed Colleen, he'd teleport into the building, track her down, and tear her limb from limb. Consequences be damned. He'd sort them out later.

"Aw, crap! Did she get hurt?" the male witch asked.

"Not hardly. She fought back. Told Mathilde off, gathered the others, and the bunch of 'em hightailed it out of here."

Thank the goddess.

Duncan shook his head. Colleen was strong, courageous, and resourceful, but still… If something hideous happened to her because he wasn't by her side, he'd never forgive himself. A sense of calm descended, welcome counterpoint to the welter of confusing feelings he'd battled since walking into Colleen's shop two days before. In that moment he knew what he needed to do. There wasn't any rush, but he'd track Titania down again, tell her he was mated to a mortal, and let the chips fall where they would. He wasn't quite sure what the process was to sever him from his immortality, but he'd do whatever he had to.

Colleen was worth it.

A smile tugged at his lips. *Now all I have to do is get her to say yes.*

He walked briskly down the steps, still shrouded in invisibility. Where would the women have gone? Supposedly, there were Irichnas nearby. Would they have gone after them? He stopped in the shadow of a stand of evergreens across from the Victorian that housed Witches' Northwest and sent tracking magic tumbling outward.

He followed it back across the street to a parking lot behind the Coven's building, which probably meant the women had left in a car. Roz must've arrived that way. It made sense they wouldn't want to abandon her vehicle. Duncan tried to imagine what he'd do in Colleen's place.

"Well, I sure as hell wouldn't chase down some demon to please Mathilde," he muttered. "Not after she laid into me."

Anger simmered. Part of him still wanted to storm Coven headquarters, solve the problem of what was wrong with Mathilde, and kick her from here to Faerie. But a bigger part wanted to find Colleen. Had the women decided to return to Fairbanks? It had to be better than two thousand miles. Quite a car trip for beings who could teleport and be there in minutes.

Something caught his attention. It was subtle, just a whiff of evil, but he stopped in his tracks, and warded himself more tightly. Was it a demon? Or Danu forbid, two of them? Before his experience yesterday, he would scarcely have noticed the faint miasma eddying in the air.

If it is a demon, what the hell do I do? Assuming I can even corral the thing, will the gatekeeper let me into Hell?

Duncan slipped between two lobes of an elaborate hedge system fronting a mansion, and borrowed plant energy to mask his own. He sent a stealthy tendril of magic toward where he'd felt the wrongness. It was definitely there, and much stronger this time. Worse, at least one hapless mortal was snared in whatever trap the demon—or demons—had set.

I have to do something. Walking away would be wrong.

He activated a telepathic version of 9-1-1, praying that at least one Sidhe would be close enough to respond.

"For the love of Danu, what is it?" A female voice, thick with annoyance, sounded in his mind.

Duncan identified himself and outlined his problem, before asking who'd responded to his summons.

"Andraste," the Celtic goddess of victory announced. That one word held such a patronizing note, Duncan winced, but the goddess wasn't done. *"I fail to see why you bothered me. We don't meddle in mortal affairs. In case you've forgotten, neither do the Sidhe."*

"That's normally true." Duncan chose his words with care. *"If we don't do something, the Irichna will overrun Earth. This has gotten bigger than just a mortals' problem. It belongs to all of us."*

Andraste was silent so long, he feared she'd severed their mind link. He readied himself to approach the demons and their prey, when he felt Celtic energy pulse near him. Duncan let go of the invisibility cloaking him just as Andraste's form materialized. Taller than him, she was built like an Amazon warrior, with broad shoulders and slim hips. Her long, blonde hair was braided into two plaits to keep it out of the way. She might have been beautiful, but for the severe planes of her ageless face.

Her sharp, blue gaze skewered him. "This grates against my better judgment, yet I am here."

"Thank you for heeding my call." Duncan bowed formally. "I had hoped for another Sidhe. That you are here is a gift, since you're far stronger than any of us."

Andraste rolled her eyes. "Pretty words from a pretty man." She stared at him with evident interest, and licked her lips. A predatory grin spread over her face. "Once we have bested this demon, we shall spend a bit of time together."

It hadn't been a question, but now wasn't the time to tell her his heart belonged to another. It might piss her off, and Duncan needed her help. "Maybe so, my lady." He bowed again.

"Heh! A spot of motivation to get this over with." Andraste's nose twitched. She craned her neck in one direction, then another. "The demon is that way." She tilted her head.

"I know. We need a plan. Do you think there might be two of them?"

The goddess eyed him as if he had the intelligence of a kumquat. "I shall immobilize the demon—and I sensed only one—for a short time. You rescue the human." She dusted her hands together. "Game over. We go home."

Duncan felt appalled, but tried to mask his concern. "The demon will just move on to the next likely human."

Andraste blew out a breath. "By then, you won't be near enough to rescue whoever is stupid enough to fall into the Irichna's trap." She shook her head, temper obviously on a very short tether. "It's damned difficult to get rid of any variety of demon, but Irichna are the absolute worst. Sorry, but I don't have time for a trip to Hell today."

Fine. I'll take what I can get.

Duncan clamped his jaws together. "Lead out."

"We go together. It's impossible to sneak up on a demon, so we'll storm the wards it's hiding behind."

Duncan hadn't considered a direct, frontal attack. "Will we have enough juice to blow right through its wards?"

She arranged her full lips in a parody of a smile. "I never fail in battle."

Duncan remembered the Irichna from yesterday, opened his mouth to issue a warning, and shut it again. Surely Andraste had faced demons before. He tightened his warding, pulled teleport magic, and joined the goddess.

In the moments it took them to get to the demon, Duncan girded himself to be prepared for anything. It didn't work. Horror filled him at the sight of the Irichna—thank Danu, there was only one—in a cowled black robe, obviously masquerading as a holy man, which was probably how he'd lured his victims. A mockery of a cross sat off to one side, with two crosspieces rather than one, and a live serpent winding its way among the staves.

Two youngish teenagers, both female, knelt before the demon, crying, begging, pleading. Blood ran down their faces and dripped to the ground. The air was thick with its coppery smell. Duncan looked closely for wounds and realized the Irichna was draining the girls' essence through their eyes, which ran red. One of the victims swayed alarmingly, her face paper white. The other put a steadying arm around her friend's shoulder.

Andraste lunged in front of the demon, hands extended, chanting furiously in Gaelic. It didn't even slow the creature down. At the shocked look on the goddess's face, Duncan knew she'd expected the thing to capitulate to her spell. She barked a word and a javelin appeared in one hand. She balanced it for a moment and then threw it at the Irichna. It went right through the demon, opening a hole in his robes, but the damage repaired itself behind the spear's passage.

Duncan deployed magic. Maybe if he mixed earth and air with her fire, they might have a chance.

Andraste had obviously been in his mind. "Do it," she hissed. "It's either that or call in reinforcements, which will turn this into an all-out war."

The demon threw back its head and laughed. It was an eerie sound, like glass scraping against itself. The cowl dropped away, revealing a face so heartbreakingly beautiful, Duncan had trouble tearing his gaze away. Blue-black hair framed Greek god features. No wonder the Irichna had been able to entice the girls mewling in fear before it. Was this the demon's true form, or merely another illusion? Ice chips skittered through Duncan's blood. His mouth was dry, his muscles so tense, they felt like rocks.

"On my count of three," Andraste shouted. "One, two…"

Duncan gave it all he had. He shoved as much as he could into the goddess's working. For one long, terrible span of time, he was afraid the best they had wouldn't be good enough, but then the Irichna's smoky eyes glazed and it wavered on its feet.

"What are you waiting for?" Andraste swatted him across the back. "Grab those girls and get them out of here. They're as good as dead, but at least they can die in better company."

Duncan swept the girls into a teleport spell and moved them to the one place he hoped might save them. Collective gasps surged around him as they materialized in the middle of the University Hospital's emergency room. With an arm supporting each girl, he pushed through double, swinging doors.

"Sir. Stop! You can't come back here," a nurse yelled at him.

Duncan spun toward her and cast an *obey me and then forget you ever saw me* spell. "Take care of these girls." He imbued his voice with an impossible to resist sweetness. "They've both lost a lot of blood."

"Yes, sir. Right away, sir."

As soon as the nurse had the girls, whose life force was indeed fading, Duncan strode from the hospital churning out *forget me* spells. He was intent on coffee and a sandwich before heading for Fairbanks, where he hoped he'd find Colleen and the other witches. If they weren't there, he'd wait for them in their shop.

Once he'd walked to the absolute rear of a huge parking lot, he glanced about and didn't see anybody. Satisfaction bit deep. When done properly, *forget me* spells made people turn the other way. Sucking in a steadying breath, he pictured a small deli in the middle of a quiet neighborhood and hoped for the best. Teleport spells were usually cooperative that way, so long as he made his needs clear.

A grove of trees materialized around him. Through their branches, he saw a diner's neon sign and grinned. The day was going pretty well, all in all. Even though he and Andraste may not have arrived in time to save the girls—and he wasn't certain they'd die, hospitals could do amazing things these days—he felt good about what they'd done. And amazed the demon hadn't gotten to him like the one the previous day.

"That's because it wasn't focused on you." Andraste stepped out of the ether and hooked an arm through his. Duncan choked back astonishment. The goddess laughed heartily. "What? You thought I wouldn't be able to find you?"

"Uh, I'm not sure I thought anything." He straightened his shoulders and tried to pull away, but she hung on.

"The Irichna didn't remain quiescent for long once you left." She shook her head until her blond braids danced around her shoulders. Furrows creased her brow. "I don't fully understand why my magic was insufficient to quell the thing."

"The witches who hunt them believe they're getting stronger. We believe the same thing."

"Mmph." She pressed her body against his side. The heat of her was electric and Duncan felt his body respond. "The demon hunt is over, at least for now. It may have been by the barest of margins, but we were victorious." She wound her other arm around him and drew her fingertips down his back.

"Shall we celebrate, pretty man?" Her nipples hardened against his chest. Andraste ground her pubes against his growing erection.

"I, er, I'm promised to another." Duncan resisted the desire to wind his arms around the goddess's body. Her lips hovered over his, so close her warm, fragrant breath bathed his face. He tried to turn his head away, but her sky blue eyes snared him.

Andraste laughed again, deep and throaty this time. "Well, I certainly won't tell her. If you keep your mouth shut, we should be in fine shape. You've had lots of women, why not me?"

He tried to utter words about honor and integrity, but his throat was thick and his cock engorged. Too late, he understood she'd spelled him. Outrage ran hot through his veins. He wrenched away from her grip, breathing as if he'd just run a race. Aroused and ashamed of his body's betrayal, Duncan put some distance between himself and the goddess, warded himself, and eyed her warily.

"I am very grateful to you for heeding my earlier summons —" he began.

"But not so grateful you'll bed me?" She quirked a blonde brow his way.

"I l-love another." His tongue stumbled over the word. The goddess surged into his head, cutting through his ward as if it weren't there.

"I see how things are." Andraste smiled knowingly. "You believe yourself in love with a mortal, yet such is forbidden to you. I can be patient, pretty man. Come find me when you need someone to pick up the pieces. These affairs are thrilling, but they never end well. Trust me. I've been there."

The air shimmered and Duncan was alone again. He dropped his head onto his palm and squeezed his eyes shut.

Andraste damn near had him. Was he truly as weak as that? First the Irichna, and now the goddess.

I have to do better. No question about it.

Gathering the shards of his dignity with difficulty, he walked slowly toward the diner. The sooner he got something to eat, the sooner he could find Colleen.

CHAPTER 11

Colleen kept an invisibility spell around Bubba. She and Jenna were waiting for Roz, who'd been inside the ferry terminal for the better part of half an hour. It was chilly and starting to drizzle. "I guess it's not the end of the world if one of us has to drive the car back to Alaska," she said.

"Yeah, but it would be so much better if this worked out for us." Jenna shivered and pulled her hood up.

"Do you have an extra coat in your rucksack?" Bubba asked.

"Ssht. No one can see you. They'll think it odd if they hear you. You're never cold."

"I am now," the changeling insisted. "Maybe I caught something from the you-know-what yesterday." Colleen exchanged worried glances with Jenna. The changeling was never sick. She dug through her bag for a sweater and handed it to Bubba.

Her thoughts drifted to Duncan. Where was he? Had Titania been generous? If not, would she ever see him again? It was closing on three in the afternoon. With luck, they'd be home well before nighttime when the Dreamers' Paths would open to her again. She elbowed Jenna. "Have you ever visited the dream world?"

The other witch's eyes narrowed. "Sure. I dream every night, but that's probably not what you mean. Are you asking about that place the dream guardian lives?"

"Yes. Dreamers' Paths. At least according to Bubba, you tread them at your own risk."

Jenna half grunted and made a face. "I had an aunt who spent a lot of time there. Too much. In the end, the place trapped her. You'll probably remember her. Rhea Whalen."

Colleen cocked her head to one side, feeling confused. From her limited experience, being forced to leave was more of a problem than being forced to stay. "Name doesn't exactly ring a bell. What do you mean?"

"She lost contact with the real world. Faded away. I'd find her body sitting in a chair, or lying on the couch, but her mind had left it." Jenna cleared her throat. "I've known a few witches with precognitive ability who visited there to check their predictions. None of them have had that problem, so maybe it was just something with Auntie Rhea."

"Humph. Any idea what percentage of witches use the Dreamers' Paths?"

"None whatsoever." Jenna stared at her intently. "Probably not very many. Why the sudden interest?"

"Because I went there last night—"

"You what?" Jenna cried and then clapped a hand over her mouth. A couple of passersby glanced sidelong at her and she subsided into mutters.

"Good to go. Finally." Roz trotted toward them. "I had to pay a good bit extra so they'd move the car from this ferry to the one in Ketchikan, but the Subaru will be at the Haines ferry terminal four days from now at six p.m."

"Our conversation's not over with," Jenna warned, shooting a meaningful glance Colleen's way.

"What conversation?" Roz raised an interested eyebrow.

"Never mind. Great news. Means we can leave." Jenna glanced around. So did Colleen. They needed somewhere their disappearance wouldn't be noticed.

"Damn! Not many places where we could just fade away." Roz chewed the jagged nail on her index finger. "Let me move the car onto the boat and leave the keys with the dude I talked to. Be right back and then we can get the rest of the show on the road."

"I don't feel good. Want to go home," Bubba whined and clung to Colleen's legs. She bent and touched his forehead. The changeling was always warm, but he did feel hotter than usual.

"What's wrong with him?" Jenna asked.

"I don't know, but it disturbs me," Colleen replied. She captured her lower lip between her teeth. Shy of hiring a taxi to take them to a more wooded area, she was fresh out of ideas for how to flicker out of sight without attracting notice. They did need to get home, though. And quickly. Before Bubba got any worse.

"I saw one of those family restrooms inside the terminal when I took a pee break," Jenna said, adding, "It's on the lower floor, over on the left hand side between the men's and women's restrooms."

"Perfect. Let's go." Colleen scooped the changeling into her arms. She stopped by the car queued up for the boat to let Roz know where they'd be and walked toward the ferry station.

Jenna caught up to Colleen and Bubba, and they squeezed through the stationhouse door. It felt wonderfully warm inside. Maybe the changeling's only problem was he'd gotten chilled. It didn't seem likely, but Colleen wasn't above hoping for miracles.

"Probably best if all of us don't go in together," Jenna murmured from behind them.

"Yeah, they'll think we're a bunch of perverts." Colleen turned right, headed down a staircase, and followed the restroom signage. She stepped to the door labeled *Families* and wiggled its knob. Locked. They milled about, trying to look inconspicuous, until an Asian mother with three children exited the small space.

Roz loped toward them, smiling. "All taken care of." She dusted her hands together.

"That's a relief. Good to have something go our way." Colleen glanced around. The restroom hallway was deserted, so she tugged the door open and gestured everyone through, locking it behind them.

"The next person won't be able to get in." Jenna reached for the lock.

Roz slapped her hand away. "It's better than having someone walk in on us when we're half here and half not."

Colleen wanted to change Bubba back to his cat form, but he shivered in her arms, and she was afraid his other form might make things worse. "You're going to have to help me, Roz."

The other witch eyed her sharply. "Sure. I'll do the whole thing. We'll come out at our house. We can regroup there."

Bubba moaned softly. He made a gagging noise, twisted in Colleen's arms, and threw up on the bathroom floor.

Colleen grabbed a paper towel and wiped the changeling's mouth. "Aw, Bubs. It will be all right. We'll be home really, really soon."

"Sorry," he mumbled. Colleen hugged him tight. She felt Roz's spell snag them and relaxed into it to maximize the other witch's magic.

The walls of their home in Fairbanks flickered a time or two, and then solidified.

Home, thank Christ!

Bubba shook and shuddered in her arms. She hurried to one of the living room couches, laid him on it, and wrapped a comforter around him. "You still feeling sick to your tummy, sweetheart?"

The changeling nodded.

"Here." Roz handed Bubba a bowl. "In case you puke again." She pushed Colleen aside, sat on the edge of the couch, and took the changeling's hands in hers. Roz was a decent healer. Colleen inhaled anxiously, barely breathing. What would the other witch find? If Bubba had inadvertently soaked in some of the Irichna's poison while the thing was in reptile form, he was probably finished.

Jenna moved close, but Colleen held a finger over her lips. Roz needed quiet to concentrate. Jenna nodded her understanding and perched on the edge of an overstuffed chair. All of them were fond of Bubba. He'd become part of their family group over the years they'd been together. The specter of possibly losing him knifed into her soul. She fought feelings of helplessness and chided herself.

Bubba was still alive. There had to be something they could do to help him.

Long moments passed before Roz let go of the changeling's hands. She moved her palm over his face in a circular motion. "Sleep," she murmured. Bubba's eyes closed. Colleen felt the other witch's spell.

Roz got heavily to her feet and motioned to them. They walked through the living room and into the kitchen, where Roz filled the teakettle with water and placed it on the stove. It was harder than hell not to mob her with questions, but

Colleen figured she was trying to make sense of whatever she'd found.

Because she had to do something, she rustled up tea herbs and placed them in a strainer that would fit into the kettle once the water had heated.

"Maybe Colleen can wait you out, but I can't," Jenna muttered. She dropped onto one of the scarred oak chairs sitting around an equally battered round oak table. "What the hell is wrong with him?"

Roz bit her lip. "Not certain. It could be one of two things." She gathered three mugs and set them on the table along with cream from the refrigerator and the sugar canister.

"Well, what are they?" Colleen snapped up the kettle, hit it with a shot of magic to make the water boil immediately, and dropped the strainer into it.

"It's been years since you found him in the barrows of Ireland. I believe that's where he draws his power from. It could be something simple, like he needs to go home to recharge."

Jenna jiggled the strainer, poured a little tea, and shook her head. "Not strong enough yet."

"How could it be?" Roz asked. "It hasn't been steeping for more than a couple of minutes."

"What's the other option?" Colleen prodded. Perfectly brewed tea was the last thing on her mind.

"He's been poisoned by an Irichna." Roz shook her head. "If that's what's wrong, all we can do is wait it out and pray he's strong enough to shake off the toxins."

Colleen walked across the kitchen and opened the cabinet where they kept the liquor. She grabbed a bottle at random, crossed back to the table, and splashed some into her mug before filling it to the top with tea.

"Good idea." Roz did the same and handed the bottle to

Jenna, who just drank from it, not bothering to dilute the spirits with tea.

The tea burned Colleen's mouth, and the liquor burned her throat. She eyed Roz. "What if his problem is a little of both?"

"What do you mean?" Roz slugged back half the liquid in her mug and grimaced. Colleen didn't blame her. Between the heat and the liquor, her throat was probably on fire.

"Well, maybe Bubba does need to go home. He's come into contact with demon poisons before, and they've never bothered him." Colleen set her mug down. "I figure it's sort of like it is with a battery. He's grown weaker, but so gradually none of us noticed—until now."

"I suppose that's possible." Roz sagged against her chair. "I think we should wait for at least a little while. I spelled him to rest. It will help him marshal his resources."

"If we wait too long, he may get too weak to travel," Jenna said.

"Yes, but what if I'm wrong and we subject him to a trip to Ireland for nothing?" Roz countered.

"How long will he sleep?" Colleen asked.

"At least an hour. Maybe two," Roz replied.

Colleen got to her feet, went to the coatrack next to the back door, and traded her jacket for a heavier one. She tugged a wool cap over her bright hair.

"Where are you going?" Jenna asked.

"I'm going to check on the shop. Besides, someone needs to bring our other car back here. It's not like we can teleport to the pharmacy and grocery store."

Roz got up, mug in hand. "I'll sit with him," she offered.

Colleen was so grateful she felt the prick of tears. "Thanks. Call me if anything happens. I can be back here immediately."

The other witch swept her into a hug and patted her back. "Don't worry, honey. It's not like he's at death's door."

"Really?"

Roz let go of her and kissed her forehead. "Really. I've never treated a changeling before, but I figure he's just like other living creatures. He'll likely still be asleep when you get back."

"Thanks."

"No thanks needed. You'd do the same for me."

"I'll make us some dinner." Jenna glanced around the kitchen. "We could all do with something hot." She stood. "Speaking of which, I'll turn up the furnace and get a fire going in the woodstove."

"You mean I'll be able to take my jacket off at some point?" Roz grinned crookedly, and Jenna slugged her in the arm.

It seemed like as good a time as any to leave. Colleen tiptoed back to the living room and blew Bubba a kiss. The changeling's color looked a little better and his chest rose and fell regularly. Maybe this wouldn't be as bad as she feared. She hesitated, and then summoned magic to teleport her to their shop. Roz was correct. Nothing for her to do at home, so she may as well take care of business.

Colleen juggled the magic that wanted to whoosh her away and called to Jenna. "Need anything else for that dinner you're putting together?"

"Nope. Good to go."

After a last, fond look at her changeling, Colleen loosed her spell. Even before the shop's walls stopped pulsating, arms closed around her and she was enveloped by Duncan's familiar scent. He rained kisses down her hair and the side of her face before closing his mouth over hers in a kiss that became hotter by the moment.

Colleen pulled away, smiling like a besotted fool. "I am so glad to see you, but we have to hurry. We can talk in the car."

"How'd you get here so fast?" He was grinning too.

"Sent the car on a ferry, actually a couple of them. We'll pick it up in Haines four days from now."

He nodded. "Ah. You teleported."

"Looks like you did too. We really do need to hurry. Bubba's sick. I just dropped by here to check on things and drive the car home."

"What do you mean sick?" A worried note ran beneath his words.

"Fever. Throwing up. Says he feels bad."

"Has he ever been sick before?"

She shook her head and stared at Duncan, sensing his apprehension. "You're not making me feel better. Come on. Car's in the back." She hurried out the shop's front door, locked it behind them, and led the way through an alley. "It's the silver 4Runner." She hit the clicker and lights flashed on the SUV. Colleen got inside, fastened her seatbelt, and waited for Duncan to do the same.

They merged into light traffic. Duncan reached across the console and laid a hand on her thigh. "It's really wonderful to see you."

Warmth, and a funny, fluttery feeling bloomed in her belly. "I was looking forward to tonight." The warmth extended to her face, and she knew she was blushing.

"So was I."

She glanced at him. "Were you planning to use the Dreamers' Paths again?"

"Of course. Last night was barely a beginning. I want more of you. Lots more."

"Did you know the Paths held danger?"

He nodded. "Of course, but I kept you safe from harm with my magic."

Her heart did a small flip-flop. She wanted to talk about the two of them, and ask if he'd tracked Titania down, but she needed to know why her comment about Bubba being ill concerned him. She placed her hand over his and squeezed. "Why'd you ask if Bubba had been sick before?"

"Because changelings don't get sick. They're immune to everything, like most magical creatures."

Fear balled in her belly. "Roz has healing ability. She thought he might need to go back to the Old Country to recharge his magic. Her other thought was the Irichna had poisoned him."

"He's fought Irichna before," Duncan pointed out.

"Yeah, that bothered me too. He's been exposed to their toxins and never had this kind of a reaction."

"Mmph."

"You're thinking something. I can't go into your head while I'm driving, it's too distracting. What do you think is wrong?"

He blew out a tight breath. "It's farfetched, but didn't it seem odd to you that Mathilde didn't go after you earlier today and at least try to compel you to stay?"

"How do you know about that?"

"I stopped by Witches' Northwest and did a spot of eavesdropping."

Colleen considered his question about Mathilde. "Now that you bring it up, I was sort of expecting her to break away from the witches who were trying to corral her and tear after us, but it never happened."

"The other witches in her Coven, at least some of them, think she's been possessed by the Irichna. If that's true, it would explain why she attacked you—and why she blew all that time grilling me. It's also possible she did something to Bubba. He wouldn't have been warded as well as the three of you."

"Shit!" Colleen yanked her hand away from his and pounded it on the steering wheel. "A magical tracking device."

"How far are we from your house?"

"Five minutes."

"We'll have to be careful. You may have unwanted company."

Colleen kicked herself for being stupid. She'd never even considered Mathilde using Bubba to follow them. "I've got to warn the others."

"No! If they've been captured and you access them telepathically, you might get snared too."

Colleen bit down hard on her lower lip, so anxious it practically ate a hole in her stomach. "Speaking of Irichna, what happened to the one in the U.K.? You know, the reason you came hunting me in the first place."

"The Sidhe are taking care of it," Duncan grunted, sounding exasperated. "I had to ask, but they understood their duty—once I rubbed their faces in it."

"Bully for them." Colleen's voice dripped sarcasm, but she didn't care. Pulling down a side street a block from her house, she shoved her car door open and got out. "We'll walk from here."

"I'll ward us." He rushed to her side of the car and pulled her close. "If it looks like we need it, can you handle an invisibility spell?"

"Yes." Her heart pounded hard. "Hurry. I couldn't stand it if anything bad happened to any of them."

CHAPTER 12

Duncan drew magic softly, subtly, to create a ward. He didn't want to alert anyone to their presence. Colleen led them to the back of a ramshackle three-story house. Lights blazed from inside. He felt her stiffen next to him just about the time he got a good, strong whiff of Irichna. She loosed a string of curses in her head, but he heard them.

He shielded his mind voice just for her. *"How many are there? I can't tell. It feels like one huge clump of evil to me."*

"Three." She paused. *"Maybe more. Hard to tell, but I sense at least three of the bastards."*

"Do we need help?"

She nodded, vibrating with outrage. *"Bubba's helpless, so either Jenna or Roz will be protecting him. At least they're all still alive."*

Hoping against hope he wouldn't raise Andraste again, Duncan transmitted a distress signal.

"Let's circle the house and see what we can." Colleen hooked an arm through his and pulled.

Because it was as good an idea as any, he followed her.

Unfortunately, the house sat high above the street. To peer into the windows, they'd have to get much closer, which didn't seem wise, since they hadn't been discovered—yet. He drew her back to where they'd started and said, *"I can get more information using magic."*

The air near them glittered oddly. Colleen raised her hands, ready to strike. "Wait," Duncan said, his voice very low. "They may be on our side."

He recognized fae energy, but not the pair who shimmered into being. Duncan draped magic about them to muffle conversation and inserted his body between Colleen and the newcomers. "Names," he barked, wondering if they were Seelie or Unseelie.

The woman's shoulder-length black hair bobbed as she shook her head in what looked like annoyance. Lines formed around the corners of her green eyes when she narrowed them in disapproval. A skintight black jumpsuit fit her like a second skin and her feet were bare. "Och aye, 'tisn't enough we heeded your call?" she asked.

"No. It isn't," Duncan snapped. "I am one of the Sidhe Elders. I do not know you."

"Duncan!" Colleen's mind voice was sharp. *"We scarcely have time for this. Either let them help us, or tell them to leave."*

The man inclined his head. Dark hair shimmied around him, falling to chest level. Eyes the color of gray smoke held an otherworldly aspect. Like all fae, he was beautiful, with a gamin's face and a perpetually youthful look. In contrast to the woman's formfitting garb, he wore a midnight blue robe, sashed with teal.

"We are dark fae, from the Unseelie Court." He held up a hand, no doubt in response to the antipathy flickering from Duncan's eyes. "Ye hold no love for us, yet we consider the

Irichna an enemy as well, or we would not have shown ourselves."

"Aye, the demons have grown powerful. 'Tis a concern for us all," the woman added. She set her hands on her hips. "What shall it be, Sidhe? Will ye swallow your misplaced pride—?"

Glass shattered. Jenna shrieked imprecations in Gaelic.

Roz shouted. "Godless fucking bastards!"

Colleen broke from behind him and sprinted for the house.

Not much reason for stealth now. "I don't have time for the formal acceptance speech," he told the fae. "Follow me. I have no idea how to weave my magic with yours."

"We will figure it out." Satisfaction ran beneath the man's low, musical voice.

Duncan had never trusted dark fae. Had he just invited the back half of a trap to snap closed behind them? He gave his thoughts a firm mental shake. The die was cast. No going back now. He reached the broken window, but Colleen was already inside, chanting like a mad thing. The fae dashed past him and catapulted through the window, graceful as gazelles. Duncan pulled magic and followed them.

The living room was a shambles. Furniture had been overturned. Broken glass littered the carpeted floor. Roz clutched Bubba in her arms. Blood ran down her face and arms. One of the Irichna stood inches from her. Duncan saw the witch's essence fading as it flowed into the demon, who lapped it like nectar. Bubba's energy just felt...wrong. Where Roz was weak, the changeling was far too strong, almost as if he were helping the Irichna, or gathering strength from it.

Makes sense if Mathilde is linked to him.

Jenna lay face down on the floor. Were they too late to save her? Duncan pushed magic forward and felt a faint pulse as her life flickered. Colleen had pounced on one of the demons. They wrestled on the floor, shifting forms so quickly he couldn't figure out quite what they were. Her clothing lay in shreds, scattered about. Obviously, she hadn't had time to take anything off before she shifted.

"We will help the changeling," the male fae said. He and the woman converged on the demon sucking the life from Roz.

Duncan raced forward. "Help the witch. I'll take the changeling. He's linked to the demons through no fault of his own." Roz's eyes widened in horror at his words and she thrust Bubba into his arms.

Duncan had just sent magic into the changeling to determine how to sever his connection with Mathilde when something hit his warding with a blast of magic from behind.

The third Irichna.

He'd forgotten Colleen said there were three. Duncan flew through the air, frantically pulling magic to soften their landing, and flopped on his stomach, right on top of the changeling.

"Ooph," Bubba grunted, but he wriggled beneath Duncan, which probably meant he wasn't injured.

"Sorry." Duncan kept his voice low. "Did I hurt you?"

"No. I'm going to crawl under the sofa," Bubba whispered against Duncan's chest in a very ancient form of Gaelic. "Do something so no one will notice me under there. I feel the wickedness inside, but I think I can keep from surrendering to it—for a little while. Help Roz and Jenna and Colleen. Especially Colleen."

Duncan shielded the changeling while he skittered beneath one of the dust covers at the back of a couch, and cast a *don't look here* spell. He also sent up a prayer to Danu to watch over the little creature until he could get back to him.

Jumping to his feet, he sent power spiraling outward. The Irichna who'd attacked him moved closer, laughing. He looked like an innocent youth, with dimpled cheeks and blond curls, dressed in dungarees and a plaid shirt. Duncan scanned the room. It was hard to tell how Jenna was, beyond the fact that she was still alive. Roz and the two fae seemed to be holding their own against the demon they faced. Roz's energy was a little stronger, but blood still dripped from open wounds criss-crossing her face and arms.

Colleen and the demon she fought had morphed into wolves, snapping, snarling, and tearing at one another. At least she didn't look wounded, and her life force pulsed strongly. Duncan reached deep, channeling power he knew about, but had never tapped before. It came from the oldest magic and was damn near uncontrollable, which was why the Sidhe left it alone. When he had it as well in hand as he could, he loosed it at the still-laughing demon, masquerading as an innocent youth.

Duncan's hair stood on end. Every nerve frazzled as power surged through him. It felt as if he'd channeled lightning. But the simpering smile on the demon's face faltered, and then winked out. The fine-boned youth's form gave way to a pock-marked ancient with open pustules marking his naked body.

Duncan understood he was seeing the demon's true form for the first time.

Because it was working, he let power flow through him, wondering how long he could serve as a conduit for an energy source designed by the Celtic gods. If Andraste had tapped into it earlier, it hadn't worked for her, but it was working for him, which was all that mattered.

His breath came in little panting gasps. All his muscles strained with the effort of channeling raw magic into the Irichna. Finally, when he knew he'd have to release his hold on the magic soon, or be consumed by it, the demon folded in upon itself, wavered, and vanished in a cloud of stinking, black-edged flames.

Duncan wanted to sink to the floor, panting, but he took stock of the others. The Irichna that had threatened Roz was gone, and the fae had closed on the battling wolves. Duncan joined them.

"Impressive, Sidhe." The woman flashed him a feral grin that twisted her beauty into something fierce.

"Aye, and can ye do it again?" the male asked.

"Good question. Maybe."

"You've got to get Colleen away from the demon first." Roz's voice sounded like river-washed gravel coated her throat. She'd picked Jenna up from the floor and laid her on a couch. Roz sat next to the other witch, hands on either side of her face. Jenna's eyelids fluttered.

One of the wolves glittered and shifted. Colleen stood, chest heaving, naked. "That was the easy part." She sidestepped the demon, which was still in wolf form, and aimed a jolt of magic its way. The two fae slid between her and the wolf. It lifted its muzzle, scenting the air, and its lupine eyes widened.

"Och aye," the female fae sneered. "Your fell companions have left. We like these odds much better."

"Give me a minute or two and I'll see he gets to Hell." Roz rose from where she'd been seated next to Jenna.

The wolf skinned its upper lip back, bared its fangs, and snarled. Gray dust rose around it. When the cloud cleared, it was gone.

Duncan blew out a weary breath. "Too fucking bad these three will live to fight another day."

"Not the one ye targeted, Sidhe," the male fae said. "I am not clear where ye sent him, but I know he is gone. I felt him dissolving. They canna return once what pins them together has failed."

The female raised her head, nose twitching. "Damn it! We are not yet clear of them."

"It's not what you think." Duncan stumbled across the room, lay on the floor, and fished Bubba's inert body from beneath the couch.

Colleen moaned and threw herself toward them, landing half on top of Duncan. "Aw, shit, shit, shit. Is he dead?" Her voice choked with emotion.

Duncan sent magic carefully into the changeling's small body. What he found wasn't encouraging. The changeling had gone deep, closing the upper levels of his mind to keep Mathilde's magic from spreading, and to deny the witch access to him. Duncan placed Bubba on the couch, awed by his courage.

"Not dead," Duncan murmured, "but not far from it. He kept his word, though. The changeling has mettle. He contained the evil inside of him, and kept Mathilde out of his mind. And out of our midst."

"What can we do?" Roz hovered. "I fear it's beyond my healing ability."

The fae drew near. "Whose creature is he?" the man demanded.

"Mine." From where she sat on the floor, Colleen settled a hand on Bubba's forehead. "Oh my God, he's cold as ice." She scooted closer, bent so her ear was against his chest, and listened. "His heart is still beating, but it's far too slow." She straightened. Her anguished gaze, eyes shiny with tears, sought Roz's. "If we'd known when we first got back here, maybe we could have—"

Duncan made a chopping motion with one hand. "What's important is what we do now." He glanced at the fae. "Are either of you healers?"

The man nodded. "Aye. That would be me."

"Can you sense a demon's marker within the changeling?" The fae nodded and Duncan congratulated himself for being correct about Mathilde's treachery. "Do you have any idea how to remove it without killing him?"

The man muttered in Gaelic, and then switched to English. "I am not certain, yet this thing must be done."

"Aye, at least if we kill him, he will die clear of demon taint," the female fae said.

"How can I help?" Colleen looked from Duncan to the two dark fae.

"Since he is yours, you must hold him," the male fae said.

"Aye, and 'tis tricky," the female added. "Ye must take care, or the evil will lodge itself within you. Because witch magic is mixed up in this, 'twill have an affinity for you and the other two witches in here." She shot meaningful looks at Roz and Jenna, who'd moved to a sitting position. Jenna's face was pale, but her hazel eyes burned with fury.

Duncan didn't like the sound of that at all. He moved to Colleen's side and wove an arm around her. "Can I do this thing in her stead?"

The male fae shook his head. "Nay. Ye may sit next to her, though, and infuse power—assuming ye have any left—into her if ye sense her weakening."

Still naked, Colleen scrambled to her feet, scooped Bubba up, and sat on the couch. Duncan took the place next to her and draped the changeling's legs over his lap.

"I'm ready," she said through bloodless lips. Duncan felt her desolation—and her guilt—in the set of her body next to his. He wanted to murmur encouragement, but Bubba's situation was grim and they both knew it. He felt Colleen ward herself and did the same.

"There is one thing else ye must know afore we begin." The male fae hunkered so his smoky eyes were on a level with Colleen's. "I canna predict exactly what will happen. Anything is possible. What is within yon changeling's body will fight to retain its hold. Your creature will struggle. He may hurt you, but ye must not let go until I tell you 'tis safe."

He switched his unnerving gaze to Duncan. "Ye are limited to infusing magic into the witch. If ye do aught else, ye will interfere with my summoning and binding spells."

Duncan nodded tersely. "I understand." Bubba's body jerked. His head lolled to one side. "Hurry," Duncan said. "I'm afraid he's dying."

Magic rose around them. It had a different feel from his own, yet it felt clean. Duncan wondered if he—and the rest of the Sidhe—had misjudged the Unseelie Court all these years. Bubba thrashed. An ungodly moan rose from him, followed by another. Colleen looked so broken, it opened a hole in Duncan's soul.

The changeling arched his back. His heels thrummed on Duncan's lap, almost as if he were having a seizure. Who knew? Maybe he was. Fae magic deepened about them. Duncan's heartbeat quickened. The Unseelie might hate demons, but they had their own agenda. He hoped to hell it didn't include shanghaiing him and Colleen for some nefarious scheme he could only guess at.

The female fae got close enough to shake a finger in front of him. "None of that," she snapped. "Weakens the spell. Ye must believe if we are to save the wee man."

Colleen turned accusing eyes on him. "If you can't help, go away." She pulled Bubba's body entirely into her arms.

Defenses leapt to his lips, but he swallowed them. "I want to stay. I'll repress my doubts."

"Is that good enough?" Colleen stared at the female fae. She hesitated for a long moment, then nodded sharply.

Duncan felt the fae's magic, which had withdrawn, thicken again. He focused on the changeling's weakening body, but kept his own magic contained. He remembered the fae's instructions: he could only shore Colleen up if her magic looked as if it were failing.

Bubba's eyes snapped open. Fire burned in their dark depths. He bared his teeth and made a lunge for Colleen's neck. She gripped him tighter and held him away from her. He writhed in her arms, growling, snapping, and drooling like a rabid dog. Colleen's expression reflected horror—and determination. Bubba laughed and gouged her, drawing blood wherever he made contact.

Duncan wanted to reach out to both of them, to soothe their pain. He ached for Colleen. If the changeling died, she'd have a hell of a time forgiving herself—if she even could.

Anguish etched deep furrows into Colleen's face. Tears flowed down her cheeks, but she held fast. Bubba raked his nails down her breasts. She tried to hold him farther out, but his arms were as long as hers.

A struggle played out on the changeling's expressive features. One moment, he looked like a small demon, the next chagrin twisted his mouth and tears dripped down his face. "Sorry, Colleen. I'm so sorry," slid out before something curved his mouth into a grin that was wickedness incarnate, and he called her a bitch and a slut.

Bubba shifted in her grip and kicked her in the stomach. She winced and moved him. Next he kicked her in the side. Duncan had never felt so helpless. Colleen's suffering ate at him. He felt it in his heart and soul and guts. He wanted to be part of whatever the fae were doing, so he could speed up the process, but the other magic-wielders hadn't requested assistance. Stepping into the middle of someone else's spell, especially when they were using unfamiliar magic, was a recipe for disaster.

Because he had to do something, he send a steadying blast of power into Colleen. Her grip on Bubba tightened, and she nodded wordless thanks. An uneven gash opened in the changeling's shoulder. Blood flowed freely, pouring onto Colleen, the couch, and the floor. Something dark and putrid followed in its wake. A form with wings and claws and sharp, pointed teeth.

"Strengthen your wards," the female fae cried and herded the shadow with a spell of her own. It moved back and forth between her hands, and then headed for her chest, but bounced off. She began a harsh chant in Gaelic that mounted in intensity until the shadow exploded, showering her and the male fae with putrid smelling bits of black goo.

Bubba's rigid body collapsed against Colleen. Both of them were crying, great choking sobs of relief, as she cradled the changeling in her arms, crooning to him.

"It is done," the male fae said. "We must leave with the tainted particles. What's left of the atrocity we removed."

"Aye," the female concurred in a strained voice. "Our task is not yet done, we must neutralize the bits so they canna reform and do further harm."

Before Duncan could thank them, the Unseelie were gone.

Colleen rocked Bubba against her. The changeling still felt weak, but he was strengthening by the moment now that Mathilde's fiendish magic was gone. Duncan plucked a blanket off the back of an overstuffed chair and tucked it around both of them.

"Thanks." Colleen was too tired to smile. "Cold in here without clothes."

Roz knelt and placed a hand over Bubba's wound, which still oozed blood and yellowish pus. "Hang on. I can fix this. Thank Danu for healing I can manage on my own," she muttered with a return of her normally acerbic wit.

"Jenna?" Colleen looked across the room and locked gazes with the other witch.

"I'm all right. Or I will be once I get this godawful mess in here cleared up."

"How long was I gone before they showed up?"

Jenna shrugged. "Not long. Five minutes, maybe."

"It was like they were right outside, heard every word, and

plotted their attack for when we'd be weakest." Roz shook her head in what looked like consternation.

"That's exactly what they did," Duncan growled, and filled them in on Mathilde's tracking device. "...I'm not certain exactly what type of magic she used, but if its design was similar to what I'm familiar with, she could see you and hear you. If it weren't for Bubba's incredible bravery, she could have used his body as a conduit right into your house, and followed the demons in here."

Colleen shivered. "That's hideous. We came here instead of our shop because we thought she didn't know where it was."

"We need to let Coven Central know so they can remove her," Roz said.

"Immediately. Before she fucks with anyone else," Jenna muttered.

"Yeah, I'm surprised she handed over that Irichna at Witches' Northwest, given she was in cahoots with them," Roz said.

"It was a diversionary tactic," Duncan said. "Had to be. Mathilde must've guessed her witches were growing suspicious."

Bubba pushed back a few inches from Colleen, moved the blanket aside, and looked at her. "Shit! Aw shit, did I do all that to you?" He pointed at the gouges on her face and arms.

He looked so distraught, Colleen almost told him one of the demons had done most of the damage, but Duncan caught her gaze and shook his head slightly. "When we begin lying, even small ones meant to soothe, we become more like our enemy. Tonight, of all nights, is a time for truth."

She smoothed the changeling's thick hair back from his low forehead. "Yes, sweetie, but I'd have tolerated much worse to save your life." Something occurred to her. "When did you first start feeling bad?"

"In the car waiting for you to come back with our breakfast."

So almost immediately after we left Witches' Northwest.

"Why didn't you say something?"

The changeling shrugged, looking sheepish. "I thought it wasn't anything. That I was just keyed up from the last demon fight. It didn't get really bad until we were waiting outside the ferry terminal."

Colleen tried for a stern face, but probably didn't do very well. "If anything like this ever happens again—"

He shot her a cowed smile and cut in with, "You'll be the very first to know."

Colleen dropped her head against the back of the couch and blew out a breath. Little clicks and clacks told her Jenna was picking things up and righting furniture. She thought she should offer to help, but was too tapped out to even say the words. She drifted for a bit with Bubba's head on her chest and Duncan's comforting presence next to her.

Duncan murmured to her in a language she didn't understand, and she felt him in her mind, patching, soothing, healing. When he withdrew, fatigue, which had surrounded her in a thick, sticky cloud, left too. Colleen turned her head to the side so she could look at him. "Thanks again."

Warmth and tenderness shone from his green eyes. "You're welcome."

"Here." Roz shoved a liquor bottle into Duncan's hand. "I've been helping myself, but you may as well too." She turned the coffee table upright and sat on it. "What's with the dark fae? I nearly had a heart attack when they showed up here. Thought I'd have two enemies to fight."

Spots of color splashed across Duncan's golden skin. "They're my doing. Colleen found me in your shop, told me about Bubba, and said we needed to hurry back here. I started thinking about the sequence of events and suspected Mathilde had something to do with Bubba's sudden illness." He stopped to take a breath. "Changelings are never sick, so I knew something had to be afoot."

Roz made a grab for the bottle and took a long swig before handing it to Colleen. "I'm missing something here. How'd we get from my question about the Unseelie to Mathilde?"

"Sorry. It's been a long day." Duncan shut his eyes for a moment and then opened them again. Colleen sensed him ordering his thoughts.

"When Colleen and I showed up at your house, she parked a little way away because I was concerned about a possible link between Bubba and Mathilde. We both scented the demons as soon as we got out of the car. I asked if we needed help. When she said we did, I put out a call. The Unseelie showed up." He threw his hands in the air. "It's always a crap shoot. The last time I requested aid, Andraste came."

Surprise shot through Colleen. "The Celtic goddess of victory?" He nodded. "Wow! Just how widespread is this, um, *come help me* signal?"

Duncan chuckled. "Damned if I know. I've only used it a handful of times in a thousand years. Each time, something different has responded. Let's see." He counted on his fingers. "So far, I've raised Sidhe, Celtic gods, a Druid, a werewolf—in human form, mind you—and now two dark fae."

Roz held her hand out for the bottle. "All righty. Back to the Unseelie. I thought they were evil."

"So did I," Duncan said. "Sidhe have steered clear of them these past few centuries."

"Do you know why?" Jenna asked. She settled next to Roz on the coffee table. It creaked alarmingly, but didn't splinter. Colleen feared it might still give way, after listening to it complain about the combined weight of the two witches.

"What happened to cleaning?" Roz asked pointedly.

Jenna jabbed her in the ribs with an elbow and pried her fingers off the whiskey bottle. "Since when do I have *housekeeper* tattooed across my forehead? The only thing left is all the broken glass. I'll use magic to get it out of here, but I need the room empty to do that, 'cause the shards will fly around like crazy." She shifted her gaze to Duncan. "The Unseelie?"

"I need to ask someone, or look them up," Duncan said. "They're definitely the mischievous branch of the fae, but they've done some pretty crass things over the years. I think the main reason we shun them is they're so unpredictable."

"You know more than you're telling us." Jenna continued to skewer him with her shrewd hazel gaze.

He grinned crookedly. "Guess keeping secrets in a houseful of witches is hopeless."

"You bet it is." Colleen snorted. "What did you leave out?"

His forehead furrowed. "Not all that much, really. Titania and Oberon oversee Faerie. The Celtic gods formed a separate pantheon, so they don't pay homage to our rulers. Mostly, they fight a lot among themselves—and give Danu fits. Ceridwen formed both branches of the fae—Seelie and Unseelie—from the same energy source. Sidhe and Daoine Sidhe are part of the Seelie Court, but we used to have a place in the Unseelie one as well."

"By that argument, you must've gotten along with the Unseelie at some point." Roz set her chin on an upraised hand.

"We did, for many years. Then they started playing tricks. Things they thought were funny, like using mirrors to confuse the routes into Faerie. We ignored them and they upped the ante. Eventually, we quit having anything to do with them. Rumor had it, they gave up on us and started harassing mortals."

"History be damned, the two who showed up tonight were

a godsend," Colleen said. Bubba shifted in her arms, mumbling sleepily about wanting to go to his bed.

"I'll take him." Roz pushed to her feet and held out her arms.

Colleen kissed the top of his head. "I'm sure glad you're still with us, Bubs."

"That makes two of us." The changeling grinned, turned, and let Roz lift him. "I could get to like all this attention."

"Don't get too used to it," Colleen admonished, but it was hard to maintain any semblance of solemnity when she was so happy. She snugged the blanket around her, leaned against Duncan, and watched Roz carry Bubba toward the stairs. "Whatever happened to that dinner you started?" she asked Jenna.

"I imagine it's still there. Maybe a bit on the thick side, but I had the heat low."

Duncan tightened his arm around her shoulders. "Hungry?"

"It's a tossup, which I want more. Food. Sleep. You." She set her mouth in a hard line. "Some reassurance we'll get at least a few hours' break before the next demon incursion."

"Guess we should sleep in shifts," Jenna suggested.

Roz tromped back into the room. "I heard that. It's a good idea. I also heard Jenna say dinner might not be entirely ruined. I'll see all of you in the kitchen. No matter what comes next, we need to eat."

"I'll second that." Jenna trailed after the other witch.

Colleen snuggled closer to Duncan. "Guess we ought to follow them."

He repositioned himself so he faced her and ran his fingertips down the side of her face. "You have cuts and gouges. Let me heal them."

"Later. It doesn't feel very important."

He brushed a knuckle over her lips. "Maybe not, but you're

important to me. I was scared for you, and for Bubba. I know how special he is to you. He's like the child you never had."

She smiled wryly. "I only just realized that in the past few days. Pretty dense of me, huh?"

"Maybe not. Admitting we care about someone makes us vulnerable, because then we shatter if we lose them."

Colleen laid a hand on the side of his face. "Earlier you said something like, tonight of all nights, is a time for truth."

"Yes, I did. Why mention it now?" He smoothed her tangled hair back from her face.

She took a deep breath, suddenly nervous about his answer to the question she hadn't asked yet. He was here, surely that meant things had gone well with Titania... "Did you talk to your queen?"

His face clouded—brows drawn into a thin line, eyes worried—and her heart seized. She looked away, fighting sudden tears.

"No, sweetheart," he said quickly. "It's not like that." He cupped her face in his hands and tipped it so she had to look at him. "I found Titania. We chatted of this and that. When I asked her about you, she said no, and vanished to end any possibility of further dialogue."

"Is that why you came to my shop? To tell me?"

"I suppose that was part of it, but the main reason I was waiting in your shop was to tell you I can't live without you. Titania's blessings don't matter. Oh, they'd make our lives easier, but we'll do all right without them. I never spent much time hobnobbing with other Sidhe." He narrowed his eyes thoughtfully. "They'll probably miss me more than I'll miss them."

Pain sluiced through her. His offer was wonderful, amazing, but she couldn't let him forsake immortality for her. She shook her head sadly. "I'm touched and flattered, but someday you'll resent having lost your immortality. And you'll blame me for it—"

Sadness rimmed his eyes with a network of fine lines. "Are you trying to tell me you don't want me? I know we've only just met, but I've never been so attracted to anyone. I can't imagine my life without you in it, Colleen. Please, please don't push me away."

The tears that had threatened a few moments before overflowed. She scrubbed her cheeks with the backs of her hands. "It would be for the best. You need someone truly immortal like you. Someone where the queen will bless your union..." Her voice ran down, overcome by a sob.

He gathered her into his arms and held her tight against him. "You're scared."

She nodded against his chest, almost too overwhelmed to form words. "It's a huge step. Relationships are hard under the best circumstances, and if you have to give up everything to have me, I just don't see how things will ever work out." Her heart ached, but what she was doing was important, necessary. Even if he couldn't see beyond today, she could, and—

"Sweetheart. Stop that." He tightened his arms around her even more. "Did it ever occur to you that after living as long as I have, immortality might have lost some of its panache? I don't care about living forever. Many of my people either go mad or fade into the *Dreaming*. What I care about is you. If Titania excommunicates me and alters something inside me that starts a more normal longevity clock ticking, it doesn't feel like a sacrifice."

She started to argue with him, tell him he wasn't thinking straight, and then she ran what he'd said through her mind. Joy, as poignant as her grief had been, burned through her like an out-of-control wildfire. She pushed back so she could look at him. "Really?" Her voice came out as a squeak.

He nodded. Tears glistened in his eyes too. "Really. I was afraid you wouldn't want me, but I vowed to sit in that shop of yours until you showed up, so I could find out for sure one way or the other. I didn't know quite what I'd do with myself if you sent me packing. Immortality would've felt particularly empty and meaningless, facing another few millennia like the last one's been." Hope illuminated his face, making his beauty even more ethereal. "If the only reason you're hedging is to save me from myself, forget it. I'm long past old enough to make my own decisions, and take full responsibility for them."

"Okay." She swallowed hard. "Last hurdle. How do you feel about Bubba?"

"I helped save him, didn't I?"

"Not what I meant. He'd have to be a part of our life."

"I wouldn't have it any other way, but I'd be a liar if I didn't admit I'm hoping we'll have other children too."

Something about the way he said *other children* melted her last reserves away and brought on a fresh spate of tears. "Christ! Look at me. I'm a maudlin mess." She snuffled. "You're right about me being scared. Hell, being responsible for me and Bubba has been hard enough."

"Darling." He pulled her against him again. "You wouldn't be responsible for me. We'll take care of each other." He laughed, sounding self-conscious. "Not that either of us has much experience in that regard, but we can learn together."

She pressed her face into the hollow between his neck and shoulder. "We'll probably make a whole lot of mistakes."

"It will be fun kissing and making up."

He tilted his head and closed his mouth over hers. The kiss started out sweet and tentative, but escalated rapidly into something with a mind of its own. His lips felt firm and demanding pressing against hers. As he plumbed her mouth with his tongue and she sparred with it, the world dropped away, leaving just him, her, and the sensations coursing through her body. Her nipples tingled, taut with need. Her crotch flooded. She wound her arms around him and slid her hands under his clothing, desperate for the feel of his skin beneath her fingers.

"Are the two of you coming to dinner?" Roz called.

Colleen broke away from their kiss long enough to call, "Just wrap whatever's left in foil. We'll get to it later."

Raucous laughter rang from the kitchen. "We'll take first watch," Jenna yelled.

"And second," Roz chimed in.

Duncan grinned. "Is there somewhere a little less public where we could go?"

She grinned back. "Why Mr. Regis, what kind of girl do you take me for?"

"It's actually Lord Regis. And the kind of girl you are is one who will be my wife."

Before she could rein in her tongue, Colleen squealed, "I accept." She rolled her eyes and felt heat suffuse her face. "Gosh, I sound about fifteen."

"I understand completely. If it didn't seem so undignified, I'd turn cartwheels across the floor." He got to his feet and pulled her after him. "Now, about that bedroom."

"Follow me." She led the way up two flights to her little room snugged beneath the old house's eaves.

CHAPTER 14

*D*uncan followed Colleen. The swing of her hips and the firm globes of her ass, outlined by the blanket wrapped around her, mesmerized him. His cock pressed uncomfortably against the front of his trousers and his throat felt dry. Heart pounding with anticipation, he walked into her cozy room and summoned his mage light, dialing it to dim, just enough to see by. A double bed with a colorful, quilted throw sat beneath the room's dormer window. An antique armoire butted against one wall. Bookshelves stretched from floor to ceiling. A computer desk was tucked into a corner, complete with an enormous screen. Some sort of tablet or e-reader lay on a bedside table, next to a softly glowing, crystal lamp. He stifled a chuckle.

Colleen turned to face him. She took him in from head to toe, and her frank gaze probably didn't miss a thing. "What's so funny?"

"I've never gotten used to the blend of old and new. Computers and witchcraft. Books, scrolls, and an e-reader, all in the same place."

"Don't you have a computer?"

"Of course I do. But it's placed out of the way where I don't have to look at it unless I want to." He shrugged, feeling sheepish. "Don't dig for meaning. Feelings don't have to make sense."

She unwound the blanket from her body, and laid it over a chair. The lines of her shoulders, arms, breasts, stomach, and hips were clean and beautiful. She was so perfectly formed, he forgot to breathe. He hastened to her side and met her ice blue gaze. "You are quite possibly the most striking woman I've ever seen."

She colored and looked away. "Oh, please. Coming on the heels of your earlier pitch about tonight being a time for truth…"

"It is the truth, at least in my eyes. No, *oh please*, about it." He ran his fingers through her thick, auburn hair, combing it back and away from her face. Tracing her cheekbones down to her neck, he murmured, "No goddess was ever more perfect. Your skin has a dusky, golden cast to it that almost sparkles. Your eyes remind me of ocean shallows in warm climates. Such a clear, pure blue." He drew his fingers down her face again. "High, defined cheekbones, a strong, determined jaw, full, kissable lips—"

"You'd better stop that. I'll become too full of myself for words."

"Somehow, I don't think that's possible." He filled his hands with her breasts. They were amazing. Full, with generous nipples, they rode high on her slender ribcage. He stood just touching her and drinking in her beauty. The moment felt magical, yet far beyond any magic he'd ever summoned. Her nipples puckered against his palms in the chill air of the room. He bent and took one in his mouth, nibbling, sucking, teasing, and was gratified when she moaned, arched her back, and buried her hands in his hair.

He moved from one breast to the other, and then back again. His cock was so swollen, it ached every time he shifted position and it rubbed against his clothes.

She tugged away from his mouth, her breath coming fast. "Let's get rid of the rest of your clothes and get under the covers. It's cold in here. The heating system doesn't include the attic."

He grinned. "We're our own heating system."

She traced the corners of his eyes. "When you smile, wonderful little lines radiate from your eyes, just like miniature sunbeams."

He felt himself blush, and his throat thickened with emotion. "I think that may be the most wonderful thing anyone's ever said to me."

"Aw, come on." She pushed his sweater off his shoulders, dropped it atop a chair, and then went to work on the buttons holding his shirt together. "You're such a handsome man. I'm sure somewhere along the line women have raved about your hair, or your eyes, or..." Her voice trailed off and it was her turn to blush.

He threw back his head and laughed as his shirt slid from his body. "Yes, I've gotten a bunch of comments about the thing you couldn't quite get around to mentioning. But it was always in the heat of passion, and I never took them seriously."

Colleen slid her hands down his bare chest and cupped his erection through his pants. "You'd better take me seriously. Your cock is amazing. Before I ran into you in my shop, I could hardly wait for bedtime to join you on the Dreamers' Paths."

A warm glow began deep in his belly that had nothing to do with his arousal. She'd been anxious for more time with him, looking forward to it. He wrapped his arms around her, glorying in the way her breasts felt crushed against his naked chest. She tilted her face up and he closed his mouth over hers.

The wonderful jasmine-rose scent of her thickened, enveloping him. She opened her mouth, welcoming him, and he deepened their kiss, while he let his hands roam down her back until they cupped her ass.

She straddled one of his legs and rubbed herself against him. From the sound of her breathing, she had to be close to release. Without breaking their kiss, he moved a hand between them, and slid it into the heat between her legs.

She writhed against his fingers, and then pulled away, panting. "If we don't lie down, I'll fall down. My legs are shaking."

He scooped her into his arms, laid her on the bed, and gazed down at her passion-splotched chest. Her nipples were tight little buds, and the red-gold curls between her legs glistened with her fluids. Duncan was so overcome by her beauty, his chest tightened. He knelt on the bed and placed his mouth over her nubbin. She laced her fingers through his hair, urging him closer.

At first, he just breathed heat into her, but her hips bucked and writhed beneath him. He licked around her sensitive tissue, then began sucking on her, while moving his fingers past her opening into her blazing hot core. She squeezed her muscles around him. Her clit stiffened in his mouth and he sucked harder. He felt the rhythmic contractions of her orgasm in his mouth and fingers as she thrust upward against him, shrieking her delight, and calling his name.

He kept sucking until the last of her spasms died away, and then strung kisses up her stomach and breasts. He straddled her body and balanced on his arms, looking down at her. What a gorgeous woman. With her auburn hair splayed around her, she looked like a Botticelli angel. She reached down, undid his pants, and captured his cock in both hands. Her touch was so incredible, he almost came. She rubbed fluid around his glans and stroked his shaft.

When she let go, he realized his eyes had been closed. He opened them, about to protest because she'd stopped touching him, but she slid from beneath him and flipped him onto his back.

"Not fair," she said. "You still have clothes on." Kneeling over him, she unlaced his shoes. They clunked when she tossed them onto the floor. He started to slide his pants down, but she batted his hands away and did it herself. His underwear followed.

She threw a leg over him, sat across his thighs, and traced the lines of his body with both hands. "Beautiful," she whispered. "So beautiful. I'll never get tired of looking at you."

He opened his mouth to correct her, to tell her that, no, she was the beautiful one, but she bent her head and took his penis into her mouth. All thoughts fled. The only thing left was the magic of her lips and teeth and tongue as they worked his shaft alongside her hands. His cock was on fire. Though he rode a ragged edge of control, it was so elusive, he didn't understand why he hadn't come yet.

"You're doing...something." His voice caught in his throat, raspy with passion.

She didn't answer. Just when he thought his balls would explode, she moved her mouth off him and positioned herself so the opening to her vault was right over his cockhead. Because she was kneeling, her body arched over him, back bent like a bow, breasts straining. He groaned at the mind-boggling feel of her, settled his hands on her hips, and plunged deep inside.

She was snug, hot, marvelous. He hit bottom, withdrew, and did it again. He wanted to be slow, elegant, but he was too aroused. Even though he'd come after being ejected by the Dreamers' Paths, he was still hotter than hell. She touched her nipples, rubbing them, then moved a hand to her clit. Watching her touch herself drove him over the edge. He groaned, unable to absorb any more stimulation. Semen raced out of him in burning jets about the time he felt her tighten around him. He'd wanted her to climax again, and she was.

He came for so long, the world shimmered and his vision dimmed. And then she was laying atop him and had pulled a quilt over them, all with him still buried within her body. He wrapped his arms around her and clenched the muscles that would make his still-rigid cock jump inside her.

"More?" She licked his neck, and then circled her tongue into his ear.

"I'll always want more." His voice was rougher than he wanted it to be.

"Good, because I will too." She nuzzled his neck. "Maybe we could get under a few layers of covers. There are a lot of them on the bed. This is Alaska."

He laughed because he felt so good and because she felt miraculous in his arms. Somehow, they separated for long enough to get into bed. Once they were nestled beneath the covers, she threw a leg over him and positioned his cock back inside her. He dimmed his mage light to a soft glow, and wrapped her in a tender embrace.

"You did something so I'd last longer," he said.

"What makes you think that?" Though her voice was muffled against his chest, he thought he detected a coy note beneath her words.

"Well, if you could make me come on demand, like you did when the demon was trying to seduce me, it makes sense you could alter things in the other direction too."

She snorted back a laugh. "Gosh, don't I get to have any secrets?"

He ran his fingers through her wonderful hair. It was like a curtain of living flame, even in the darkened room. "You can have all the secrets you want, darling. Making love with you was unbelievable. I've never been so high."

"No complaints?"

"How could you even ask?"

She snuggled closer against him. "Making love with you was stupendous, astounding, better than my wildest expectations. I could stay in this bedroom with you for a year, and still not feel like leaving your side."

"There's a *but* hovering nearby, just beneath those lovely thoughts."

She swatted his back gently. "No fair, you've been peeking inside my head. The *but* is this: we need to sit with Roz and Jenna soon and map our strategy. The demons haven't gone away—except maybe that one you vaporized with magic."

He wanted to talk about a lot of things, like how much he loved her and where they'd live, and maybe even adding a second changeling to keep Bubba company, but all that would have to wait. Colleen was right. They needed to outline the next few days. If they couldn't get the Irichna under better control, all his other plans would never happen.

"We'll hold a war council in the morning," he said. "It can't be far off."

She nodded. "Yes, first thing. Hopefully, one of the others will have alerted Coven Central about Mathilde."

"What exactly is that?"

"It's like a governing board. It doesn't have any real power, but they do convene a tribunal periodically, and it's where witches who have misbehaved go to answer for their sins."

"You said they don't have any power. So how can they mete out punishment?"

She rolled onto her side and propped her head on an upraised palm. "They don't have any power over how the

Covens manage their affairs, but they do have the authority to excommunicate—or even kill—miscreant witches."

"If they don't discipline Mathilde, my first order of business will be killing her."

Colleen drew her eyebrows together into a serious line. "Normally, I'm pretty pacifistic, except where demons are concerned. But after what she did to Bubba, I'm all over wanting vengeance." She squeezed her eyes shut. When she opened them, she murmured, "If you hadn't been in my shop, I would've traipsed back into the house, big as you please, and gotten trapped along with Jenna, Roz, and Bubba."

He'd come to the same conclusion hours ago, but hadn't wanted to say anything. After what just passed between them, he tried for a supportive, positive spin. "The three of you are strong, plus three is a power number. You might have prevailed."

A corner of her mouth turned downward. "It's a nice thought, but unlikely. Thanks for the vote of confidence, though."

"Anytime." He kept stroking her hair. "Sleep, love. I don't need much. I'll watch over us."

"Bubba's in the little room right across the hall," she said sleepily.

"Never fear." He kissed her forehead. "I'll keep an eye on him too."

Colleen closed her eyes. He added a bit of a spell to her body's own process, and felt her relax in his arms. As he held her, he swore to any deity who might be listening that he'd protect her until the end of time. Maybe she sensed his thoughts, because her lips curved into the softest of smiles.

❦

COLLEEN POURED herself another cup of coffee, and put another waffle in the toaster for Bubba. The changeling looked himself this morning. For that fact, so did she. Duncan had healed her cuts and bruises while she slept. She poured syrup on the waffle and put it in front of the changeling, who smiled his thanks and started eating. Colleen pulled out her chair and joined the others sitting around the round oak table in the kitchen. She stared at the dregs of breakfast on her plate and decided she'd had enough.

"I still can't get over that it's ten in the morning and still dark outside," Duncan said. "What time does it get light here?"

"This time of year, near the winter solstice, we're lucky if it's light from eleven until two or three."

"Four hours?" He poured more coffee, added cream, and drank from his mug.

"Sometimes as little as three. We're pretty far north," Jenna said.

Colleen blew out a breath. They could talk about the weather forever, but it was a smokescreen to avoid what they needed to discuss. She cleared her throat meaningfully. "Did either of you raise Coven Central?"

Roz's jaw tightened. Colleen didn't bother snooping in her mind. "When were you going to tell me?" she demanded.

"Roz and I talked about it," Jenna cut in. "We'd decided after breakfast was time enough."

Colleen waited, but neither witch offered anything further. Finally, she said, "Is one of you going to tell me, or do I need to raid your thoughts?"

"It wasn't particularly pretty—" Roz began.

Colleen rolled her eyes. "Yes, I already gathered that. I've also figured out they refused to rein in Mathilde, but why?"

"It was odd," Jenna said, her hazel eyes serious. "Roz and I used the conference call feature on my cellphone so we could both talk with them. They didn't exactly cop to it, but I'm certain this isn't the first complaint they've had about her."

Roz worried her lower lip between her teeth. "Not only that. I almost caught a whiff of fear. Like they're afraid if they force her to answer for her sins, something terrible will happen to them."

"What'd they tell you to do?" Colleen asked.

"Walk away, and keep as much distance between us and her as we can," Roz answered.

"They sound about as useful as the Sidhe council," Duncan muttered. "Lots of talk, but when it comes down to it, they rarely take any significant action." He met Colleen's gaze. "What are we going to do?"

Roz and Jenna stared at her. "That's a very good question," Roz said through tight lips.

"I want to go back there and kill Mathilde," Bubba said around a mouthful of waffle.

Duncan reached over and ruffled the changeling's hair. "Interesting. You and I are in full agreement."

Roz's eyes widened. "Do you think that's wise?" She aimed her question at Colleen, who took her time answering.

"If the witches in Mathilde's Coven are correct, and she's truly in league with the Irichna, I don't see where we have a choice. Her linkage with them will strengthen their ability to breach the veil between the borderworld where they live and Earth." She slapped her palm against her forehead. "Shit! Not sure why I didn't think of this before, but Mathilde might be the reason the demons have been gaining strength."

Duncan smacked a hand against the tabletop, making the dishes rattle. "Humph. I didn't think of that, either, but it's as good an explanation as any."

"How do you want to do this?" Jenna asked, her voice carefully neutral.

"I'm going to kill her. With a silver knife. Carve her up in little pieces and feed her to the demons she sold us out to." Bubba doubled up a fist and brought it down on the table much harder than Duncan had. Dishes and silver jangled against one another. "She used me and almost killed all of you because I didn't ward myself better."

Colleen understood revenge, and the sweet taste of victory when an enemy fell. Every time the gates in the lowest level of Hell slammed shut, with a demon on the other side, she felt richly compensated for the risks she'd taken.

"I know you want retribution," she told the changeling, "but I think our best ally will be stealth. We need to get inside Witches' Northwest, kill her, and get out, without anyone knowing we were there."

"I agree." Duncan nodded.

"So do we," Jenna and Roz said in unison.

Roz snorted. "Yeah, the last thing we need is someone turning us in to Coven Central, especially after they told us to walk away from the problem."

"Don't you suppose they'll know we did it?" Colleen asked.

"Probably," Duncan said. "But if they're anything like the Sidhe, they'll look the other way, while being privately grateful someone had the balls to step up to the plate and do something they were afraid to tackle."

Colleen poked him with an elbow. "And here you got on me for mixing witchcraft and computers." She gave him a long, thoughtful look. "I suspect you have a television in a closet somewhere and have spent hours watching war movies and sporting events. That suggestion had military tactics stamped all over it."

Color spread over his face, and he bowed his head. "You got me. Guilty as charged." He looked up and grinned, turning his features into something profanely beautiful. "In my defense, though, I was plotting battle strategy long before TV or video games were invented. Dungeons and Dragons too. Where do you think they got their ideas from?"

"Jesus!" Jenna pushed to her feet. "You're too good looking for your own good, Sidhe. Let's get moving before I duke it out with Colleen for your attention."

Bubba stiffened, half rising from his chair. "You leave him alone. He's Colleen's."

"I know that, honey. I was joking." Jenna ferried plates to the ledge, tweaking the changeling's ear as she waltzed past. Bubba settled back into his chair mumbling about how he'd never understand witches.

Roz chuckled softly and waggled her brows. "If you're ever up for a threesome—" she poked Duncan in the side "—don't be shy about speaking up."

"You'll be the first to know, but wouldn't that be a foursome?" He nudged her back, and everyone dissolved into laughter.

"Math was never Roz's strong suit," Jenna choked out between chortles.

Colleen got up to help clear the table and wash dishes. At least the mood in the room was lighter. They had a big job ahead of them—one fraught with danger—and any joy they could grab hold of had to be a plus.

CHAPTER 15

Duncan watched a gradually lighter sky emerge. Nearly noon and it was finally light outside. If it was important to Colleen, they could stay in Alaska, but he hoped she'd want to visit his home in Northern England too. Maybe they could spend chunks of the winter there… Winter days were short in the U.K. but nothing like this.

She came up from behind and wrapped her arms around him, hooking his shoulders. "About ready to leave?"

He untangled himself and turned to face her. "Yes. I still think it would be better if just you and I went."

"You can't leave me behind." Bubba stalked up to them. "I'm the one she hurt."

Duncan hunkered next to the changeling. "I want to be sure you're safe, little man."

Bubba bristled. "I may be small, but everyone here treats me like a child. I'm not. I'm much older than any of the witches."

Colleen sat on the floor next to them and looked at Duncan. "Last night, you said both halves of Faerie were formed from similar magic. Where did changelings come from?"

"You don't have to ask him," Bubba huffed. "I know the history of my race."

Colleen smiled. "You're a born storyteller, sweetie. How about an abbreviated version. We really do need to get going."

The changeling nodded, looking serious. "We were the spirits in the hills and barrows of the Old Country. Someone, I think Ceridwen, breathed life into us and gave us form, but we retained the earth and root essences from our home. It's why we share some of the demons' power."

Duncan shifted so he sat too. "Changelings are a blend of magics from Ceridwen's kettle and the natural world." He patted Bubba's shoulder. "It's the mix that makes you strong and able to shape shift."

Bubba shot him a solemn look. "Don't forget your promise."

"I won't. I've already told the Sidhe council they should free your Scottish kinsmen."

"If they don't, can you?"

Duncan considered it. "Maybe. If I can locate the threads that bind them."

Colleen laid a hand on his leg. "If they're just going to excommunicate you anyway—"

"What?" Bubba cut in. "Why? What did you do? They can't excom—" he stumbled over the word and forged on "—you until the changelings are out from under that Sidhe spell."

"My sin was falling in love with Colleen."

The changeling's eyes widened. "Ooooh. Because she's not Sidhe?"

Duncan nodded solemnly. The more time he spent with the changeling, the better he liked him, and the angrier he grew at his kin for shackling their power.

Roz bustled up. Dark circles ringed her eyes. "I'm ready. Let's get this over with."

Duncan pushed to his feet and offered Colleen a hand up. "Call Jenna. Let's go over this one more time. There are lots of holes in the plan we hatched after breakfast. We need to plug as many of them as we can."

Colleen cupped a hand over her mouth. "Jenna."

"Be right there," sounded from upstairs. Footsteps clattered down the risers.

He waited until they were all together. "Jenna and Roz. You'll show up at the front door and tell whoever answers you've rethought their demon problem and are back to help."

Roz cracked a feral smile. "That part shouldn't be a problem. They'll even believe us."

"Especially after we tell them we sensed a demon leaving their building," Jenna added. "And we want to talk with as many of them as we can, to see if anyone had run-ins with it."

"We would have gone after it without stopping to talk with them first," Roz went on, "except we wanted to reassure them. Just in case the demon had done harm."

"Excellent." Colleen knit her fingers together, hands in front of her. "While you've got a bunch of them busy in the front hall, Duncan, Bubba, and I will teleport into Mathilde's room, kill her, and leave."

"These are the possible weak spots." Duncan counted on his fingers. "One. They may not allow Jenna and Roz in. I'm sure the Irichna let Mathilde know what happened here. Plus, she must know we obliterated the black magic she stuffed into Bubba."

"We can still divert them with some level of conversation," Jenna said.

"Two." Duncan raised another finger. "Mathilde may have some sort of direct conduit to the Irichna. If she does, she'll summon them to protect her. They'll dance to her tune because they want all of you dead."

"That would be a pretty big problem," Colleen said. "Even if we kill Mathilde, we'd be stuck with God-knows-how-many demons."

"Do you suppose the Unseelie would help out again?" Roz asked.

"Even if they would," Duncan replied, "they're sometimes not reliable. They were wonderful last night, but that doesn't mean they'd bring the same level of enthusiasm to the next confrontation, even if the same pair showed up, which is scarcely a given. I can certainly put out a call for help, but it's anyone's guess who will show up."

Colleen blew out a tense-sounding breath. "We can't control all the variables, but what else is new? We don't have that luxury when we go after the Irichna. We'll just have to play some of this by ear."

"You can always call us telepathically if you have more than one demon to deal with," Roz said.

After Duncan's experience channeling arcane magic, he was certain he'd be able to knock out at least one demon. "We'll manage," he said with a terse set to his mouth. "We've got to do something, before Mathilde spreads her poison farther. Hope-fully, she hasn't already." He took a breath. "I haven't wanted to say anything, but it's possible some of the witches at Coven Central have been seduced by whatever she offered. We need to slam that door before Mathilde gathers more witches to help the Irichna."

"I want to kill her," Bubba insisted. "Me."

Colleen dropped a hand on his shoulder. "You will mind me. You will remain either within my warding, or one I set around you. Are we clear on that?"

"No." He set his shoulders stubbornly. "Make me a cat once

we're there. Lots of cats live in that house. The witches will never know I'm not one of them."

Colleen shook her head. "Too risky."

Duncan stepped into the breach. "It's not all that bad an idea—"

"Whose side are you on?" Colleen sounded outraged. She made a grab for the changeling and lifted him into her arms.

He writhed, but stopped shy of kicking her. "Put me down. I'm not your child. You only think of me that way." She gave him an odd look before setting him on the floor.

"I'm on our side," Duncan said. "Bubba is correct. Mathilde won't be paying much attention to a cat. I don't think she saw Bubba in cat form last time we were there, and even if she did it's unlikely she made the connection, unless she actually saw him shift."

"She didn't," Bubba said.

"Why do you want to be a cat?" Colleen asked. Her forehead furrowed in worry, and small lines formed around her mouth.

"I can leap onto her and bite through the big blood vessels in her neck."

"You could," Duncan said, "but she'll be trying to funnel magic to kill you."

"Your job will be to make sure she doesn't." Bubba sidled over to Colleen. "If I'm skilled enough to help you herd demons into Hell, I'm good enough to help with Mathilde. Demons are much more dangerous than she is."

Duncan waited. He'd horned in enough, perhaps more than he should have, judging from the stiff set of Colleen's shoulders. She knelt and looked the changeling in the eye. "Maybe I'm still shaken from what happened yesterday and how close I came to losing you forever. I know you want to be part of this, and not just hide behind a ward. And I understand why." She inhaled sharply. "I'll change you before we leave."

"Thanks, Colleen." His dark eyes shone. "I won't let you down."

"Just don't die, goddammit," she hissed and got to her feet.

"Why does he need your magic to shift to a cat, but he can shift to other forms to fight demons?" Duncan asked.

"I borrow power from the demons." Bubba looked proud of himself. "They're easy to tap into, because I have some demon blood."

"Technically," Colleen said thoughtfully, "what you have in spades is earth magic. Demons have a bit of it too. It's not exactly the same as having demon blood."

"Can we hold the philosophical discussion later?" Roz summoned magic. The air shimmered with it. "Let's go. If we're lucky, we'll be back here in time for dinner."

"Sure you're okay teleporting you and Jenna?" Colleen asked.

"Of course. It's Jenna who can't teleport worth a shit."

Jenna rolled her eyes. "Thanks. I've been practicing. I even think I can feed power into your spell." The two witches glittered, faded, and vanished.

If they weren't back in time for dinner, something would have gone horribly wrong, but Duncan didn't say that. Instead, he pulled magic, enveloped Colleen and Bubba—who'd morphed into a cat—and moved them to a wooded glen behind the Witches' Northwest's building. They'd decided to come out there and magically case the building to pinpoint Mathilde's location, before putting their plan into motion.

Jenna and Roz were using tree energy to shield their presence. "Good idea," Duncan whispered to Colleen. "Take the changeling and join them. I'll be right back."

"Where are you going?" She kept her voice very low.

"To figure out where Mathilde is. I can do it faster than any of you since my magic is different." He waited for her to argue with him, but she tightened her hold on Bubba and moved deeper into the shadows, near the other witches.

Duncan muted his power and draped himself with invisibility. Having different magic was both blessing and curse in that he'd stick out like a sore thumb if anyone were looking.

There's the ticket. Maybe no one will be.

Mathilde was narcissistic enough, it would probably never occur to her to watch her back. She'd assume Colleen would complain to Coven Central, and for some reason she had them in her back pocket. He wondered again why the other witches literally let her get away with murder.

Maybe she threatened to sic the Irichna on them…

He sent subtle threads of magic up and outward, circling the house and searching for demon taint. He wasn't disappointed. Demon miasma was concentrated at the far end of the top floor. Near as he could tell, it was very close to the room where he'd met with the witches and been questioned. The stench had been quashed by some sort of spell, but it was obvious enough to him. He wondered why the witches who lived there hadn't noticed and then decided it was subtle enough, maybe they'd accommodated to its presence.

He balled his hands into fists and reined in his anger. Bubba had been vocal about wanting to kill Mathilde, but Duncan wanted to rip her limb from limb with his bare hands for the pain she'd caused Colleen.

Maybe we'll both get our wish.

In the interest of being thorough, he did a cursory search of the rest of the house. Most of the witches were on the main floor. He supposed it could be time for a midday meal, which would work in their favor if it meant Mathilde was alone.

They hadn't discussed how to deal with any other witches

who might serve as Mathilde's bodyguards, mainly because he figured they'd switch allegiance in a heartbeat once their mistress summoned a demon—unless they'd already been turned. He and the witches had tightened the flaws in their plan, but like Colleen had said, they couldn't control every unknown. Duncan hastened back to the others and told them what he'd found.

"No time like the present," Roz said. She and Jenna headed for the front steps.

Duncan drew power to teleport himself, Colleen, and Bubba to the west end of the top floor. He stabilized warding about them as soon as their molecules settled. As a precaution, they'd decided on maintaining silence, since there was a chance Mathilde—or the demons—could intercept even shielded mind speech.

Bubba mewed softly. Colleen set him down. He scented the air and padded to a closed door. Duncan nodded grimly. The changeling was sharp. He'd picked the right place. Colleen quirked a brow and pointed. He gave her a thumbs up and sent magic to blow the lock.

He and Colleen stepped through the open door.

Mathilde sat before a sewing machine, bright fabric spilling over her lap. She glanced up. "You could have knocked."

"We could have," Colleen agreed.

Duncan glanced about for Bubba, but didn't see him. "Would you have let us in?" he asked.

Mathilde twisted her mouth into a grimace. "Probably. It's nearly impossible to keep a determined magic wielder out." She gave a little push and yards of fabric slithered to the ground in a shiny, multi-colored heap. The mistress of Witches' Northwest flowed to her feet, hands at her sides, but Duncan felt the subtle shift when she began amassing power.

Colleen must've felt it too. "I wouldn't if I were you," she growled.

"Wouldn't what, dear?" The magic swirling about Mathilde thickened.

"You're opening a path for the Irichna." Colleen raised her hands. Power shot from them, forming a shell around Mathilde.

The crone rolled her eyes. "Oh, please. An acolyte could chew her way through that." She stepped away from Colleen's working. With dogged determination, Colleen lobbed more magic her way.

Duncan didn't see any reason to tarry. The longer they did, the bigger the chance Mathilde could summon reinforcements. He tried to be subtle about gathering power. So long as Mathilde's attention was focused on Colleen, there was the barest chance she might not notice, but the old witch's head snapped about.

"Oh no, you don't," she snarled.

Bubba streaked from somewhere behind Mathilde and jumped onto her back, digging his claws in deep. The witch shrieked and reached for the cat, but his jaws closed around the side of her neck. He bit deep and shook his head from side-to-side.

Blood geysered everywhere. Bright red, but with threads of black woven in.

Mathilde chanted furiously. Colleen dove at her and slapped her across the face. She twisted the other witch's arms behind her. Duncan heard bones snap and leapt into the fray. He wrapped Mathilde's arms with magic so she couldn't use her hands. It would truncate, but not eliminate, her ability to call for power.

Bubba, whose hold on the witch had been firm, suddenly jumped to the floor hissing and spitting. Blood continued to spurt from the hole in Mathilde's neck, so the changeling must have punctured an artery, but she didn't seem to be weakening.

The cat yowled. His form glistened, taking on a liquid aspect. When it solidified, he was the same snake with arms Duncan remembered from when they'd chivvied the demon to Hell.

"Shit!" Colleen shouted. "Strengthen your wards. If Bubba could do that, Irichna have to be close."

Duncan channeled magic as hard and fast as he could, until breath clotted in his throat and his heart pounded. It passed through Mathilde, without phasing her. "Danu's tits!" Frustration tightened his muscles into knots. "Isn't there something we can do to kill her before she lets them through?"

"Apparently not," Colleen grunted through clenched teeth.

Bubba rose on his coils like a cobra, his body shifting from side to side.

Duncan felt foul energy barrel toward them with the power of a runaway train. Mathilde's body made a hideous, wrenching sound and burst, showering them with blood, bone, and sinew. He wiped bloody debris out of his eyes, and cursed. Where Mathilde had stood, an Irichna leered at them. A second one popped out of the ether, followed by a third. This time, they all looked the same. Tall and thin, they were swathed in hooded black robes. Eerie yellow eyes smoldered with fiery rims. Skeletal hands, flesh barely covering bone, reached toward them hungrily.

"Fuck!" Duncan grabbed Colleen and tried to shove her behind him, but she wouldn't cooperate.

One of the demons closed on Bubba, sneering, but the changeling held his ground, snake's tongue whipping in and out of his wedge-shaped mouth.

"At least Mathilde won't be a problem anymore," Colleen

muttered. "The shape she's in, no one could resurrect what's left."

Footsteps pounded down the hallway. Jenna and Roz burst into the room, followed by as many witches as could cram their way inside.

Roz moved to one side of Colleen, Jenna the other, displacing Duncan. Colleen motioned Duncan behind her. He shook his head and edged to where he'd presumably have a direct line to channel killing power into the demons. His words clinched it. "Keep a path clear between me and them," he growled.

"Good grief, what the fuck happened in here?" Jenna pointed at splintered bones and clumps of tissue.

"Later," Colleen gritted.

"What can we do?" one of the witches standing just inside the room asked.

"Where's Mathilde?" another demanded, shifting nervously from foot to foot as her gaze darted about the room. Colleen started to answer, but Roz saved her the trouble.

"Get iron manacles, chains, whatever you have," Roz snapped, sidestepping the questions about Mathilde and the gore splattered on the walls and floor.

Duncan winced, probably at the mention of iron. Colleen

set her mouth in a hard line. Nothing she could do about his sensitivity to metal. He'd have to suffer it being close to him, or come up with an equally potent tool against the Irichna.

She glanced his way. "Do you need to leave?"

"I'll manage." He looked so determined—and so fierce—she wanted to wrap her arms around him, but now wasn't the time.

Colleen tore her attention away from Duncan and glanced from one demon to the next. They stared back at her implacably, easy in their bodies, apparently not the least bit worried about whatever puny magic she and her cronies might dish out.

Metal clanked and creaked from the doorway. Several witches tossed a collection of handcuffs, leg irons, and chains in front of Colleen. The demons drew back a couple of paces, hissing.

"How'd you get the manacles on the one I escorted to Hell?" Colleen asked.

"We didn't," a male witch said.

"It was Mathilde," another concurred. The demons snarled and snapped amongst themselves in a guttural language, apparently pissed Mathilde had sold one of them down the river.

"At least all that metal forms a temporary barrier," Jenna muttered. She rocked back on her heels, her gaze never leaving the demons.

As if to prove her wrong, one of the Irichna leapt high into the air and dive-bombed her, cutting through the witch's warding as if it weren't there. Jenna shrieked. A hole opened from her shoulder and spread down one arm. Blood flowed freely as she grappled with the demon, trying to keep its mouth away from hers so it couldn't suck her soul from her body.

Colleen hurled magic into the demon, but it didn't even loosen its hold on Jenna. Desperation filled her, along with fury. She launched herself at the pair, intent on saving her friend.

All hell broke loose.

Magic flew every which way as everyone jumped into the battle.

Duncan looked absolutely green, probably from the pile of iron five feet from him, but his face was carved into resolute lines as he channeled power, presumably from the source he'd tapped into at her house. It flowed through him and straight into one of the two demons still on the far side of the manacles.

Colleen shouted at Roz. "Keep the third one off my back while I help Jenna."

"You got it."

Colleen sent more power spinning into the demon atop Jenna from pointblank range. Bubba slithered over and attached himself to the creature's back. He wrapped his four arms around the thing and cut into it with his pincer-like claws. Where he tore through skin, black ichor oozed. It smelled like a cross between road kill and sulfur. Colleen's stomach curdled into a nauseated ball, but she swallowed down bile. There'd be time to throw up later—if there was a later. She snapped up a set of handcuffs and slapped them around the demon's wrists while he grappled behind his back to displace the changeling.

The Irichna bellowed in pain and outrage, its voice so eerie it iced her blood. In a distant, disembodied corner of her brain, she wondered if she'd ever be able to get warm again.

Bubba moved far faster than she would have thought possible, slithering beyond the range of the demon's feet, which had turned into hooves with razor sharp edges. The Irichna surged to its feet, and in a double-jointed move that defied physiology, he swung his manacled arms over his head so they sat in front of his body.

At least Jenna was free. She stumbled to her feet, looking dazed. Blood still ran down her front. "Thanks. How the fuck will we corral the rest of them?"

"I haven't got a clue." Colleen glanced at Roz. "How are you doing?"

"Okay. Every once in a while he ups the ante, but so far, it's been manageable. I think he's waiting to see what happens with the other two. Dirty cocksucker!" She returned her full attention to the demon. "Bastard! Take that." Power blazed from her hands, but the demon skinned bloodless lips back from yellowed teeth and laughed.

Colleen shifted her gaze to Duncan. Color had drained from his face, but the demon he'd been pouring magic into had developed an insubstantial, almost translucent, look. Duncan made a feral, grunting sound, pushed power hard, and the Irichna disappeared. She started to congratulate him, but he slid to the floor, barely breathing.

"Shit!" Colleen ran to him and knelt by his side. He might be immortal, but that didn't mean other bad things couldn't happen. Bubba hissed, long and low. Jenna screamed a warning.

Because her awareness was focused on Duncan, she hadn't been paying attention to the manacled demon. Somehow, it had gotten behind her. It snugged the handcuffs against her throat and pulled hard. She writhed, trying to escape, but it was too close and too strong. Metal bands dug into her throat, cutting off her airway. She heard pathetic choking noises and realized they were coming from her. Dark spots danced through her vision. The demon bent her head back. Its face was inches from hers. If she didn't do something, it would have her. Mouth atop hers, it would absorb her soul. If that happened, she'd join their ranks.

"Nooooo," she shrieked with what little air she had left.

Jenna hurled herself at the demon, tackling it from the side. Colleen's head snapped back with a crack that reverberated through her skull, but at least she could breathe again. She shot to her feet and stumbled away from where Jenna and the demon rolled around on the floor. Bubba slithered up the demon's body and buried his fangs in its neck.

Duncan opened his eyes, took in the scene, and roared his displeasure. He bounded to his feet. The air crackled with power as he summoned killing magic. He held it between his hands, apparently so overcome with the energy, he couldn't speak, but he tilted his head toward the demon.

Colleen understood the problem. "Bubba! Jenna!" she cried. "Let go now!" They did, rolling and skidding out of the way, just as Duncan released a stunning blast of magic into the Irichna. The room pulsed with light so bright, it looked like lightning had struck. Colleen squinted, trying to see. Maybe because this demon was partially bound with iron, which had to have muted its magic, it vanished much faster than the first one had.

Magic pulsed from Roz's hands. She taunted the third demon. "How about a one way ticket to Hell, buddy, with me as your escort? My partners here will bind you and then we'll take a little trip."

"We're on it," Colleen said and plucked a set of handcuffs from the pile. She smiled grimly. One demon felt imminently manageable—so long as he didn't summon reinforcements.

Jenna grabbed a set of leg irons. She and Colleen converged on the last demon. It eyed them balefully. The changeling, still in snake form, glided between them, hissing. With a long, snarling hoot, the demon became less substantial. Colleen tried to snap manacles on it, but they cut through empty air. She blinked hard, willing it to remain, but the last vestiges of the thing shimmered into nothingness.

"Fuck!!" Roz screeched.

"Slimy, craven bastard." Jenna brandished a fist at the place the demon had stood.

Colleen shook her head to clear a sudden dizziness that threatened to engulf her. She forced deep, healing breaths, willing oxygen to the very bottom of her lungs. Maybe it would cut through the stench of demon that still hung heavy the room.

Duncan stumbled to a window and heaved it open. He bent his upper body, shoving it outside, and Colleen heard him gulping air that wasn't tainted by iron. However bad she might be feeling, he was probably much worse. She thrust her own discomfort aside, raced to him, and put an arm around his waist.

"Are you all right? Christ! I was worried sick when you passed out."

He made a sound between a snort and a grunt. "I did not *pass out*. I was merely resting."

She blew out an amused breath. "Yeah, right. Your eyes were closed and you were barely breathing. In my book. That's passed out."

"Whatever." He turned his head, looked at her, and winked. "All's well that ends well, sweetheart. We'll live to fight another day." He ginned up what was probably meant to be a lascivious grin, but he was still a bit green about the gills. "I want to wrap my arms around you and hold you, but you've got to get all that iron out of here first."

She leaned into him, reveling in how good he felt, then let go and turned to face the rest of the witches who'd gathered around Roz, Jenna, and Bubba. "How about if you get that iron out of here, then we can all go downstairs and sort things out."

"Are they coming back?" one of the witches asked.

She didn't have to define who she meant by *they*. Colleen knew.

"Probably, but not today," Roz said.

"And not necessarily back here," Jenna added.

"Yes, that's one of the things we need to discuss," Colleen cut in too tired to be anything other than forthright.

Bubba slithered over to her and rubbed his reptilian head against her leg. She eyed him. "No demons to borrow power from, huh?" His snake's tongue flashed out. Maybe he was agreeing, or laughing. She'd have to ask him once he could talk again. "What'll it be, Bubs? Cat?" The snake shook his head. Colleen flicked magic his way, surprised she had enough left to do anything. The changeling morphed back to his gnome's body and shook himself.

"I helped." Pride rang in his voice.

"Yes." Colleen smiled at him. "You did. A lot."

"What is he?" a witch asked.

"Who cares? I'd say he's pretty handy," another witch chimed in.

"Yes," said a third. "Whatever he is, I want one."

Bubba drew himself up. "I'm a changeling, and we pick our magical partners." He shot Colleen a look. "Before you start nagging, you don't have to remind me. I'll get my clothes out of your bag."

"I'll get them," Roz said and plucked Colleen's backpack from where it was partially buried beneath the bloody remains of Mathilde's body.

"Ewwww. Not sure I want anything out of there." Bubba screwed up his face in disgust.

"Everything inside is fine," Roz informed him. She reached into the bag and handed him a shirt and pants. The witch snorted and smoothed a hand down her still-intact clothing. "At least none of us had to shift."

Colleen rubbed her throat. It felt swollen and bruised from where the demon had nearly strangled her. She would've shifted then if she could, but magic required air, and the demon had caught her unawares. "We can talk about changelings downstairs too," she told the witches. "Let's move the iron, so Duncan, my, um sort of fiancé, can leave this room without fainting again."

"I like the sound of what you called me, minus the qualifier." Duncan turned so the open window was at his back and smiled broadly. "Leave a man a spot of pride, would you? I know you're teasing, but I did not faint. That vein of magic I borrowed liberally from is like harnessing lightning. Takes damn near everything out of me. Having enough iron to shoe an entire cavalry troop right next to me didn't help."

"Point taken. I'll stand down." Colleen laughed, but it made her throat hurt. She exchanged glances with Roz and Jenna. "Well, gals, we did it again."

"Me too," Bubba said.

"You too." Colleen squatted and held out her arms. The changeling trotted to her and gave her a hug.

"We barely did it," Roz conceded.

"By the skin of our teeth," Jenna muttered.

"Doesn't matter." The fierce undercurrent in Colleen's voice surprised her. "Like Duncan just told me, we'll live to fight another day." Bubba let go and she straightened.

The Coven witches grabbed armfuls of iron and left the

room. Finally, only the five of them were left. "Shall we?" Colleen said.

"Absolutely." Duncan moved to her side, draped an arm around her shoulders, and pulled her against him. "I want to figure out what this group knows about Mathilde and her link to the Irichna."

"We all do. You two can play kissy-face later," Roz growled. "Do you want this?" She waved Colleen's blood and gore splattered rucksack in the air.

"Nope. Think it's time to buy another one."

Roz snorted. "Somehow I thought you'd see it that way." She scooped the rest of Colleen's things out of it, dropped the backpack into a waste can, and led the way downstairs.

"Why'd you say that about playing kissy-face? We weren't doing anything," Colleen asked, as she made her way down several flights of stairs.

"You were thinking about it," Jenna answered before Roz had a chance. "Keep moving. I want to find somewhere to sit. I'm about done in."

"Here's your stuff." Roz handed the backpack's contents to Colleen.

"Thanks." She stacked her clothes and wallet on a carved, antique table before following Roz from the bottom of the stairs to a large dining room. The witches had been busy. A buffet table was laden with cheese, crackers, cookies, tea and coffee pots, and a staggering array of liquor bottles. Colleen placed a few slices of cheese and some soft cookies on a plate. Figuring something warm would soothe her inflamed throat, she poured a cup of tea and added honey to it.

"Between that plate and cup, it looks like you're out of hands," Duncan noted. "Would you like me to pour us a glass of something alcoholic?"

"Sure. I don't have a preference. Just pick something."

Eventually, they worked their way into a luxurious meeting room lined with rows of chairs and small tables. A fire burned merrily in a huge stone fireplace that took up one end of the cozy space. Old-fashioned chandeliers were festooned with unlit candles. Witches motioned them to a raised dais catty-corner from the fireplace.

Colleen trudged across the room. Setting her plate and cup down, she took a long drink of tea. The warm liquid and honey helped a lot. She dropped onto a padded chair. Duncan sat on one side, Bubba on her other. Roz and Jenna settled in the seats next to Bubba.

"Whew!" Jenna toed off her shoes. "My feet are killing me."

Colleen glanced under the table. "It's your penchant for high heels. Now if you'd develop a taste for nice, practical boots…"

Jenna ignored her, spread a cracker with cream cheese, and popped it into her mouth. Her wounds were looking better, so she must've had enough magic left to focus healing energy on her neck and arm.

"Old argument?" Duncan asked archly and quirked a brow.

"Very old." Colleen drank more of her tea.

A buzzing, whispery noise filled the room. One of the witches Colleen remembered from the tribunal that had grilled Duncan walked to the front of the room, mounted the dais, and raised her hands for silence. The hall quieted instantly. The witch turned and bowed to Colleen. Her long black hair swept the floor. Brilliant blue eyes glowed in her olive-skinned face. About five feet eight, with a willowy build, she could've been anywhere from thirty to a hundred or more. Witches didn't show age, unless they wanted to. Rather than the robes she'd worn the other day, she was dressed in a long, black skirt and a multicolored top, hand painted with runic symbols.

"I am Naomi, second in command here. First, I wish to thank you. You saved many of us from certain death."

Colleen rose and bowed in return. "You are most welcome." She remained on her feet and waited. Naomi must have questions—lots of them.

"Is Mathilde going to return?" Naomi's voice was stern, but worry flickered in the depths of her eyes.

"No. She's dead." Colleen reached for her cup, but Duncan gave her the glass with whiskey in it. She took a tentative sip, unsure how liquor would react with her sore throat. It wasn't as bad as she feared, and she only sputtered a little.

Naomi squared her slender shoulders. "Probably not supper conversation, but how do you know Mathilde is dead?"

Colleen considered her answer and then decided to ask a question of her own. "Did you know Mathilde parlayed with the Irichna?" She sent a truth spell to eddy between them.

The other witch's eyes widened, and then she nodded her understanding.

"I didn't know, not for certain, but I suspected something was wrong. Mathilde hadn't been herself for months, maybe as much as a couple of years. The changes were so slight at first, I barely noticed them." She shrugged. "One subtle change, piled atop another, added up. A group of us—" she spread her arms to encompass the witches scattered through the room "—were getting closer to a direct confrontation. We asked Coven Central for help, but they turned us down."

"Funny. The same thing happened to us," Roz said.

Naomi focused her intense blue gaze on Roz. "Recently?"

"Very. Between our last visit here and this one."

Naomi drew her dark brows together. "That doesn't seem right," she murmured.

"No shit." Roz said succinctly. "We wondered just what

Mathilde threatened that would intimidate such a powerful group of witches."

"Maybe you should ask them?" Duncan spoke up. "Seems safe enough now that Mathilde's been reduced to that pile of bone chips and protoplasm in the upstairs room."

"Goddess be praised," ran through the assemblage along with, "So that's what all that was."

Naomi pounded on a table for order and got it. "We will gather her remains and burn them. I need volunteers." A few hands shot up. "Thank you." Naomi scanned the group. "To respect who Mathilde once was, we will hold a ceremonial farewell at dawn tomorrow. Those of you who wish to can meet behind the house half an hour before sunrise."

Colleen took another sip from the glass in her hands. She waited until Naomi turned back to her and said, "We'll be leaving soon."

Naomi pressed her lips together and nodded. "I understand how tired you must be, and I would never hold you against your will, but I'm hoping you won't go before you tell us how vulnerable we are to another demon attack. It's clear to me now that Mathilde opened some sort of pathway between their world and this house. I need to know how to close it, permanently."

"We want to know more about the changeling too," someone called out.

Bubba broke off shoveling food into his mouth long enough to wave enthusiastically and answer, "Glad to oblige."

Duncan got to his feet, ruffled the changeling's hair, and hooked an arm through Colleen's. He sucked in an audible breath. "I suppose I should have discussed this with you first, but I didn't." He turned his clear, green gaze toward Naomi. "Colleen has agreed to be my wife—"

Heat whooshed from her chest all the way to the top of her head. "I—I may have in a private moment, but, but…"

He moved his arm around her waist, snugging her close. "But nothing. I'm about to ask for Naomi's blessing. If she agrees, my next request will be if someone here would perform whatever is traditional among you to bind couples in marriage. Would this help?" He sank to one knee before her and placed a hand over his heart. "Colleen Kelly, you'd make me the happiest man alive if—"

A titter began in one corner of the room, spreading rapidly, along with a chorus of *oohs* and *aahs*. Witches surged to their feet and moved closer. A smattering of applause broke out.

"Oh for Pete's sake, get up would you?" Colleen grabbed one of his hands and tugged hard. Despite her embarrassment, her heart cracked open, overflowing with joy. Duncan was amazing. Not only was he drop dead gorgeous. He was funny and kind and considerate. Good at anticipating her needs too. And he understood her amazingly well, probably because he spent so much time in her head…like he probably was right this minute.

"Oops." She eyed him through downcast lashes.

He grinned and gestured with both hands, looking both innocent and guilty as sin, all at the same time. "Why of course I was in your mind, but I'm all those things and more. Keep your thoughts coming, darling. Nectar to my heart, balm to my soul."

Colleen couldn't help herself. She laughed, ignoring her lacerated throat. "Egotistical beast." She mock swatted him. "Now that you've had a turn through my head, will you please get up?"

Duncan flowed to his feet, and walked to Naomi. "Would you bless us and marry us, even though I'm not one of you?"

The witch's blue eyes twinkled. "It would be my pleasure, but we must wait until the signs are auspicious."

He cocked his head to one side. "How will you figure that out?"

She crooked a finger at him. "Once we're done asking questions, and you're done answering them and eating, you and Colleen will join me for a Tarot session. If the cards are good to you, I'll cast your astrological charts and check their synastry."

*D*uncan was tired, and anxious to be alone with Colleen. Night had arrived hours ago and was nearly spent. Though he was a veteran of many marathon Sidhe meetings, nonetheless he'd been ready to bid the Coven witches farewell hours ago. Colleen leaned heavily against him as they walked across the lush, damp lawn in search of their lodging.

"I can't believe how wiped out I am," she murmured.

"You have every right to be. We didn't get much sleep last night, and you've fought Irichna twice in twenty-four hours." He kissed her forehead. "My brave darling. Once we're inside, I'll see what I can do about healing your throat. It's bruised up something fierce."

"That would be nice. It hurts."

He twisted the skeleton key in the lock and pushed open the door to one of several guest cottages scattered about the grounds of the Witches' Northwest compound. Jenna, Roz, and Bubba were in the cottage right next to them, presumably already asleep, since they'd excused themselves once the Coven witches had run out of questions.

The Coven spent hours asking about everything from ways to ensure Mathilde's gateway could be well and truly closed, to how they could rustle up a dozen changelings.

Once he and Colleen were finally done with that, they'd trailed after Naomi. True to her word, she'd cast several Tarot spreads before moving to her computer and asking them for birth data for her astrology program. He'd told her he was nearly certain her computer program wouldn't include his birthdate, but she'd arched a brow, said many witches were quite old, and muttered something about extrapolation based on planetary cycles. A few key strokes later, she'd declared him and Colleen a perfect match, and set their nuptials for ten days hence, during the winter solstice.

Sometime between now and then, he'd have to find Titania and square things with her. And then there was the follow-up Sidhe council meeting where he'd promised to make a good faith effort to show up with the witches in tow. It would be a busy few days.

Colleen fired her mage light, gazed around the cottage, and gasped. "Oh my. This is charming. Like a hobbit hole."

"Without the tiny, round doors, fortunately."

Duncan pulled the door shut behind them and sent magic skittering across the room to light a fire. Someone had thoughtfully laid raw materials for it in the rustic stone fireplace, and the tinder flared quickly. The cottage was cozy, with knotty pine walls, and overstuffed chintz furniture. Rag rugs were placed strategically on a polished, hardwood floor. An inviting bed, strewn with plump pillows and comforters, was visible through an open doorway. A second door probably led into a bathroom.

He moved behind Colleen and wrapped his arms around

her. She leaned into him, her head tilted back. Oberon's balls, but she felt good against him. "Would you like a bath?" he asked. "I'm presuming there's a tub, but I'm not certain."

She turned her head and nuzzled his neck. "I want it all. You. Bath. Neck healing. Sleep." Her eyes fluttered shut. "Now if I could just stay awake for half of that, I'll be doing good."

Protectiveness shot through him, so fierce and sweet it shocked him. He'd make sure she had everything she wanted. Always. He tightened his arms around her. "My feelings won't be hurt if you drift off. We've had a hell of a couple of days here. Let's check out the bathroom. We both still stink of Irichna."

She narrowed her eyes and sniffed audibly. "Now that you mention it, I guess we do. I'd sort of adapted."

He unwrapped his arms, took her hand, and guided her across the room. The fire was already putting out a pleasant, crackly warmth. She turned the knob and pushed the bathroom door open. It was his turn to gasp. An inlaid marble tub was sunk into the floor, deep enough to thoroughly immerse themselves in. He bent, turned on the taps, and closed the drain. Hot water, with a distinct mineral smell, ran into the tub. The remainder of the bathroom was tiled in glittery, gold-toned granite.

"So that's what she meant about tapping into a natural hot spring." Colleen closed the bathroom door to keep the steam inside.

"I wasn't listening. You can tell me, but later." Duncan returned to her side and gently laid a hand on her throat. "Hush, this will only take a moment." He sent magic into her, assessing damage, and fixing broken places as he went. The injury was mostly at a surface level, but many cells had burst, causing a bruise to form from beneath her chin all the way down her neck. He summoned his own mage light and made it bright so he could assess the results of his efforts.

Colleen's eyes were closed, her head tilted backward as he worked. Soon the creamy tones of her skin returned.

"There. All done," he said, adding, "You'll need to drink a lot of water to flush the debris out of your body."

"Thanks." She opened her eyes and met his gaze. "Feels better already."

He brushed a knuckle over her lips, and then kissed her softly. "Tub's getting full. We probably should get in."

"You just want to see me naked." She grinned, and ran her tongue over her lips.

"Yes." He grinned back. "That too." He tugged her top over her head and unhooked her bra. He wanted to kiss her breasts, but lovemaking could wait—at least until they got into the water and sluiced off the top layer of grime.

She bent and unlaced her boots. He did the same and toed his off. His sweater and shirt came next. Colleen walked up behind him and ran her hands down his back. "I'll never get used to how stunning you are. I've never seen skin like yours. I swear it would glow, even if we didn't have the mage lights going."

A warm, fluttery feeling moved through his insides. Deep joy that she found him pleasing suffused him with emotions he had no name for. She reached around and unfastened his pants. They pooled around his feet and he stepped out of them. He gave his underwear a shove and they followed. By the time he turned to face Colleen, she was naked too.

Water was just lapping over the edges of the tub. He scooped their clothes off the floor and laid everything over a padded bench next to one wall. The bathroom floor had two drains, but there was no point getting their clothes soaked when the tub overflowed—and it would once they got in.

She turned off the water, sat on the tub's rounded edge, and eased into the steaming water. "Heavenly," she pronounced. "The minerals are a godsend."

He joined her, sitting across from her in the oblong tub. True to his prediction, water ran over the lip of the tub and into the drains. Their legs intertwined. He pulled one of her feet into his lap and massaged the instep. "What was that about a natural hot spring?"

She smiled shyly. Her hair drifted in the water like ruddy sea anemones. "Naomi, or maybe one other others, said this property sits atop a huge mineral pool. They pipe all their hot water from it."

"Convenient."

"Yup. We witches are a crafty bunch." She shoved her other foot into his lap and he rubbed both of them. Their proximity to his cock gave it ideas. It stiffened, floating in the hot water. Tired as he was, lust pierced him.

He cleared his throat. "Before I'm lost to your charms, and I forget everything, one of the reasons I was waiting for you in Fairbanks was to escort you and Jenna and Roz back to the U.K. for a Sidhe council meeting."

Her eyes, which had been sitting at half-mast, flew open. "Why do they need us?"

"I told them they needed to take back responsibility for the Irichna—"

"And they told you they needed our blood to get the genetic code," she cut in. The soft line of her mouth dissolved into a resolute expression. "What if we're willing to share, but don't want to give up our demon assassin job?"

Duncan snorted back a laugh. "In the first place, I'm not at all certain any of the Sidhe want the Irichna back in their laps. If they accede, it will be because of guilt. Somehow, I don't think they'll fight you if you still want to ferry demons through Hell to the Ninth Circle."

She inhaled thoughtfully, and then shook her head. "I'm so tired, it's hard to think straight. Roz and Jenna need to speak for themselves. I have no right to make that decision for them. I don't know why I'd be so attached to facing down danger again and again, but I am."

Duncan understood, or he thought he did. It was all about adding purpose and meaning in a life, about being an integral part of something important. The Sidhe lost far more than they realized when they drafted the witches. He held his peace, though, snagged a fragrant bar of soap, and began washing her legs. She found another bar of soap and returned his ministrations. Wherever she touched him, his skin caught fire.

"Turn around," he said, his voice rougher than he'd meant because he was so aroused.

She came to him and nestled in his arms with her back against his chest. He wet, soaped, and rinsed her hair, while his cock pressed against the mounded curves of her ass. It took forever before the water ran clear. Satisfied he'd done a credible job washing her hair, he turned her in his arms and brought his mouth down on hers. She returned his kiss hungrily, opening her mouth to him, and teasing with her tongue.

She urged him away from the side of the tub, and wrapped her legs around his waist and her arms around his shoulders. His cockhead hovered at the circle of her entrance for several long, delicious moments while they kissed. Her peaked nipples pressed into his chest, and she writhed against him, moaned, and let her body slide down his shaft. The heat inside her made the water's warmth pale by comparison.

It was all he could do to keep from exploding the minute he hit bottom and she clenched her muscles around him. Colleen hooked her arms beneath his and grasped his shoulders. She rubbed her breasts against his chest in a little circular motion that made her nipples even harder. He dropped his hands to her hips and set a rhythm that might—maybe—let him last past a dozen strokes.

Colleen had other ideas about the tempo she wanted. She bucked against him and pressed her clit against his pubic bone. Rocking against him, crying, shrieking, she came, one set of spasms starting up almost before the last subsided. He hung on as long as he could, but somewhere after her third peak, his balls snugged against his body, and he knew he'd passed the point of controlling anything.

Semen juddered from him. A feral cry split the air. It took long moments before he understood it had come from him. Her pussy tightened around him once again and he knew she was coming. He kept on thrusting until their last shudders died away.

They sat clasped in one another's arms for long moments breathing each other in. Jasmine, rose, musk, and steam. He stroked her damp hair and kicked his inner barriers wide open to a love so deep, and so pervasive, it filled every molecule of his being with longing.

"I love you too," she murmured and moved back enough to smile crookedly. Her face was blotchy with the heat of their lust. "Two can play that mind reading game, plus I thought I should tell you in case we face the Irichna again, and don't come up quite so lucky."

He placed a hand on either side of her face. "Nothing bad will ever happen to you. Not on my watch."

She crinkled her nose. "A Neanderthal attitude. Just what I like in my men."

"What did you call me?" But then he dissolved in laughter.

"Let's get your hair washed and get out of here. Water's

getting cold. We could warm it with magic, but it would be better to get into bed." She scooted off his cock, moved behind him, and poured water through his hair. He started to protest that he could wash his own hair, but in the end he let her do it because he loved the feel of her hands on his body.

He opened the drain, got out of the tub, and helped her out. Colleen was so weary, she swayed on her feet when he wrapped her in a fluffy, white terrycloth towel. He blotted the water from her and swathed her hair in another towel. She started unsteadily for the door, but he scooped her up and carried her to the bed.

"I'll be right there." He strung kisses down her neck before laying her down. "Just as soon as I'm a bit drier myself."

Her mage light winked out. He went back to the bathroom, made sure they hadn't forgotten to do something critical, and grabbed a towel for himself. By the time he returned to their bed, she was sound asleep. His cock twitched, wanting more, but he told it to stand down. Morning would be plenty of time.

Careful not to wake her, he got into bed, dialed his mage light back to the barest glow, and watched her sleep until darkness took him as well.

～

A SHARP TAPPING on the door brought him flying out of bed. Duncan sent magic surging outward and started breathing again once he recognized Jenna, Roz, and Bubba's energy.

"It's okay," Colleen said sleepily and patted his arm. "The bad guys don't usually knock."

"If I hadn't been so deep asleep, I'd have realized that." He snapped up a towel, wrapped it around himself, and strode to the door.

"It's about time." Bubba pushed past Duncan once the door was open. "Colleen," he called. "Where are you?"

"In here, sweetie." The changeling made a beeline for the bedroom. Springs creaked, and Duncan assumed Bubba had jumped onto the bed.

Roz gaped at him, open-mouthed. "Good God," she said. "What a hunk you are."

Jenna snorted and licked her lips. "Christ on a crutch, you aren't kidding. Maybe Colleen would consider sharing."

"In a pig's eye," Colleen yelled from the bedroom. She came into view, also draped in a towel. "Thank Danu." She strode to Duncan's side, bare feet slapping the polished wooden floor. "From the sound of things, I figured you'd lost that towel somewhere between our bed and the door."

"Where's Bubba?" Duncan looked over a shoulder and laughed. "I should have guessed. Bouncing on the bed."

"Colleen," Roz said in a wheedling tone and gazed meaningfully at Duncan. "Remember all the favors I've done you."

Colleen eyed the other witch. "Sharing my husband-to-be feels like a lot bigger favor than you loaning me your favorite black skirt."

Roz shrugged and balanced her hands in front of her like a scale. "Favorite skirt. Favorite man. Not all that much difference…" Colleen growled. Roz broke into a broad grin. "I'm just teasing, sweetie. Don't know what I'd do with a Sidhe."

"I do," Jenna cut in. "From the rumors I've heard—" She caught herself midsentence and stopped talking. Her face reddened.

Bubba trotted to Colleen and inserted his body between her and Duncan. "I'm hungry. Is there any food in here?"

Roz held out her arms and the changeling came to her. She lifted him and kissed the tip of his nose. "How about this? We'll go out on the porch and let them get dressed. Then we'll all go to the main house for breakfast."

Duncan glanced out a window. "Closer to lunch time, isn't it?"

"Whatever. When you keep the hours we do, food is food. Doesn't matter how you label the meal." Roz turned. "See you guys in a couple of minutes."

"That won't leave us any time for a midday roll in the hay," Colleen said archly.

Jenna slugged her in the arm. "Nope, it won't. Nothing like rubbing your good fortune in the faces of your two sex-starved sisters." She wrapped her arms around Colleen and kissed her on both cheeks. "Kidding aside. I'm so happy for you. Can Roz and I be bridesmaids?"

Colleen laid her cheek next to Jenna's. "I'd be honored. So would Duncan, but before the wedding, it looks as if we'll all be taking a trip to the U.K."

Jenna drew back. "What? Why?"

"Tell you once I've got some clothes on."

Duncan dressed quickly, wishing he had fresh clothes that didn't reek of demon stench. He experimented with varying degrees of magic, but couldn't quite rid his trousers of the smell.

Colleen gathered the few things from her backpack and picked up her wallet. "Ready?"

He nodded. "I can't wait until we have a long, uninterrupted stretch of time together. Like a year, maybe. Or a century."

She stretched on tiptoe and kissed his cheek. "That will never happen. We have Bubba." She laid a hand over her midsection. "And maybe another small, dependent soul, since we weren't careful. Not that I couldn't do something about things like that if you didn't want to be a daddy quite yet, but…"

Love filled him and spilled over. He wove his arms around her and drew her close. "I do want children. Never felt that way before, but I want them with you. No worries, darling. You're not pregnant. Not yet, anyway, but you just say the word." He drew back so he could meet her gaze. "I control when my seed creates life."

"Let's at least get on the far side of the next couple of weeks." Her blue eyes twinkled for a moment, then sheened with worry.

He took her hand. "Come on. Bubba sounded desperate for food."

"He's always desperate for food." Colleen grinned.

"Yes." The changeling's voice sounded from their front porch. "Come on. Hurry."

They walked across the grounds to the main house and settled at a corner table in the large dining room. Witches brought them enough food to satisfy twice as many people, along with coffee and a fragrant, herbal tea.

"What were you telling Jenna about us going to England?" Roz asked.

Colleen looked at Duncan. "This is your dog and pony show. How about if you explain it. I was pretty tired when you told me last night."

"It was actually early this morning." He set his fork down. "Be glad to." He outlined having called the Sidhe council meeting and what had transpired. "In any event, they're considering taking back some—or maybe all—of the responsibility for the Irichna. They asked that I bring all of you to the next meeting. Let's see." Duncan thought about it. "It's in about four days, taking the eight hour time difference into consideration."

Roz drew her dark brows together. "What if we don't want to give up stalking and killing demons?"

"Funny," Colleen said, "but I asked the same question."

Jenna kept her gaze on her plate. Duncan stayed out of her mind. It was clear she was torn. At length she looked up. "Some days I'm sick of being scared to death. Of wondering whether today will be the day when some demon does me in, or sucks the soul out of me and makes me one of them." She took a breath. "On the other hand, I don't know what I'd do with myself if I wasn't with you two." She tipped her chin at Colleen and Roz.

"And me," Bubba piped up. "Don't forget me."

"Yes, hon. You too." Jenna reached over and patted his shoulder. "Even though I got really excited at the possibility of getting out from under killing Irichna, the more I thought about it, the more I came around to deciding I'm okay sharing our job with the Sidhe, but not okay with them just swooping in and taking over for us."

Colleen blew out a breath. Duncan knew she'd been worried. He'd seen it in her mind. She placed her hand in his lap and grasped one of his. "When do we leave?"

"Soon," he replied. "I'm assuming you'll want to take a few clothes along, which means we need to swing through Fairbanks."

Colleen looked sheepish. "I hadn't even considered that, but of course we'll need something beyond what we have on."

Roz snorted. "I'd settle for something clean at this point."

Jenna glanced at her clothing. It had huge rents and blood-stains from her battle with the demon. "Clean and without holes." She amended Roz's statement.

"How are we going to get back to the Old Country?" Bubba asked. "It's a really, really long way."

"Teleporting all of us might be a little much, even for me,"

Duncan admitted. "I can gin up a glamour to make Bubba look more human, and I'll secure airline tickets for us. Do all of you have passports?"

Jenna nodded. "I do."

"So do Roz and I," Colleen said. She bit her lip and looked at Bubba.

"What's a passport?" he asked, sitting up straighter.

Naomi drifted by, pulled up a chair, and sat. "Do you have everything you need?"

"I need a passport, whatever that is," Bubba said and ate another forkful of scrambled eggs.

Naomi grinned and shoved her long hair behind her shoulders. "Well, you've come to the right place, little man. I'm sure we can come up with something that will work for you."

"Good to know. How'd Mathilde's funeral go?" Colleen asked.

Naomi worried her bottom lip between her teeth. "About twenty of us showed up to bid her farewell. I'm certain I sensed Irichna hovering. They apparently didn't want someone they'd used as a vessel purified during our cremation rites."

"I didn't feel anything demon-wise when we walked over here," Roz said. "And I did check."

"You probably wouldn't have," Naomi said. "They left as soon as Mathilde's remains caught fire, and we added incense and sacred herbs."

"Maybe the demons are gone for now, but they're not really gone," Bubba said sadly.

Duncan blew out a tense breath. Not only were the demons not gone, they felt more intrusive than ever.

They teleported to Fairbanks so she, Jenna, and Roz could pack a few things for themselves and Bubba. There hadn't been time to stop in Haines and pick up their Subaru. Colleen hoped to hell the ferry authorities wouldn't tow it before one of them had a chance to retrieve the damn thing.

They'd boarded a jet in Anchorage that took them back to Seattle. From there, they caught an over-the-pole flight for London. Duncan told them it would've been closer to his home if they'd been able to land in Glasgow, but that would have meant flying across the U.S. to one of the eastern seaboard cities, and then catching an additional flight, which would have taken longer.

Since Colleen had done very little in the way of international travel, she let him make all the arrangements, trusting he knew what he was doing. It actually felt really, really good to be taken care of. She'd expended so much effort holding men at arm's length, she was surprised how quickly Duncan wormed his way around her barriers. It felt as if they'd been together for years, not a scant span of days. He felt solid and warm and comfortable, and she didn't think she'd ever get enough of his nakedness pressed against her, filling her until her world shattered into streaming bits of ecstasy.

Colleen dozed on and off through much of the plane ride. Duncan had bought first class seats, and they were plush and comfortable. Fortunately, Bubba slept too. When he was awake, he wanted to stroll up and down the aisles, striking up conversations with strangers. The changeling's glamour was amazingly effective. He appeared about seventeen, with attractive, longish black hair, dark eyes, and a broad-shouldered, lanky build. In jeans, T-shirt, and a sweater, he looked like prime daughter-date material. Colleen smiled to herself. It had taken Duncan a few passes before he was satisfied with Bubba's glamour. She could see its edges, but they'd be invisible to mortal eyes.

One of the flight attendants announced they'd be landing in London in about thirty minutes. Colleen stretched her arms over her head, and rotated her shoulder blades.

Duncan placed a hand on her leg. "Did you get some decent sleep?"

"Uh-huh." She glanced about for Bubba, relieved when she saw him across the aisle, seated next to Jenna.

"I've been keeping an eye on him. Here." Duncan handed her a bottle of mineral water. "The air in these jets really dries you out. Have a drink."

"What happens once we land?"

"After we clear customs, a car should be waiting for us."

She grinned. "Were you a travel agent in another life?"

He grinned back. "You have no idea."

She leaned against him. Despite teleporting them to Alaska and being in terminals or on planes for the last twenty-four hours, give or take, he looked amazingly fresh. "Did you get any rest?"

"I'm fine. I can get most of what I need with catnaps. One eye open and all that."

"I'm trying not to feel too safe and comfortable around you, but you're making it damned difficult."

"Colleen, my sweet." He turned her face so she had to look at him. "I want you to be safe and comfortable and pampered. My goal in life—"

"Ssht." She waved him to silence, and heat spread upward from the open neck of her stretchy top. "People will hear you."

"Not a problem, dearie." The woman in the next row leaned forward. "I'm hoping Charles here—" she jabbed a portly man sitting next to her "—will get some ideas. He's a dear, sweet fellow, but romance is scarcely his strong suit."

Duncan closed his mouth over hers in a brief, sweet kiss that promised much more. He leaned back, looking satisfied, and murmured. "Got to set a good example."

Colleen laughed. "I shouldn't encourage you. You're incorrigible as it is."

The plane touched down uneventfully. Duncan went through one customs line, the rest of them another with their U.S. passports. Colleen breathed a sigh of relief when the agent stamped Bubba's and told them to enjoy their stay in the U.K. Though the Witches' Northwest Coven forger had seemed extremely competent, and Bubba's passport looked just like a real one, Colleen hadn't been certain there wasn't some electronic way to determine his was a fake. It had passed muster in Seattle boarding the International flight, but this was a whole different country.

Duncan herded them through the terminal to the spot designated for private ground transportation. A shiny, silver

Rolls SUV waited, complete with a uniformed driver who bowed.

"Welcome home, Lord Regis." He held the back door open. "Don't give your bags another thought, ladies. I'll stow them in the boot." Dressed in a black suit jacket, black pants, and a monogrammed jacket, presumably carrying the Regis coat of arms, the driver's longish tawny hair was drawn into a queue. Like Duncan, he was classically handsome, with defined cheekbones and a strong chin.

Bubba strode to the chauffeur and fingered the insignia on his breast pocket. His eyes widened. The chauffeur shook his head almost imperceptibly. "I can see you too," he murmured. "Be a good man and get into the car so we can leave."

"Can I sit in front with you?"

"Of course." The man's eyes twinkled. Colleen realized with a start that they were silver.

She sent a tendril of magic snaking outward to take a closer look. Sure enough, the driver was Sidhe. He winked at her and made shooing motions with both hands. Once they were settled, the chauffeur took his place behind the right hand drive steering wheel and ferried the luxury car out of the airport.

"Quite a show, Tristan." Duncan clapped a hand on the driver's shoulder. "Good job."

The other Sidhe shrugged. "What's life without a spot of playacting here and there? You're cutting things a bit close. The meeting at Ronin's is tomorrow afternoon."

"Best we could do," Duncan said. "Let me introduce everyone. The stalwart fellow sharing the front seat with you is Niall Eoghan, but the witches call him Bubba."

Tristan glanced at the changeling. "Irish?"

Bubba drew himself up. "What else? You cut the balls out from under my Scottish kin."

Tristan winced. "So we did. Sorry. I do believe that's been rectified."

"What? When?" Bubba's voice rang with excitement.

"In the third seat," Duncan went on smoothly before Bubba could ask any more questions, "are Jenna Neil and Roxanne Lantry, better known as Roz."

"Pleased to meet you." Tristan made eye contact via the rearview mirror.

"Next to me," Duncan went on, "is Colleen Kelly, my fiancée."

A shocked look bloomed on Tristan's face. He exchanged it for neutrality, but not before Colleen noticed. "You've discussed this with Titania—or Oberon?" Tristan asked.

"In a manner of speaking." Duncan's tone didn't invite further questions.

"Damn it!" Colleen shook her head. Distress soured her stomach. "I told you this was going to cause problems for you —a whole bunch of them."

"It's not that," Tristan cut in. "I was just startled, and it's rare that anything surprises me." Horns blared, and he returned his attention to the dense London traffic, after narrowly avoiding being sideswiped. "Actually, I think it's excellent news. I'm chuffed, truly pleased, for both of you."

Colleen narrowed her eyes. "The two of you seem like close buddies. How are the rest of the Sidhe going to feel?"

"What difference does it make?" Duncan tried to wrap an arm around her, but she shook him off.

"The difference it makes is you have a life here. You want me to share it, but if your kin take the same stand as Titania, we won't have much in the way of friends."

"So? Means fewer visitors." Roz chuckled lewdly. "You'd just have to get out of bed to answer the door."

"I have it." Jenna snapped her fingers and elbowed Roz.

"You and I can hang out here, snag ourselves some Sidhe studs, and then it won't seem so unusual. If there were three witch-Sidhe couples, the stuffed shirts would have to accept us."

Tristan snickered. He seemed to be trying to control it, but in moments he was laughing so hard, he wiped tears from his face. His silvery gaze flickered in the rearview mirror. "I'm guessing if I asked you to supper, Miss Jenna, you wouldn't turn me down."

"Ooooh." Jenna leaned forward. "Better watch it, Bubba. I'll displace you from that front seat so I can paw at Tristan."

He snorted. "You can paw at me all you want later. I adore female attention. Right now, we need to talk about tomorrow, while we're alone."

"What do you know?" Duncan asked. Colleen felt tension radiate from him. She could relate, since her anxiety was reaching critical mass too.

"Not much. The others suspect you and I talk, so I've had to be sly about gathering information. From what I've been able to glean, the majority are ready to resume their demon assassin duties."

"Not without us," Colleen snapped.

"Yes," Roz seconded. "We'll welcome assistance, but we're not willing to totally step aside."

"That will probably work," Tristan said thoughtfully, "given how ambivalent some of my kinsmen are."

"What about my kin?" Bubba spoke up. "You said something earlier about recti— Uh, something or other."

"The consensus is we did changelings a disservice."

Bubba bounced against his seatbelt. "You'll free them and return their power?"

Tristan smiled. He was just as beautiful as Duncan, but in a more robust way, with his ruddy skin tones and tawny hair. "We already have."

Bubba screeched and pounded the dashboard with a fist. "Stop the car. Let me out."

Duncan angled his body forward and placed his hands on the changeling's shoulders. He flicked a bit of magic and the glamour dissipated. "You can do all the running about and high-fiving you want, once we get closer to the northlands. You'd be hard-pressed to find anyone to celebrate with this far south."

Colleen leaned forward and ruffled the changeling's hair. His joy was contagious. "Happy for you, Bubs. Would you like to spend some time here celebrating?"

He twisted in his seat and met her gaze. "Are you offering to undo the binding?"

Well, am I?

Colleen nodded. Her throat thickened. She loved the changeling, but part of loving someone was not being selfish. The changeling drew his brows together. "Do you want to get rid of me now that you have Duncan?"

"Oh no, sweetie! I just want you to be happy is all. You're a big part of my life and I'd miss you terribly."

Duncan nodded. "Before Colleen accepted me, she made certain I'd welcome you as part of our family."

"Really?" Bubba glanced from one of them to the other. For the first time, he looked like the ancient creature he was.

"Really." Duncan squeezed the changeling's shoulders.

"You're telling the truth. I can tell." Bubba set his mouth in a determined line and reached over the seatback for Colleen. She took his hand. "I want to spend a little bit of time with my kinfolk, but I wish to maintain our bond. Can't let you fight Irichna without me."

Colleen wove her way between Duncan's arms and hugged Bubba. His clothing that was far too big for his natural form slipped from his shoulders. "Thank you. I didn't want you to go away, but I would never hold you against your will."

The changeling quirked a brow. "One tiny thing?"

"Certainly." Duncan nodded.

"I never figured out why the witches started calling me Bubba, but I want everyone to use my real name. Bubba sounds like a cat."

"Which is exactly how you ended up with it," Roz said.

"There must be cats named Niall somewhere." He moved away from the jungle of Colleen and Duncan's arms and stared at Roz.

"I'm sure there are." The witch blew him a kiss. "We'll do our best to remember, but after forty years, it may take a bit of time before we're all on line with your real name, every single time."

"I can wait," he said solemnly. "So long as you're trying."

DUNCAN AND TRISTAN guided the three witches and the changeling into Ronin's mansion the following afternoon, nodding to various Sidhe and making introductions as they moved from the lushly manicured grounds to inside the imposing home.

"Now remember." Colleen focused her mind voice just for Duncan. *"No introducing me as your fiancée."*

"But I'm proud of you," he replied out loud.

"You promised." She tapped his chest with an index finger.

"What I promised was to not say anything until after the meeting was over."

"It would be better if you didn't say anything at all." Rather than agreeing like she hoped he would, Duncan just looked at her, an enigmatic expression on his face.

"Wow!" Roz craned her neck from side to side. "Here I thought Duncan's place was grand. This looks like a castle."

A corner of Duncan's mouth twisted downward. "Once upon a time, it was, but so was my manor house. The English countryside never suffered for lack of castles. Let's sit there." He pointed to a row of elegantly padded chairs in an enormous room paneled with dark wainscoting and hung with cut crystal chandeliers. Liveried servants flitted about offering champagne flutes and hors d'oeuvres.

Jenna slid into a seat. "I didn't get a chance to ask last night—"

"Because you were so busy *chatting* with Tristan," Roz noted snidely.

"You're just jealous," Jenna sniped back.

"Damn straight I am." Roz snorted. "Nothing like being surrounded by the sounds of people fucking when you're by yourself."

"You didn't have to listen. Besides, we weren't fucking, or even kissing. Keep your mind out of the gutter." Jenna tried for a superior look, but failed. The corners of her mouth twitched.

"Witches have sharp ears," Roz said and sat next to Colleen.

"Yes, especially when they augment their hearing with magic." Jenna glanced sidelong at the other witch, clearly pleased she was gaining the upper hand, albeit slowly.

"Keep your eyes open, Roz," Duncan said. He looked as if he was struggling to suppress a smile. "You may find an eligible bachelor or two in the group."

"How long have you lived in your house?" Jenna asked. "It was what I tried to ask before Roz interrupted."

"Since the fifteen hundreds. Of course I've had it modernized. Several times, actually."

Fifteen hundreds!

Breath whooshed out of Colleen's lungs. It was easy to

forget just how old Duncan was. Beyond an overarching impression that he lived in a museum, she hadn't really had time to explore any of the rambling multi-story mansion beyond his bedroom.

"So," Jenna pressed on, "all those paintings and sculptures and knickknacks that look antique—"

"—were new when I bought them," he finished for her.

"My home is just outside Richmond." Tristan smiled at Jenna and took the chair next to her. "It's not as grand as Duncan's or Ronin's, but we Sidhe do like our creature comforts."

Jenna leaned into him. "I'm sure you do. Sheesh, I was comparing all this elegance to our place in Fairbanks…" She rolled her eyes and let her words trail off.

Tristan started to say something, but Duncan shushed him.

Ronin strode to the front of the room. With iridescent robes flowing around him and shiny dark hair, he cut a fine figure. "Thank you all for coming." His melodious voice reached every corner of the vast room. Colleen figured he'd boosted it with magic. "Special thanks to our guests." He bowed toward the witches and changeling.

Colleen inclined her head. So did Jenna and Roz, but Niall simply glowered.

Ronin cleared his throat. "We have had many productive meetings this past week." He shot Duncan a glance, but Colleen couldn't interpret it. "All our elders but for Lord Regis were in attendance. He was absent because his task was to bring the witches here. Let me address things one at a time. We returned sovereignty to the changelings two days ago and have pledged our assistance until their magic is fully restored."

"About time," Niall muttered *sotto voce*.

"Hush," Duncan whispered. "That's as close to an apology as you're likely to get."

Ronin glanced their way, but didn't comment. He extended his arms. "Would the witches be so kind as to step forward?"

It was more command than question. Colleen rose. So did Jenna and Roz. Together, they walked to the front of the room and stood before Ronin, waiting. Colleen considered bowing, but didn't. She didn't want to appear subservient in any way.

Ronin dropped his arms to his sides. His probing, blue gaze roved from one witch to the next. "We may have made an error in tasking you with the Irichna. We stand ready to resume our duties in that regard."

Colleen exchanged glances with Roz and Jenna. She squared her shoulders and looked Ronin right in the eye. "We've discussed it. While we are extremely grateful for your offer, the demons are stronger than ever."

"We are willing to share the responsibility." Roz put her hands on her hips. She too, focused her dark gaze on the Sidhe. He stared back. Something electric passed between them. Colleen readied magic, just in case things got out of hand.

"Yes," Jenna cut in. "Share it, not give it up entirely."

Ronin's mouth softened from its customary stern line, which might mean the Sidhe leader was pleased. Perhaps this was the outcome he'd hoped for.

"I believe we can accommodate your request. We will need a bit of your blood, however."

"Not a problem. Looks to me like we have a deal."

Colleen extended a hand. After a long moment, Ronin clasped it and shook. Roz and Jenna held their hands out as well. Ronin clung to Roz's a shade too long, or maybe she clung to his. Colleen suppressed a knowing grin. She'd known Roz too long not to recognize when the other witch was trolling for a date.

A collective sigh surged through the room.

Roz ran her fingers across Ronin's palm before releasing

him, and quirked an inquisitive brow. "Will every Sidhe in here be able to fight demons?"

Ronin shook his head. "No. It never worked that way before. We have, or we used to have," he corrected himself, "a warrior class. They will be the ones who volunteer to resorb the genetic code."

Colleen picked up the direction of Roz's thoughts. "I'm assuming there are more Sidhe than those in this room."

"Yes. Perhaps triple this number," Ronin concurred.

"If half of you took back the genetics to fight demons," Colleen said, "we'd have them on the run in no time, plus Duncan uncovered a source of magic that allowed him to send them packing, and he hasn't had any genetic alterations at all."

Gasps escalated into a sibilant rustling that became nearly deafening. "Duncan." Ronin's voice was sharp, rising above the din. "Come up here."

Colleen walked back to where Duncan sat and crooked a finger. "Sorry. Didn't mean to blow your cover," she murmured.

"You're in for it now, old chap." Tristan clapped Duncan's shoulder.

He got to his feet and joined Colleen. "Should have told you to keep quiet," he whispered.

"I have very good ears." Ronin's voice carried across the room.

Colleen bit back laughter. Duncan made a grab for her hand, but she trotted ahead of him. Together, they walked briskly to where Ronin stood.

The crowd quieted. Duncan turned so he faced everyone. "It's quite simple, really. I tapped into the ancient power source that we normally eschew because it's so hard to control. You know, the one they teach us about when we're young, and then tell us never to use."

"And?" Ronin's eyes blazed with something wild and barely constrained.

Duncan shrugged. "The power is there. Just like it's always been. It's hideous to manage, but it does seem to force demons back to their borderworlds. If you believe the dark fae, it extinguishes the Irichna, but I'm not so sure about that." He grinned. "I'm still here to tell about it, so it doesn't force us into the *Dreaming*."

"The Unseelie? Where do they come into play?" Ronin laid a hand on Duncan's arm. The wild look in his eyes shone hotly. "I have a feeling you haven't told us quite everything."

"You'd be correct," Duncan said, "but when would I have had a chance?"

"You haven't, but you'll make time to tell me everything." Ronin's voice rang with command, and Colleen caught a glimpse of just how powerful he was.

She took a deep breath. Getting to know the Sidhe would be an adventure in and of itself.

"My lord." Duncan inclined his head. "I'm sure we'll work something out."

"Ronin can wait. Teach us how to access that power," someone cried. "It's been so long since I learned about it, I've forgotten."

"Yes. Immediately," another Sidhe demanded.

"I'll do what I can," Duncan said. "Colleen and I are due back in Seattle on December twenty-first for our wedding."

Sidhe surged to their feet and rushed forward with hugs, kisses, and good wishes. Questions bounced about the room. Had he told Oberon? Titania? Did they give their blessings?

"I asked you not to do that." Colleen spoke low into his ear.

"And I said I wouldn't until the meeting was over." He drew her against him. "It's looking pretty much over to me. People want to congratulate us. I say we let them."

"I thought you said they'd shun you because of Titania, that she'd excommunicate you or something."

He smiled, appearing so happy and relieved, it touched her heart. "Looks as if I was wrong about part of it. Titania may try to bar me from Sidhe society, but it appears my kinfolk will ignore her."

"So." Ronin held his ground against the Sidhe forming a tight circle around them. "I'll forgive you for the short notice, if you invite us to your nuptials."

"Of course—" Duncan began.

"We need to at least ask Naomi," Colleen interrupted, concerned about taking advantage of the Witches' Northwest Coven's hospitality. She scanned the group. "There must be around eighty of you here. If the other two-thirds of you came too, that would be over two hundred extra people. It's not the sort of thing you can just spring on someone without lots of notice."

"Tell her we'll cater your wedding." Ronin waved an airy hand. "Besides, I need time with Duncan. If I have to chase him across the Atlantic to get it, I'll do so." He eyed the witches. "Besides, it's high time our races got to know one another better."

"Is that so?" Roz's old sarcastic tone was back in spades. "If you really mean it, there are Covens right here in the U.K. where you could begin."

Ronin gazed at her and placed a hand under her arm. "Come sit with me, my dear. You can fill me in on who I need to talk with to begin mending bridges."

CHAPTER 19

Colleen lolled on a plush sofa in one the many downstairs rooms in Duncan's house. She sipped from a snifter of Armagnac and sighed heavily. "I can hardly believe we're alone for a few hours."

Duncan settled next to her and swirled the liquor in his own snifter. The amber liquid gave off a heady fragrance. "Well, we are. Bubba, er Niall, is with a group of Scottish changelings, probably getting shit-faced. Jenna went shopping, and—" he rolled his eyes "—unbelievable as it may seem, we left Roz at Ronin's chatting with a group of Sidhe council members."

"Why is that unbelievable?"

"I told you the Sidhe are unbearably insular, plus Ronin has ignored the human race since the fourteen hundreds."

"What happened then?"

"A mortal woman died delivering his child. The babe died too. He always blamed himself for falling in love outside our ranks."

"That's horrible. No wonder he comes off as a pompous

prig. It's a defense mechanism to keep people away. I almost feel sorry for him."

"Don't. He's had more than his share of women since then. He just never let himself get attached again." Duncan sipped his brandy. "He may be arrogant, and a bit of a pain in the ass, but he's been a good leader, all in all."

Colleen leaned against him. "Probably no one else wanted the job. I'm beginning to see where immortality's not all it's cracked up to be." She wriggled, trying to loosen stiff muscles. "All I have to say is he'd better not patronize the witches in Seattle, or he'll have to answer to me."

Duncan laughed, the sound deep and rich. When he could talk again, he said, "It would be amusing to see the two of you square off against one another, but I have a feeling it won't come to that."

"No fair. You've been peeking inside my mind." He adopted an innocent look, all wide eyes. She elbowed him and said, "On a more serious note, we have until what? Day after tomorrow, and then we have to leave?"

"Something like that. Did you phone Naomi?"

"Uh-huh."

"What'd she say?"

"After she got over not being able to talk at all, she said she was sure they'd figure something out. I guess they've had as many as five hundred people there before for ceremonies."

Concern flitted across his perfect features. "Did you tell her the Sidhe will take care of all the food?"

"I did. I think she was more shocked that the Sidhe wanted to visit her Coven than anything else. You haven't exactly been the most approachable group."

He nodded his understanding. "No, we haven't." Duncan set his snifter down, and took hers, setting it on the coffee table alongside his. He opened his arms. "Rather than rehashing history, I'd like to make better use of this little sliver of private time that fell into our laps."

She winked. "Just what did you have in mind...my lord?"

"I can come up with a French maid's outfit if you're going to talk like that."

"Really? Who was the last one to wear it?"

In one lightning fast move, he scooped her into his arms and closed his mouth over hers. He licked the seam between her lips, probing for entrance, and she opened her mouth to him. He tasted wonderful, sweet like the brandy and fresh like wheat fields she remembered from her childhood in eastern Washington. The more they made love—and they'd even managed to squeeze into the tiny jetliner bathroom by using magic to make the flight attendant look the other way—the faster she responded to his advances. Her nipples pebbled and her crotch flooded with heat. She pushed her hands under his shirt, frantic for the feel of his skin. Fingertips connecting, she reeled from the larger-than-life reality of him: hot, silky, electric, and all hers. Her breathing quickened, and her throat clotted with desire.

He broke their kiss and licked his way down her neck. Where he touched her, she felt supercharged, alive. No matter how much he caressed her, she always wanted more. She arched against him, moaning low in the back of her throat.

"I love it when you make that sound," he said, hands tightening on her back. "You sound like a lioness purring."

He rucked her shirt out of the way and reached behind her to unhook her bra. She moved it above her breasts and he settled in to suckle her. He was so skilled, licking, sucking, biting, nibbling, she sometimes came without any additional stimulation. From the hot tightness spooling between her legs, this was looking like one of those times. She writhed and rubbed her thighs together. Anticipation of sensation added spice to her peaks when they cascaded through her, leaving her breathless and satiated.

She repositioned herself so she could cradle his cock in her hands. The heat of him through his pants seared her. She wanted to take him into her mouth and do some serious licking and sucking of her own. She'd just begun to unfasten his trousers when something in the air shifted and changed.

Her eyes snapped wide open. "What was that?"

He lifted his mouth from her breasts. "What was what, darling?"

"You're as lost in rut as I am. I felt…something just a few seconds ago." She straightened and pulled her top down, scanning the room for clues.

"You're being silly—" he began, and then broke off. "Damn it!" He drew away from her, rearranged his cock, and zipped his pants back up.

"Who's here? Or who will be?" She reached behind herself to hook her bra.

"Titania," he said through gritted teeth and shook his head. "I'd meant to track her down, but what with all the Sidhe clamoring to know about that power source I tapped into, and Ronin wanting a full report on the dark fae, I ran out of time."

"Excuses, excuses," an airy voice trilled. A coruscation flashed in the air and a tall, emaciated woman, with silver hair to the floor, stepped from its glow. "Lovely. Perfect." She clapped her hands together. "I'd hoped to find the two of you —alone."

Duncan scrambled to his feet and bowed. "Your Highness. Welcome to my home. May I offer you refreshments?"

Because Colleen wasn't certain of the correct protocol, and because she didn't owe any allegiance to the Faerie queen, she remained seated. Wary and watchful, but seated.

"Thank you." Titania swept the room with her pale blue gaze. "Whatever you're having will be fine."

"It's Armagnac. I have mead if you'd prefer." Duncan straightened and stood, looking at his queen.

"I would prefer it. You know me too well, dear boy."

"Back in a moment." He trotted from the room.

Colleen winced. There was something patronizing about Titania's tone that grated on her nerves. As if the monarch had read her thoughts, she turned to face her. "You don't like me."

Aw shit, here it comes.

Colleen got to her feet, so they'd be more equally matched. "Why should I?" she countered. "Duncan came to you and said he wanted to marry me. You not only withheld your blessing, you vanished so he couldn't discuss it further."

Titania winced. "Ach, he told you that, did he?"

"Why wouldn't he? Lovers shouldn't hold secrets, at least not ones of that nature. Plus," Colleen forged on, "you put Duncan in a really difficult position. He had to choose between his kinsmen and me." She put her hands on her hips. "That wasn't fair."

Duncan walked back into the room. He handed a glass of mead to Titania and strode to Colleen's side. "Darling. It's all right. You don't have to defend me." He glanced at his queen with eyes that looked weary and wounded. "You sought me out for a reason, my liege. Tell me what you wish of me."

She furled her silver brows. "I actually wanted several things. I wanted to meet the woman you were willing to place above allegiance to your people."

Colleen smiled coldly. "Here I am. Do you think I'm worth it?"

"It's not wise to bait her," Duncan murmured.

Titania smiled too, but it was reminiscent of a scimitar. "I could flay the skin off your body."

"Feed me to the Irichna?" Colleen inquired caustically. "I've been there more times than I can count. You don't scare me. But I am angry you caused Duncan pain."

Titania fixed her unearthly gaze on Duncan. "She doesn't understand us."

He blew out a breath. "She understands me. I'm not certain about the rest of us."

"That was the second thing I wanted." Titania forged ahead, making Colleen think the queen lacked even the barest rudiments of how to conduct a two-way conversation. "When you sought me out, there was only one witch-Sidhe pair, now there seem to be three." She spread almost translucent fingers before her. "Why are you making my life so trying? Ronin, in particular, is nearly impossible to control. I have no idea what he sees in that black-haired hag, but—"

"Now you hold on a fucking minute." Colleen's blood heated with outrage, and her temper shot over the top. "Roxanne Lantry is one of the strongest, most courageous women I know. I will not stand by and hear her slandered. Do I make myself clear?" She sucked air and forged ahead. "Plus, at least so far all Jenna and Roz have done is talk with some of your precious Sidhe males. That scarcely makes them couples."

Titania rolled her eyes and fanned herself with one hand. "What a feisty bunch you are. I had witches pegged as a docile lot who cast runes around a fire and chanted up homilies."

"You had us pegged wrong." Colleen bit her lower lip. She wanted to slug Titania, but figured it wouldn't go over well. Damn royalty anyway. They treated whomever they wanted like crap, and got away with it—every time.

Duncan looked miserable. He moved between Colleen and the Queen of Faerie. "Titania, you cannot deal rudely with my wife-to-be. She will soon be the lady of this manor." He inhaled raggedly. "If you came here to sever my ties with Faerie and relieve me of my immortality, please get on with it."

"Presenting yourself to me like a plucked goose, are you?"

"This isn't funny," Colleen snapped. "He's doing the best he can. I don't fully understand all your rules, or I'd help him."

Titania snapped her fingers in front of Colleen. "Oberon's breath, woman. Stand down. Show some respect. I'm many thousands of years old."

"If you want respect from me," Colleen said evenly, wondering where her courage was coming from, "you'll have to earn it. I have a funny way of not respecting people who treat those I love badly."

Duncan turned to her. His mouth twisted into an expression she couldn't read. "I love you for being fierce and trying to protect me, but let's hear Titania out. She'll tell us what she wants eventually."

"Indeed I will," the queen huffed.

Colleen opened her mouth, but Duncan shook his head. She balled her hands into fists so hard her nails dug into her palms. While she waited for the queen to spit out what she wanted, Colleen made a conscious effort to unkink her aching hands.

"Much better." Titania frowned. "I was beginning to wonder if you could remain silent, or if you always had to have the last word." She flicked a finger toward Colleen. "Always having to win isn't a good trait in a woman."

"So it's better in a man?"

Duncan's mouth twitched. In moments, he started to laugh. After a long, awkward moment, Titania joined in. Colleen just watched, open mouthed, wondering what was so funny.

Titania took a substantial gulp from the glass in her hand, and then set it down. "You may not like me," she said to Colleen, "but I think I'm going to like you very much. I was testing your mettle. You not only passed—" the queen snorted "—you surpassed my wildest expectations of what you'd be like. You're tough, gutsy, and apparently not afraid to stand up to anyone."

Colleen swallowed outrage so she wouldn't lope across the room and deck the Queen of Faerie. "That...that—" she waved her arms at a loss for words "—was all just a test?"

Titania nodded, her blue eyes guileless.

"You're not going to excommunicate Duncan, or take away his immortality?" A complex array of emotions buffeted Colleen. Gratitude sparred with anger that the queen hadn't been more direct.

"No. I'm not planning to do any of those things." Titania shifted her gaze to Duncan. "At least not today, but if you do something to anger me in the future..."

Joy, so primal it was painful to look at, bloomed on his face. Colleen blanched as the depth of his feelings for her slammed home in raw, visceral Technicolor. She meant everything to him, enough for him to be willing to walk away from home, hearth, and kin.

"Thank you, my liege." He bowed low.

Colleen's anger evaporated in the face of Duncan's obvious relief. Courtesy of her blow-hot, blow-out, Irish temper, she'd always been quick to flare up, but equally quick to let things go. She faced Titania and bowed too. "Thank you."

The queen smiled broadly. "Now that we have the preliminaries out of the way, aren't you going to invite me to share your evening meal? I want to hear all about the upcoming wedding." She skewered Colleen with her unnerving gaze. "You must tell me more about witches. I had no idea you were such a captivating group."

Colleen wiped the grin that wanted to surface off her face.

"We can be enchanting, tenacious as all get out, and harder than hell to get rid of."

Duncan stammered a garbled mixture of words in English and Gaelic. Colleen had a hard time following him, but thought he was asking for a rain check on dinner.

"Pfft." The queen waved a hand toward him. "I know the two of you were rutting when I showed up. The air in here positively reeks of lust, but you have company now, so sex will have to wait."

"It's fine," Colleen said. "I'd like to get to know Titania, and I'd be honored to share a meal with her."

"Truly?" Duncan looked at her, his eyes glowing with love and relief.

"Truly." Colleen glanced about. "Which way is the kitchen? I can probably cook something once I know what I have to work with."

Duncan draped an arm around her. "No need for that. Sidhe servants are invisible until we need them. I'll take care of ordering up a meal." He laid his cheek against Colleen's and strode from the room.

"Excellent." Titania clapped her hands together. "Shall we wait in here or in your dining room?"

Colleen felt herself blush. "'Fraid I don't know where that is, either. I haven't been here very long."

"I suspect that rascal of a Sidhe has kept you in his bedchamber the entire time." Titania laughed, the sound reminiscent of wind chimes. "I remember what it was like to be young, with my juices flowing." She picked up her glass, settled on a leather settee, and patted the spot next to her. "Come sit. We can chat until Duncan returns, and afterward too. I'm looking forward to getting to know you."

To her surprise, Colleen realized she felt the same way.

Suspicion flared. Had the queen trapped her in some kind of spell? "Did you do something?"

Titania met her gaze. "You tell me. Did I?"

Colleen fanned magic through the room, and relaxed. When she smiled, it felt genuine. "Guess not."

"You have a great deal of common sense, my dear. It came to the fore and told you I could be trusted."

"Is that what happened?"

Titania nodded. The wisdom of the ages shone from the depths of her ancient eyes.

"The odd part," Colleen grinned, "is I believe you."

"No reason not to. Now tell me all about witches, my dear. Especially the ones who seem to have my Sidhe council in thrall…"

"If it's an unusual event for your subjects to talk to anyone outside their ranks, it might seem like that to you, but Ceridwen made us all…" Colleen chatted on, finding Titania easy to talk with.

When Duncan returned a little later to usher them to supper, the Queen of Fairie was starting to feel like a friend.

THIS IS the end of *Witch's Bounty*. The story continues in *Witch's Bane*, Roz and Ronin's story. Read on for a sample.

ABOUT THE AUTHOR

Ann Gimpel is a national bestselling author. A lifelong aficionado of the unusual, she began writing speculative fiction a few years ago. Since then her short fiction has appeared in a number of webzines and anthologies. Her longer books run the gamut from urban fantasy to paranormal romance. Once upon a time, she nurtured clients, now she nurtures dark, gritty fantasy stories that push hard against reality. When she's not writing, she's in the backcountry getting down and dirty with her camera. She's published over fifty books to date, with several more planned for 2018 and beyond. A husband, grown children, grandchildren, and wolf hybrids round out her family.

Keep up with her at www.anngimpel.com or http://anngimpel.blogspot.com

If you enjoyed what you read, get in line for special offers and pre-release special reads. Sign up for Ann's newsletter on her website or her blog.

WITCH'S BANE, CHAPTER ONE

Roxanne Lantry—Roz to everyone who knew her—paced up and down the sodden lawn outside the huge old Victorian that housed the Witches' Northwest Coven headquarters in Seattle. Rain pelted her from beneath a gunmetal sky, but it was better out here than inside. She fought an unfamiliar thickening at the back of her throat and balled her hands into fists.

"I will not cry," she muttered to an inquisitive ground squirrel that ran across her boot tops, but telling herself and controlling her emotions were two different things.

One of her two best friends, Colleen Kelly, would be getting married in less than half an hour. Roz had been inside, in the midst of all the bride-craziness, but seeing Colleen swathed in cream-colored lace sent her into a tailspin.

What the fuck is wrong with me?

She kicked at a hummock of grass and yelped when it didn't move, but the pain from her stubbed toes helped her focus. If she was honest, not an easy task when men were involved, she knew exactly what was bothering her.

"Yeah," she mouthed the words, lecturing herself. "Two failed marriages and a whole bunch of loser dudes before, after, and in between. I'm jealous and I need a good, swift boot in the backside. Just because Colleen finally stumbled across Mr. Right doesn't lower my odds of ever finding someone who's gorgeous and magical and worships me."

Now if I could only believe that...

Roz was happy for Colleen and Duncan, the Daoine Sidhe she was marrying. They made a great couple, but surely there was enough connubial bliss in the universe to sprinkle a little her way too. Her last go-round with a strikingly handsome Oklahoman she'd met online had ended in fireworks when he'd admitted all he really wanted was to tap into her magical ability. When the rubber met the road, he didn't even like women. Her stomach churned. She hated being made a fool of. She'd turned the guy in to his Coven for false advertising and laying a trap to delude a fellow magic wielder, but she doubted they'd done much to censure him.

Water dripped off her nose. She stuck out her lower lip and blew upward, but the rain kept on dripping. Roz shook her fist at the low-hanging clouds, recognizing it for displacement activity. What she really wanted to do was pound her fist through the Oklahoman's nice, straight nose.

Enough of this. Give it a rest. That happened months ago.

For Christ's sake, I need to get moving, go inside, and trade my jeans and serape for fancy duds.

Roz took a few deep breaths to settle her angst. She couldn't show her tear-stained face to the world. She'd never live it down. When she closed her eyes, the Oklahoma asshole formed behind her lids, taunting her. Roz clenched her jaw and summoned a calming spell. It seemed like cheating, but time was short. As the wispy edges of magic caught her up, they soothed her frazzled nerves and she turned hard right and headed for the house at a brisk trot.

She, Colleen, and Jenna Neil were the last of a long line of demon assassins. Witches with specialized powers, they lured Irichna demons, immobilized them, and sent them packing to the netherworld. When things worked right, she and her sister witches—along with Colleen's familiar—shanghaied the demons and locked them behind the gate guarding the Ninth Circle of Hell.

The demons didn't go without a fight, though, which was what had killed off the other demon assassin witches. It didn't help that demons as a group had been gathering power these last fifty years or so. Witches lived a long time, but they were far from immortal, and demon assassination ability was genetic. She, Jenna, or Colleen would have to produce children or that strain of magic would die out. None of them had a shred of domesticity, so no one had signed up for motherhood. At least not yet.

I can't put two weeks together without a major demon battle these days. How the hell could I take time off to raise a kid?

Rain ran down her neck and Roz shivered. Thinking about demons chilled her bones. Realizing she'd stopped walking, she plodded toward the house again and forced her thoughts to the magicians' supply store she owned with Colleen and Jenna in Fairbanks, Alaska.

The other two witches had moved there months ahead of her. She hated the idea of all that snow and cold and winter nights that lasted twenty hours, but she'd boxed herself into a dicey situation and hadn't had much choice. Her temper, never very controllable on a good day, had gotten the better of her, and she made short work of her cheating husband and his two —yup, count 'em—girlfriends. After that, she'd packed up and headed her aging Subaru north. Next stop, Fairbanks...

That had happened a few years ago. So many, it was almost time to move on before anyone noticed she and the other witches didn't seem to grow any older.

Roz shook her head, not wanting to go there, either. She forced her mind back to the special skill she shared with Colleen and Jenna. She hated to admit it, but demons held the high cards these days, and she had no idea how to even the odds.

Aren't I just the queen of cheerful?

She gave herself a mental shake with instructions to snap out of her funk.

Roz made it to the huge house and tugged on one of the ground level doors. When it didn't open, she hit it with a jolt of magic, and the deadbolt snicked aside. She stopped long enough to shake water off her and then loped down a long corridor with a concrete floor toward one of the old mansion's many stairwells. Fluorescent lights, recessed into the ceiling, gave off a sickly yellow gleam that matched her sour mood.

She'd just begun climbing upward when a rush of footsteps sounded from the hallway below.

"There you are," Bubba, Colleen's familiar, cried out and leapt up the stairs after her.

Roz glanced over a shoulder and saw he was in his normal form: a three-foot-tall changeling with oversized feet, long arms, and a bow-legged gait. His shaggy, black hair had been brushed until it shone, and his dark eyes glittered mischievously. Colleen had a hell of a time keeping him dressed, but today he sported black pants and a black jacket over a white shirt.

"Yes," Roz countered, still feeling out of sorts. "Here I am. The question is why aren't you upstairs with everyone else?"

"Colleen got worried. She sent me to hunt you down."

Bubba crossed his arms over his chest, looking pleased with himself.

Roz rolled her eyes. "Bubba, look—"

"Uh-uh." He uncrossed his arms and waggled a finger at her. "Niall. Remember, you all promised to use my real name from now on."

"So we did. Crap! I don't have time for this." She unkinked her neck and trudged upward.

"No kidding," he agreed. "Everyone's here, and you're not even dressed yet."

Rather than focus on her shortcomings, Roz changed the subject. "You're looking pretty spiffy, bud."

"Do you like it?"

"What I saw of it. It's sort of like a black tuxedo, but with Velcro instead of buttons."

"I hate buttons."

Roz grinned in spite of herself. "I know you do, sweetie."

She came to the third floor landing and pushed the stairwell door open, holding it for the changeling. "Run and tell Colleen I'll be there in about fifteen minutes." Without waiting for an answer, she walked briskly halfway down the long hall and let herself into her bedroom. Locking the door behind her, she unlaced her wet boots and toed them off. Next she shucked her sodden clothes, ducked into the bathroom, and gathered strands of coal black hair, pulling it into a ponytail with both hands. Once she had her hair together, she wrapped her head in a towel. She didn't believe in hair dryers, so once she'd soaked as much water as she could into the towel, she grabbed her comb, made several sections, and plaited her knee-length, straight-as-a-stick hair, weaving it into a pseudo-French braid.

Before she left the bathroom, she inspected her face in the mirror. She never wore makeup because it made her look like a clown. Her bronzed skin and stark bone structure declared her Native American blood more clearly than words could have. She smoothed her eyebrows with a few drops of water and considered which of two outfits to wear. Colleen had said it didn't matter to her, so long as Roz didn't show up in her usual tattered blue jeans and combat boots.

With a snort of amusement, she padded back into the bedroom and pulled a long, beaded black buckskin skirt off a hanger. She stepped into it and laced the side fastening. Next came a turquoise deerskin top, also beaded, that clung to her like a second skin. In addition to not bothering with makeup, she also didn't care for underthings, so the outline of her breasts was clearly visible through the soft leather. She slipped a heavy silver and turquoise necklace over her head, arranging her braid on top of it, and grabbed a matching ring off the dresser.

The only thing left was her moccasins. Roz wriggled her feet into them, enjoying the way the deerskin warmed and hugged her feet. Jenna always wore high heels, but Roz had never understood how she could tolerate them. They'd had a few heated discussions years ago before Roz finally gave up.

"To each her own," she told the mirror. Satisfied she looked presentable, she focused the threads of her calming spell, strengthened it a bit to make certain she'd last through the ceremony without breaking down and bawling like an idiot, and let herself into the hallway.

The buzz of a crowd reached her from the main floor. She glanced toward the stairs and then the other way, wondering if Colleen was still up here. Figuring it couldn't hurt to find out, she walked two doors down and knocked. The door flew open almost immediately and she looked into an accusing set of pale blue eyes.

"It's about fucking time," Colleen exclaimed. Auburn hair with lily of the valley woven into it swirled around her, falling to waist level. At six feet, Colleen was normally a good four inches shorter than Roz, but today she wore heels and they were of a height.

"Huh?" Roz murmured, confused. "I almost went downstairs. I had no idea you were waiting for me."

"We'd planned to all go down together." Colleen sounded sullen. "You know, like a proper wedding party."

"If we were all that proper," Roz said, "Jenna and I would be wearing matching—"

Jenna made chopping motions with both hands and unfolded her well-rounded frame from off the bed. Blonde hair, hacked off at shoulder level, framed a gamine's face with shrewd, hazel eyes. Rather than her standard, thrift store couture, today she wore a short beige silk skirt, a lacy blouse, and her trademark high-heeled boots. Huge, golden hoops graced her ears.

She walked to Roz's side and looped an arm through hers. "Don't think anything of it. The bride—" she waved an airy hand Colleen's way "—has been antsy as a scalded cat all day."

Colleen closed her teeth together with an audible clack. "Maybe I'm making a mistake."

Roz and Jenna turned to stare at her. "What?" Jenna asked, incredulous.

"Hey, if you don't want him—" Roz began.

"No shit," Jenna interrupted. "Tall, blond, drop dead gorgeous. Those green eyes are to die for and those shoulders." She made panting noises. "The couple of times I saw him without a shirt, I almost came just watching his muscles rustle beneath his skin when he walked."

Colleen rolled her eyes. "You two are impossible. Can't a bride have a case of jitters without her two closest friends turning into vultures?"

"No." Roz looked down her nose at Colleen. "Considering

how long and hard I've hunted for decent partner material..." She let her words trail off before the extent of her jealousy leaked out.

The door blew inward and Bubba marched in, hands on his hips. "Come on. Everyone's ready." He lowered his voice, but not by much. "I think Duncan's worried that you—" he pointed at Colleen "—got cold feet."

"She nearly did," Jenna muttered.

"Aw, crap. Guess I need to go tell everyone the wedding's off." Bubba did an about face, but before he could sprint through the open door, Colleen snatched him up.

"You'll do no such thing." She swallowed audibly. "I'm ready. I guess."

"Let go of me." Bubba writhed in her grasp.

"Not before you promise to keep your mouth shut."

Roz smirked. Circumspection was not exactly the changeling's long suit. She walked to Bubba's other side. "I'll take him." She held out her arms.

"I can walk," the changeling said with a great deal of dignity, "as soon as Colleen lets go of me."

"You haven't promised," Colleen said. "Please, sweetie. It's important to me. A girl needs to have some things stay private."

He blew out an annoyed sounding breath. "All right. I promise." Colleen relaxed her grip. Shaking himself like a dog might have, the gnome-like changeling chuckled. "Too bad. Something like that's a prime piece of gossip."

Colleen broke into a broad grin. "Right up your alley, eh?"

Roz made shooing motions. "Let's get going. You don't want all that food the Sidhe catered to get cold do you?"

"I don't care about food," Colleen mumbled. "I'm so nervous I probably won't be able to eat a thing."

"Well I do," Jenna said. "I'm with Roz. Let's get this show on the road."

"Have a couple belts of whiskey," Roz suggested. "It'll do wonders for your nerves."

The hallway air brightened and shimmered. When it cleared, Titania, Queen of Faerie, shook floor-length silvery hair out of her ice blue eyes and pushed it over her shoulders. A diaphanous gown, more jewels than fabric, floated around her tall, thin frame. "Is there some problem?" she inquired with asperity, and her gaze zeroed in on Colleen.

Colleen half curtseyed.

Roz considered it, but didn't because Titania wasn't her queen.

"No problem at all." Colleen inclined her head. "We were just on our way."

The Queen of Faerie's severe expression softened. "Thank the goddess. For a minute there, I was afraid you were going to break Duncan's heart." She strode forward and thumped Colleen's chest with a bony forefinger. "If you ever hurt that boy, I'll hunt you down and make you very sorry."

"That *boy*—" Colleen held the queen's gaze "—is a thousand-year-old man."

Titania furled her perfect silver brows. "Details. Besides, it's rude to contradict me. Privilege of age and rank and all that. Let's go. I haven't performed a marriage in centuries. I'm quite looking forward to it."

Colleen's eyes widened. "I thought Naomi, the leader of this Coven, was going to join Duncan and me."

"We both have roles to play." Titania's mouth twitched. "Surely you didn't think I'd let one of my own be bound in marriage without my magic involved."

"I have no idea what I thought," Colleen managed, but she looked ready to throttle the queen.

Before things got any tenser and Colleen started in about it being *her* wedding, Roz herded them out the door and down the hallway. Colleen stopped for a moment at the head of the stairway, tension rolling off her in waves.

Roz wrapped an arm around her. "It will be fine," she whispered. "Just fine." After a quick hug, she let go.

As if those six words did the trick—or maybe it was the hug—Colleen swept down the long, curved staircase, looking regal. Roz, Jenna, and Titania jostled one another as they made their way down the twenty-five steps. Bubba made an end run around them and fell in behind Colleen, where he picked up her lace train.

They marched through the dining area where caterers and witches bustled about laying out a spread of food that smelled delicious, into a large, luxurious room that took up much of the bottom floor of the old Victorian. At one point, they'd talked about having the ceremony outside, but the weather put the kibosh on that idea. Roz wondered why they'd wasted their breath even considering an out-of-doors event. It was the winter solstice in Seattle. She bet there'd never been one when it wasn't raining like crazy—or snowing.

Chairs lined the wood-paneled great room, and a fire burned merrily in a huge stone fireplace that took up one end of the sumptuous space. Old-fashioned chandeliers were festooned with hundreds of blazing candles. Witches sat on one side of a center aisle, Daoine Sidhe on the other. Roz guessed between three and four hundred people were in attendance—more Sidhe than witches. Everyone turned in their seats to stare at Colleen, and a collective *aaaaah* surged through the room.

Roz clamped down on a grin. Colleen really did make a lovely bride, with her Irish complexion and red tresses. The creamy lace dress was perfect. White would have made her look washed out. Titania strode around all of them and took her place at the head of the room. Roz noted with amusement that Naomi held her ground when Titania tried to push her to one side.

Before she and Jenna left Colleen to find their seats, her gaze landed on Duncan—Lord Regis—and her heart nearly stopped. All Sidhe had an ethereal beauty, but Duncan practically glowed. Dressed in a black tuxedo with a crimson cummerbund and diamond studs, he cut an impressive figure with his high forehead, sculpted cheekbones, and strong jaw. Longish blond hair had been braided in tight rows, but the severe style suited him and make him look like an ancient warrior.

Roz averted her gaze, afraid he'd catch her staring, but he only had eyes for his bride. She said a quick prayer asking the goddess's blessing on their union and turned toward the witches' side of the room.

Because Ronin came up from her other side, she didn't notice the Sidhe leader until he wove an arm around her shoulders. "I saved you a chair next to me."

Her heart slammed into double-time rhythm. She'd met Ronin two weeks before at his castle in northern England, and they'd shared several spirited conversations over meals. Something magical and electric had sparked between them, but she'd chalked it up to everyone's emotions running full tilt. She'd just escaped demons by the skin of her teeth, and he was dealing with shame or guilt—or whatever he felt—about forcing witches into being demon assassins two centuries before. While his attentiveness had been welcome—and more than a little flattering—she'd been more focused on her relief at being alive than anything else. Besides, after the Oklahoman, she'd sworn off men—forever.

Ronin smiled, not looking anything but glad to see her, and

her heart did a funny little flip-flop, in addition to beating much too fast. Dark hair hung loose to his shoulders, and his blue eyes twinkled warmly. Every bit as handsome as Duncan, he was dressed in formal clothing, black with a blue cummerbund, and what might have been ruby studs.

"I can't," she whispered. "I'm supposed to sit over there." She gestured in the general direction of the witches' side of the room.

"No one will notice," he assured her and hooked his hand beneath her arm.

Roz didn't fully understand why she let him guide her to a padded straight-backed chair near the front of the room and help her into it, but there was something irresistible about his energy. Too late, she recognized a mild compulsion spell. Anger spiked, but now wasn't the place to give in to it. With every shred of self-discipline at her disposal, she forced her attention to Duncan and Colleen reciting their vows, and to Naomi, who'd muscled her way in before Titania could get rolling.

When Ronin draped an arm around her shoulders, she shot him a harsh look that made him move it damned fast. *Good,* she thought. *It's about time the Sidhe realize their days of pushing witches around are over.* Yes, he was gorgeous, and he seemed interested in her, but the last thing she needed was some overbearing mage mucking things up. She still wasn't quite certain how Colleen's marriage to Duncan would impact her and Jenna. They'd always been kind of like The Three Musketeers, demon style. The permanent addition of a Sidhe was bound to have some effect. Exactly what was hard to gauge.

Who am I kidding? We didn't just get Duncan. We're stuck with his kinfolk now too. All of them.

She bit back a sigh. If the series of meetings a couple of weeks before in the U.K. was any indication, she, Jenna, and

Colleen would have to fight to be recognized as anything remotely close to equal.

Roz snuck a glance at Ronin. He sat straight in his seat, his profile heartbreakingly beautiful. His long-fingered hands were clasped together in his lap. She couldn't stop herself from wondering what they'd feel like stroking her body. Warm. Electric. Compelling.

Maybe I should give him a chance, a tiny, inner voice piped up.

Bosh.

Roz tried for a stern note, but the other part of her brain wouldn't shut up.

onin Redstone unwound his arm from Roz and gripped his hands together in his lap to lessen the temptation to touch her again. Where he figured most of the guests were anxious to see the bride, he'd been waiting for Roz. Feeling like a prime idiot, but unable to stop himself, he'd bounced to his feet the moment she entered the room. Not sure how she'd take his interest, he'd spun the mildest of spells to coerce her to sit near him.

He pressed his lips into a flat line as he wrestled with his thoughts. Ever since he'd met the tall, imposing witch at his home in northern England, he'd been able to think of little else. She even entered his dreams with her silky black hair, pronounced cheekbones, and hawk-like nose. In those dreams, she was naked, her bronze skin glimmering in moonlight.

Her heady scent, pine forests and jasmine, tickled his nostrils and made him wonder what she'd feel like in his arms. Once he kicked the door open to that slippery slope, his cock sprang to life, clearly eager to find out. He tried to clip his libido before things whirled out of control and she noticed his arousal, but his cock wasn't in the mood for negotiation—or retreat. He wove the tiniest don't look here spell and draped his lower body with it.

In years past, he'd simply have created a love charm, imbued it with compulsion, and bedded her. That probably wasn't a good idea, though. Roz would sense his magic, be outraged he tried to coerce her, and that would be the last he ever saw of the striking witch. Never mind, she had good reason to not want much to do with him since he was one of the key players who'd foisted demon assassination onto the witches two hundred years ago.

He tightened his jaw muscles. Who could have guessed his little machination to get his kin out from under a highly unpleasant task would nearly be the death of the few witches who'd inherited the power through a magical version of gene splicing? Of course, he'd also been the one to send Duncan to fetch one of the witches to quell a demon uprising in the U.K. last month. That was how they'd discovered only three of the special witches remained...

No wonder she's not overly fond of me.

Ronin grimaced, not liking the truth in his thoughts. An inner voice huffed, reminding him it wasn't his fault the witches in question hadn't produced more offspring, but he shushed it.

Surely I can at least charm Roz out of that sour expression on her face.

He forced his breathing into a regular pattern and glanced toward Duncan and Colleen at the front of the room. The resident witch had completed her part of the ceremony, and Titania was speaking in Gaelic so old he had trouble following it. The Sidhe binding ceremony lasted at least half an hour, so he let his thoughts drift. Anywhere but to his cock, which still throbbed uncomfortably.

As de facto leader for the Sidhe, a post he held more because no one else wanted it than because of any special skills on his part, he sensed they stood at the brink of a cataclysmic event. Abbadon and his henchmen, the Irichna demons, had grown appallingly strong. Capturing them one at a time and shepherding them to the Ninth Circle of Hell where they were trapped for all eternity wasn't a workable solution anymore. There were too many of them, and maybe not enough space in the bottom of Hell.

Because he was afraid of a firm answer regarding Hell's demon storage capacity, he hadn't asked Titania, though surely she'd know. If they couldn't dump Irichna behind the Ninth Circle's gate, he had no idea what they'd do with them. And if Abbadon consolidated his full power, Earth would be laid to waste. Ronin clamped his jaws together. Apocalypse didn't come close to describing what would happen if Abbadon was freed from protecting his demons and could concentrate on taking over Earth.

In addition to not inquiring too closely about the Irichna, I also haven't asked about Oberon.

Ronin grimaced again. If the King of Faerie were truly so tired of immortality he'd let himself fade into the Dreaming, Ronin didn't want to know about that, either.

When did I turn into such a craven that I avoid unpleasant answers?

Even though he wasn't expecting one, a response popped up anyway. He'd loved a human woman once, but she'd died bearing their son, who'd perished right along with her. The major vessel serving her heart had ruptured, and no amount of Sidhe magic could heal her or breathe life into their dead child. Ronin withdrew from the other Sidhe after that, mostly because he didn't want to hear their lectures about the whole debacle being his own fault. They weren't supposed to mate outside their blood. He had, and it hadn't ended well. No one to blame but himself.

When he finally picked up the reins of command a couple of centuries later—or maybe it had been three—he held himself aloof and avoided confrontations with anyone, about anything.

He ground his jaws harder. His internal inventory was damned depressing. It forced him to take a harsh look at himself, and he didn't like what he saw. He glanced at Titania. She clasped Duncan's and Colleen's hands between her own, and his eyes widened. Had he truly spent the entire ceremony sunk in memories and self-pity?

It would appear so, he thought dryly.

In moments, Titania would utter the final words, Duncan would kiss Colleen, and the ritual would be done. He barely had time to wonder why Titania hadn't kicked up more of a fuss about Duncan marrying a mortal, when the bridal pair kissed.

The tiniest sigh escaped Roz, and he glanced sidelong at her. Her full lips were parted in half a smile, and she looked captivated by the traditional ceremony that had unfolded, mostly without him paying one whit of attention to it.

She leaned toward him, her earlier ire apparently forgotten. "They make such a lovely couple," she whispered.

Ronin narrowed his eyes and looked hard at Duncan and Colleen, wrapped in one another's arms and kissing enthusiastically. He didn't know about the lovely couple part, because he didn't view the world that way.

"They do look happy," he whispered back because he thought he ought to say something.

Bubba, who'd been standing off to one side, made a grab for a bag Ronin hadn't noticed before. The changeling reached inside, and Ronin's internal alarm went off. The changeling was about to throw something at the couple. Had the creature been co-opted by demons? It wasn't unheard of since their race contained a smattering of demon blood. Afraid if he hesitated he'd be too late, Ronin pulled strong magic and rose to his feet.

Before he could loose it, Roz fastened a hand around his lower arm. "It's just rice," she said, her voice still low. "He's going to throw rice at them. Stand down."

Ronin met her dark, luminous gaze. "What sort of custom is that?" he demanded. Magic thrummed around him, making the air shimmer in iridescent hues. The changeling indeed tossed rice high in the air, showering everyone within a ten-foot radius of him, laughed uproariously, and then did it again.

"An old one." Roz tugged on his arm and he sat reluctantly. "Bubba adores Colleen. He's laid his life on the line for her a bazillion times. He'd never hurt her."

"Better safe than sorry," Ronin muttered, feeling like an ass. "How was I to know?"

"It's okay." She let go of his arm and patted one of his hands.

As long as he was in an apologizing mood—they were rare for him—Ronin exhaled sharply and said, "I'm sorry I, um, suggested you sit next to me."

She cocked her head to one side and quirked a brow. "If you'd only suggested, it would've been fine, but you did a tad more than that."

Flutes and guitars began to play Mendelssohn's "Wedding March." Colleen and Duncan turned and floated up the center aisle with Bubba right behind, still throwing rice. Even Ronin had to admit they looked radiant. He'd known Duncan his entire life, and he'd never seen his fellow Sidhe look so carefree and besotted with joy. In one wild, unrestrained moment, before he glossed his emotions over with rationality, he wanted the same for himself.

Ronin felt Roz's gaze still on him and knew he couldn't ignore her comment. "You're right," he said stiffly. "I did do more than that."

She repositioned herself so he had to look at her. "Why?"

Because I've wanted to strip you naked and worship your body from the day I met you.

He cloaked his mind, hoping he'd been fast enough and she hadn't read his thoughts. "I'm not quite sure." He stumbled over the words, because they weren't the truth.

Her dark gaze never left him as she weighed his statement. Finally, she nodded, almost to herself. "When you figure it out," she said and winked broadly, "be sure to let me know."

Heat rose from his neck and swooshed over the top of his head. Damn! He was a Sidhe and a warrior. It was unseemly to blush like a love-struck maid. He opened his mouth to stammer some sort of reply, but she got up, along with the rest of the guests.

"Come on," she said. "I'm starving."

He'd been afraid the second the ceremony was over, she'd race away from him as far and as fast as she could, but she'd just invited him to eat with her, at least he thought she had. He bit back a smile until just the edges of his mouth twitched. Maybe she didn't abhor him as much as it seemed when she'd shot him that poisonous look once she sensed his magic.

I learned something. I have to ask her, not simply push her to do what I want.

Ronin hurried after her swishing skirt, not wanting to lose her in the crowd. He could always locate her, but the less magic he used until she got to know him, the better.

* * * *

Roz caught up to Jenna just inside the dining area and hugged her. "Wasn't it just perfect?" she gushed, still caught up in the mystical pull of dual wedding ceremonies.

Jenna hugged her back and nodded. She disentangled herself and eyed her friend. "What the hell, Roz? It isn't like you to fall all over yourself."

Roz settled her face into its usual, stern planes. "There. Is that better?"

Jenna grinned. "Yup. There's the grumpy old witch I know and love. What happened to you anyway? I looked back and you were trailing after that hunky Sidhe."

"He snared me in a spell."

"Ooooh." Jenna clapped her hands together. "He must be interested." She leaned close. "What did he do during the ceremony?"

Roz felt her face redden. "Nothing. I got mad at him once I realized he'd bamboozled me. Hush. Here he comes."

"Awesome." Jenna practically vibrated with enthusiasm. "He can eat with us."

"I already invited him."

A knowing look crossed Jenna's face and she opened her mouth, but Roz hissed, "Can it, sister," just before turning to Ronin and asking, "Where would you like to sit?"

He half-bowed—a courtly, old world gesture that drove home just how old he really was—lifted Jenna's hand to his lips, and said, "Nice to see you again, Miss Jenna. Anywhere the two of you wish to settle is fine with me."

"Maybe we should get our food first," Jenna suggested brightly, "since the tables will fill fast."

"Good idea," Roz snapped, feeling unaccountably jealous. Ronin hadn't kissed her hand, but he'd been quick enough to snatch Jenna's.

"If you don't want him..." Jenna spoke in their telepathic speech.

"I thought you were interested in Tristan." Roz led the way to a buffet table and picked up a plate.

Jenna smirked. "I am, but he's not here."

"Any slut in a storm." Roz shot a meaningful look Jenna's way.

Jenna laughed, grabbed a plate, and agreed far too cheerfully. "Guilty as charged."

"Guilty of what?" Ronin glanced up from the buffet table.

"Ask Roz," Jenna countered still grinning like a mischievous cat.

Since she wanted to cut this conversation off at the knees, Roz turned her back on both of them. She dished up an interesting looking salad, brimming with shrimp and crab, and followed it with a few slices of rare beef and a roll. They found a table beneath a leaded glass window and laid their plates down.

"I'll get us something to drink." Ronin smiled. "Preferences?"

"What are you getting?" Roz asked, avoiding Jenna's gaze.

"Mead," he answered. "It's what I prefer."

"I'll take Irish whiskey," Jenna trilled and settled into her seat.

"Just bring me a glass of one or the other," Roz muttered. "I'm not picky." As soon as Ronin was out of earshot, or close enough, she glared at Jenna. "Leave him alone."

"But you're not even sure you're interested in him," Jenna protested.

"And how would you know that?" Roz stuffed a forkful of salad into her mouth, chewed with a vengeance, and swallowed.

The other witch dropped her gaze, looking sheepish. "I, um, peeked."

Roz slammed a fist on the table hard enough the dishes rattled. "You looked inside my head without asking?"

"'Fraid so. Sorry." Jenna started eating with a studied nonchalance.

Roz exhaled and then did it again. Both of them were lonely—had been for years. Getting angry with her longtime friend wouldn't serve any purpose other than creating bad water under the bridge that they'd have to clear at some point.

"Jenna." Roz touched the other witch's arm. "It's the wedding ceremonies. Both of them, witch and Sidhe. The ancient magic in the bindings makes us want what Colleen and Duncan have."

"I suppose you're right." Jenna's hazel gaze met hers and she looked repentant, her brows drawn together. "I'm sorry."

"Me too." Roz smiled crookedly. "Let's not fight. Not today."

Ronin plunked two bottles on the table. Glasses were already there, along with silverware. "Here you go." He folded his tall frame into a chair and reached for the mead. "Did you decide which you want?" he asked Roz.

"I'll try mead." She held her glass toward him, and he filled it with amber liquid that smelled heavenly. She took a sip and rolled it around her tongue before swallowing. "Interesting. I've never had honey wine before."

"I'm glad you like it." Ronin filled his own glass. "It's a traditional libation for my people."

Jenna tipped the Irish whiskey into her glass and drank. "So…" She skewered Ronin with her hazel gaze. "Where's Tristan? I thought he was coming to the wedding."

Ronin pressed his lips together, looking uncomfortable. "Deciding who had to remain in the Old Country was quite a task." He rolled his deep blue eyes. "Everyone wanted to come to the wedding, but we had to leave a sufficient number of us in Britain."

"Why?" Roz asked, and then she knew the answer and mumbled, "Never mind."

Demons were running amok through the northern English countryside. It was why Duncan had sought out Colleen in the first place. And why the three witches planned to return to England just as soon after the wedding as they could manage.

"Exactly." Ronin set his glass down and laid a hand over hers. "Better not to speak of evil out loud. It tempts fate—and not in good ways."

"Is Tristan one of the men holding down the fort?" Jenna pressed.

Ronin nodded. "I'm certain he'd rather be here with you."

Jenna ducked her head, but Roz saw a flush spread upward from her neck. "That's a nice thing for you to say," Jenna murmured, "but he and I barely know one another—"

"Ronin." Two male Sidhe that Roz didn't know converged on their table. Ronin raised a questioning brow, and she caught the magic of telepathic speech, though she had no idea what they said to one another.

"If you ladies will excuse me." Ronin flowed to his feet in a supple motion and walked briskly from the room with the other Sidhe.

"Wonder what that was about?" Jenna gazed after them. "Those other two were pretty damned gorgeous too."

Roz smirked. "All Sidhe are stunning, or did you miss that little detail?"

"Whatever. I'd take any of them in my bed at this point."

Roz would too, but the one she wanted was Ronin. Though she didn't have much of an idea regarding Sidhe mores, she was pretty sure it would muck up her chances with Ronin if she had a roll in the hay with whoever asked her first. She went to work on the rest of her meal, feeling thoughtful.

Bubba trotted over, grabbed the whiskey bottle, and drank deeply. He wiped his mouth with the back of one hand. "I'm having a great time," the changeling announced.

"You're getting drunk," Jenna observed.

"You should know." He glared meaningfully at her from beneath his thick eyebrows.

"Sometimes I do drink too much," she agreed and belted back half her glass of whiskey.

"I'm happy for Colleen and Duncan." Bubba danced a small jig and took another swallow from the bottle still clutched in his hand.

"We are too, sweetie," Roz said. Her head snapped up. "Shit!"

"What?" Jenna glanced around, clearly searching for what had alarmed Roz.

Nostrils twitching, Roz surged to her feet and raked the corners of the room for what she was sure she'd smelled. She didn't see anything, but the smell didn't go away.

"Demons!" Bubba barked and craned his neck from side to side. "Where are they?"

Jenna bolted up from the table and joined Roz. "It makes sense," she said through clenched jaws. "All three of us are here."

Bubba took off for the dais at the head of the room. "Gotta warn Colleen," he cried over one shoulder.

"Yes," Roz growled. "We need to warn everyone."

"Do you suppose that was why those Sidhe came for Ronin?" Jenna asked.

"Does it matter?" Roz shot back.

Jenna shook her head. "Let's get Colleen. If we have to fight, we're stronger together."

Roz couldn't agree more, so she pulled her skirts aside and sprinted after the changeling.

www.ingramcontent.com/pod-product-compliance
Lightning Source LLC
Chambersburg PA
CBHW071243190726

48292CB00007B/2388